THE LOST AND FOUND STORIES
OF MORLEY CALLAGHAN

Jacket painting, *Green Cityscape* (1966), by Philip Surrey, C.M., R.C.A., LL.D. Born in Calgary in 1910, Surrey studied under LeMoine FitzGerald, Frederick Varley, and Jock Macdonald. He has been in many group shows and has had twenty one-man exhibitions, including a solo retrospective at the Musée du Québec (1966), and another at Montreal's Musée d'art contemporain (1971) which travelled to the Canadian Cultural Centre in Paris in 1972. His work is in many collections, including the National Gallery of Canada, the Montreal Museum of Fine Arts, the Art Gallery of Ontario, the Art Gallery of Windsor, the Winnipeg Art Gallery, and the Edmonton Art Gallery. Mr. Surrey lives in Montreal.

It is our intention, with the International Fiction List, to seek out and publish fine fiction—new works as well as classics—by authors from around the world. Authors shortly to be published in the International Fiction List include: Antonine Maillet, Barry Callaghan, and Thomas Keneally.

Books now available in the International Fiction List

THE INTERNATIONAL FICTION LIST

*I looked in the mirror on the wall and rubbed my
hand softly over my face. It was not a flabby face...*
(From "Rendezvous")

DRAWING BY GEORGE GROSZ

THE LOST AND FOUND STORIES
OF MORLEY CALLAGHAN

Lester & Orpen Dennys/Exile Editions

FIRST EDITION

Canadian Cataloguing in Publication Data

Callaghan, Morley, 1903–
    The lost and found stories of Morley Callaghan

ISBN 0-88619-079-7 (bound). - ISBN 0-88619-081-9 (pbk.)

I. Title.

PS8505.A41L59 1985   C813'.52   C85-099101-3
PR9199.3.C343L59 1985

Design and series design by Spencer/Francey Incorporated
Set in 12 pt. Stempel Garamond OS by Tumax Typesetting

George Grosz illustrations by permission of the Estate of George
Grosz, Princeton, New Jersey

Printed and bound in Canada by
T.H. Best for
Exile Editions Ltd.
69 Sullivan Street
Toronto, Canada M5T 1C2
and for
Lester & Orpen Dennys Ltd.
78 Sullivan Street
Toronto, Canada M5T 1C2

He was watching his father as if at last he understood everything his father felt. . .
                    (From "A Boy Grows Older")

THE LOST AND FOUND STORIES
OF MORLEY CALLAGHAN

CONTENTS

Foreword

It was just after Christmas and we were standing in the dining room. My father said that back in the 1950s he had probably left two or three stories out of his big *Morley Callaghan's Stories*, which included 57 stories. "I got bored I guess ... I just said, 'That's enough,' and let it go at that."

"Where do you think they are?"

"Over there, I think. With the bills."

He was pointing at a small mound of brown and blue envelopes – unopened telephone and gas bills. Months go by and Morley doesn't pay his bills. I don't know how he gets away with it. They don't cut off his phone or his gas. They don't even prod him, and he just goes on stacking his little mounds, and then after six months or so, these get swept – along with letters and notes – into big manila envelopes or old used padded Jiffy bags, and it all gets put away somewhere. It is his comfortable clutter in a big house that has to be big.

I looked for the three stories and they were there, with one – "The Fugitive" – in the onionskin manuscript my mother had typed years ago.

"What else do you think you've got hidden away?"

"I don't know."

"You want to look?"

We went up to the old linen closet, closed for years off the back stairs. The cupboards, with their little iron button-latches on the doors, were piled with broken Christmas decorations, an old pair of boy's hockey shoulder pads, frayed curtains, and cardboard boxes. The boxes hadn't been touched in thirty years. The flaps and the papers on top were heavy with dark dust and, inside, the papers and magazines were jammed and rolled and bunched in no order at all.

As I rummaged through them, with Morley standing behind me chuffing on his pipe, muttering that he was sure there was nothing anybody would care about in the boxes, I found a letter from Sinclair Lewis, and then the proofs of a piece Edmund Wilson had written about his work – with Wilson's corrections in the margins – and the manuscript of *More Joy in Heaven.*

"Why, I thought I'd lost that years ago."

"And what's this?"

"Oh, that's *John O'London's Weekly*, an English magazine. They used to print a lot of my work."

"Well," I said, lifting the brittle brown newsprint into the air, "it says here you wrote a story called, "The Fiddler on Twenty-Third Street.""

"I never wrote any such story. Not with that title."

"You sure did."

"I wonder if it's any good?"

After an afternoon of sifting, shuffling, and thumbing through dirt, crumbling book reviews, and old, worthless gold penny mining stocks, I'd found letters from his friends in Paris, the manuscripts of all his 1930s novels, the manuscript of an abandoned novel from the forties that he'd forgotten all about, photographs of himself with mother in Montreal, with Madame Thérèse Casgrain, and Slitkin and Slotkin, the famous old saloon keepers, and some twenty short stories.

He seldom remembered the titles and couldn't remember most of the stories. "You see," he said, "in those days I was living only off the stories I wrote and sold. I had to get the money to keep us. I was the only guy I knew of in America somehow selling my non-commercial stories in the great commercial market and staying alive."

But the stories brought back forgotten memories – a memory of Max Perkins would come back to him as I held up an old orange *Scribners* magazine, or of George Grosz, as I brushed off a floppy *Esquire* dated 1937 and found that a story of his had been illustrated by Grosz. "Yes, I was supposed to go and meet Grosz one night with my old pal Norman Matson, but we got talking and never got there."

Soon, the old magazines – the staid *Yale Review* and *Harper's Bazaar* with line drawings of lean elegant women on slick heavy paper, and *The Saturday Evening Post* with a water color of a fanged dog frightening a boy, *Cosmopolitan* and a pristine page of print from *The New Yorker*, *The North American Review* and *Weekend* with garish pulp drawings of wide open faces full of wonder at the possibilities of life – were all there, big magazines that were meant to be spread open just as families and life were meant to be big and open back then in hard mean secretive times. His stories had been printed everywhere all through the thirties, forties, and fifties, stories that seem, deceptively, so easily told about the little moments that are so big in everyone's life.

"Well, there they are," I said.

"I suppose so," he said.

But week after week I kept coming back, finding another story and then another in a box in another room,

3

and then one night, just as he'd finished tinkering with a few of the stories – and while I was upstairs trying to find a George Grosz drawing he was sure he'd put somewhere – I came across a manuscript that had never been published, "A Couple of Million Dollars."

"You should stop," he said, as he sat down and read the story.

"I should say so," I said, wiping the dust off my hands.

"But they're all pretty darn good," he said.

"Yes."

The next night, as we went on looking for the Grosz drawing, he reached for some small colored sheets of children's scribbler paper that were sticking out between two books on a bottom shelf. They were the titles to another twenty-five stories. "Where are they?" I cried. He didn't know. He couldn't remember the stories.

"Cut it out," I said. "This has got to stop."

"Perhaps it will," he said, as he sat in the lamplight, his elbow on the desk beside a mound of old telephone and gas bills I'd never seen before.

Barry Callaghan
1985

Introduction

WALKING THE CITY STREETS IN THE AFTERNOONS, I WAS always working on a story. Not a real story – just the beginning of one. It was as if I was trying to remember something someone had told me so that my imagination would be set off. Though no one ever tells me a complete story, often something is said that shows me the aroused wonder in the person telling me about the incident. I would try to let this wonder grow, not forcing the story, just waiting, while I walked alone watching faces on the street. Or, maybe this would happen after meeting someone and having an idle conversation. Then, maybe two hours later, and without any concentration on my part, that unfinished incident would have progressed astonishingly, joining with another incident, becoming a form – a real story. And I remember once hurrying into a quick-lunch, getting a coffee, taking out a pad I had in my pocket and beginning to write. I had three coffees while writing steadily, and then, since it was six o'clock, I hurried home and, before dinner, finished the story. But most stories don't come that easily. I saw stories everywhere – in churches, saloons, the prize-fight ring, the dance hall… in whores and saints, young lovers, boys growing up – always the boy on the threshold of some sobering knowledge about the world; the half-beaten man striving for a little dignity; and always the devastating influence of money and the rich and poor. I say I saw stories everywhere – and this is the mystery for the writer; most of the time I didn't know I had seen the story when it had been right under my eye. I had to wait for months until something else happened that made me remember, and then, what had been stored up far back in my imagination was suddenly there as something I had not been able to see before.

I can give an idea of the way a writer's mind works. Take the story "Loppy Phelan's Double Shoot." It had its beginning in my only encounter with the rather fabulous "Indian" naturalist, Grey Owl. After a great success in England, where he was treated as a wonderman of the Canadian forests, he came to Toronto. His publisher, Hugh Eayrs of Macmillan, had a dinner at the York Club in his honor. About ten of the local literati, all in black tie dinner dress, broke bread with Grey Owl in the high-ceilinged, solemn York Club. Grey Owl, tall and handsome and with his long black hair in an Indian braid, was also in dinner dress. I sat directly across the table from him and as the fine dinner progressed, I watched him. He became aware that I was studying his face carefully. Once, as I turned quickly, I saw that he was eying me thoughtfully. When we all rose from the table, Hugh Eayrs, opulent and good-humored, asked me, "Well, what do you think?" Smiling, I said, "Well, I don't know, but I'll tell you one thing. He is no Indian." "Are you so sure?" he said, but he laughed good-naturedly.

Whether or not he was an Indian was unimportant to me at the time. Then, one day some fifteen years later, I had got some news from Collingwood where I had spent my boyhood summers, and I sat remembering the boys I played with and how we all used to go to the fairgrounds to watch the town ball team play a team from one of the American ships tied up at the grain elevator. Then, suddenly, I remembered that character, Loppy Phelan, a pitcher, and how the boys all claimed he could throw a double shoot, a curveball that actually zig-zagged its way to the plate. Well, the boys saw what they wanted to see, and that night long after, thinking about Loppy and the kids – I suddenly remembered my dinner with Grey Owl. The recollection of Grey Owl was stored up there back in my memory as if waiting to be used when the time came for me to write about Loppy Phelan.

And sometimes it happened that I was lucky enough to recognize at once that I had walked right in on a drama in progress, and indeed, might be helping to shape the story. In the depths of the great depression, I had a good close friend who, after enjoying some rich halcyon days in Montreal dealing in stocks and bonds, had lost everything. Dead broke, and of course finding himself being avoided by old fairweather friends, he had come to Toronto. Here, after a year or two, he had begun to get his life together and was earning a frugal living. He had a big front room in an old rooming house. When I walked in on him one evening, I found he had a visitor, a thin gaunt man with a persistent nervous smile. This visitor, from Montreal, had also been in the stock and bond business before the crash. From then on, whenever I called for my friend, this fellow would be in the room, lying on the bed, smoking or reading or having a drink. When my friend and I went out, he would auto-matically trail along, not after me, but after our friend, as if he was scared he might get separated from him. I used to wonder if he was scared that someone pursuing him might get to him quickly if he was left alone. I wrote his story and called it "The Fugitive."

Through those years, I was often writing about people who, when they came into my life, had no real interest for me – not at the time anyway. Yet it seems that they got tucked away in my mind, waiting. At drinking parties around town, I used to encounter occasionally a plump, very soft-faced, broad-smiling, amiable fellow in the advertising business. He drank too much. He bored me. I avoided him. I only had one conversation with him. I forgot about it till the day I read in the newspaper that he had died. That conversation, that one conversation – with me – and why me? Oh, I remembered it. I wrote the story "Rendezvous."

I know that over the years – and even now, walking the streets, watching and listening or meeting hundreds of new people and getting mysteriously involved with them – faces, voices, and what happened, all seem to fade out; yet I know none of it does. It's there, all there in a way I don't understand, stored away, being nourished, until something new happens, someone new is met. Then, suddenly, the something new seems to belong to a stored-up and suddenly remembered thing and I have to write a story. Anyway, that's the way it was with the writing of these stories.

Morley Callaghan

1985

An Enemy of the People

IT IS TRUE THAT LUELLA STEVENS AT SIXTY-EIGHT WAS A little too old to be singing in the choir of our church, but no one in the parish remembered when she had not sung her solo at the eleven o'clock mass. Any one who glanced up at the delicate face and the detached expression of this plainly dressed, frail little woman realized that if the parish had ever had large attendances at mass, then she, with the possible exception of old Catherine Hogan who played the organ, was the only one who could remember them. For a long time everybody was glad to have Luella Stevens up in the choir.

The new, poorer people in town, or the farmers who drove in to church on Sundays, were uneasy when talking to Luella Stevens because she would never let them forget that she came from an old and once influential family. She had been the only daughter of a doctor. She lived alone now in an unpretentious brick cottage. People used to make up stories about how pretty she had been once, and how she had been in love years ago with a man who had gone to Chicago and become a wealthy merchant and the father of a large family. For a great many years afterwards, they said, she had cherished her secret of unfulfilled love until it was too late to bother with any one else. Then her father had died, the people she had grown up with had gone away or were dead, too. The town had begun to decline and the only place that remained for Luella through the years, as it had been in her youth, as it had been for her family and the man who had been her lover and gone to Chicago, was the parish church and the choir with Catherine Hogan at the organ.

Yet there was no longer any use pretending that Luella had the beautiful voice of her youth. After mass on Sundays old parishioners like Mrs. Todd, the stout, stubborn-faced wife of the town flour-and-feed merchant, began to say, "My goodness, did you hear Luella Stevens today? I declare upon my soul she was positively shouting. Her voice is gone completely. Some one ought to tell the poor woman."

When this was said, prominent ladies of the parish, standing on the sidewalk under the trees in front of the church, nodded their heads gravely as if at last a scandal of tremendous importance had crept into the stagnant life of the town. Those who hardly ever listened to the choir made up their minds to listen eagerly the next Sunday.

Not knowing that her neighbors were now listening to her with a new rapt attention, Luella stood up on Sunday and, with as much confidence as she had ever had during the last thirty-five years, shouted at the top of her voice. Luella was aware, of course, that her voice was no longer a girl's voice, but by attacking the high notes with an extra enthusiasm she imagined she got over them very nicely. On this Sunday, those who had come to pass judgment on frail Luella Stevens turned in their pews and gawked up at her aristocratic old face and soon their own faces were full of indignation at the way she was shouting. The fidgeting young ladies of the choir were aware that at last, judging by the way heads kept turning round, people were noticing

Luella; they were so embarrassed that they dropped their own voices in shame and sang so listlessly that the young priest, Father Malone, who had been in the parish only a year, looked up, wondering what was the matter.

After that mass, Mrs. Todd went around to the priest's house to speak to Father Malone. The priest confessed frankly that he thought Luella Stevens's voice disrupted the whole choir. The wife of the flour-and-feed merchant and the priest shook their heads sadly, talked in a low grave tone, and wondered who ought to speak to Luella. "Catherine Hogan is the one, she's been there as long as Luella," Mrs. Todd said in triumph. "A splendid suggestion," said the priest. He thanked Mrs. Todd warmly for her exemplary interest in the matter and then accepted an invitation to play cards next Tuesday night with her husband and their family.

So, one Sunday when the two old women, Catherine Hogan and Luella Stevens, were on their way home from church, they got into a discussion about church music and their own choir in particular. Catherine Hogan, the organist, was stooped and withered compared with Luella, who walked proudly upright. "Did you ever think, Luella, of letting some of the younger girls take some of the solos you've had so long?" Catherine asked. "Just so there'll be some chance for their advancement."

"It never entered my head," Luella said.

"There are those, and mind now, I'm not saying who they are, who think your voice isn't what it was, Luella, and that you shouldn't be singing so much at your age."

"At my age, Catherine Hogan? And doesn't any one seem to remember that you, at seventy-two, are four years older than I am? Where's your own memory, Catherine? Why, when I was a child I always thought you were too old for me to play with. You know you were always far ahead of me in school like one of the older girls. I've always thought of you like that and will to my dying day. Isn't your own eyesight failing you, Catherine?"

Catherine Hogan was full of rage, knowing Luella was deliberately making her out to be an old woman when everybody in town knew she could play the organ blind-folded, that it didn't matter if she had to be carried into the choir on a bed with her eyesight gone, she would still know the music. She was so offended she made up her mind never to mention the subject to Luella again.

When she was alone in her cottage, cooking her dinner, Luella, muttering to herself, said, "Old Catherine's mind must be wandering, the poor thing." She simply could not bear to think of leaving the choir. Instead of eating the food she had cooked she sat at the end of the table remembering all the tiffs she had had with Catherine in the last forty years; she thought of jealous women, of newer ones in the parish scheming to have their daughters take her place in the choir, and she grew frightened, wondering what there would be left in her life if her enemies were successful. She stood rigid, her lips began to move and soon she was giving every one in the parish who had ever displeased her a thorough tongue lashing.

On Sunday, as if to threaten those who would deprive her of her rightful place, she gave full throat to her favorite hymn, singing more bravely than ever. Yet never was it so apparent as on that morning that the woman was simply shouting, that the last bit of sweetness had gone forever from her voice. Young people, who by this time had taken an interest in the matter, began to snicker. Mrs. Todd and Mr. J. T. Higgins, the undertaker, turned and looked up at Luella with a withering severity, and then, glancing at each other and screwing up their lips in disgust, they felt they positively despised the arrogant woman. The whole congregation, looking up at Luella when she had finished singing, began to feel that somehow she was making a shameful mockery of them all by refusing to retire. When they bent their heads piously to pray they felt she really had become their enemy.

After the mass the priest, a tall man with powerful shoulders and a blunt nervous way of speaking, was white-faced, and when he left the altar he fumbled with his vestments, calling sharply to the altar boys who were beside him, "Quick, go up to the choir and tell Miss Stevens I want to speak to her."

When Miss Stevens came in, smiling benevolently at the young priest because she was always anxious to help, he stopped pacing up and down and dropped his hands to his sides. He wanted to blurt out, "You've become a perfect nuisance, I tell you. You distract me. I can't offer up the mass. I can't pray and listen to your terrible shouting," but controlling himself and taking a deep breath, he said, "Miss Stevens, I noticed for the first time today that your voice was failing. I noticed your voice distinctly. Perhaps you feel you've served the choir long enough."

"For over thirty years," she said coldly.

"Yes, indeed. I believe you're sixty-eight."

"Catherine Hogan was seventy-two last July," Luella said triumphantly.

"I don't care how old Catherine Hogan is," the priest, who was exasperated, said. "I don't want to be harsh. I'd like to have you pick up the suggestion yourself. However, I'll say frankly I think you ought to leave the choir."

"I understand," Luella said tartly. Bowing coldly, she went out. She meant she understood that those who were scheming for her position were now successful, and with her head tossing, she walked past the little crowd of people standing in the sunlight in front of the church, not noticing how outraged they were as they stared at her.

It was only when she was going down the old gray dust road, the road she had taken every Sunday of her life, that she began to feel frightened. By the time she got to the bridge over the Swinnerton's Creek, she was dazed. Leaning against the rail, she trembled and looked back over the road she had come. It had gotten so that now there was only one main road in her life, the road from her cottage to the church. She wondered what had happened to her life, for though she had stood on this bridge often when she was a little girl, and often, too, when she was in love, and many times afterwards when she was alone, she had never had such a helpless feeling as she had now.

Luella Stevens went a little late to mass the next Sunday. She went in timidly like a stranger entering a great cathedral in a foreign city and she stood in the last pew at the back of the church. Those around her, who noticed her, could hardly stop smiling and nudging each other, and if they hadn't been praying they would have burst into loud, hearty laughter. But Luella felt lost down at the back of the church: she couldn't remember the last time she had been there, it was so long ago.

Everything went peacefully except that when it was time for her solo Luella began to hum, and then, mechanically, she began to sing, though she kept her voice as low as possible.

A week later she moved up a little closer to the altar where she could feel more at home, and she hummed and hummed and even sang a little louder. Mr. J. T. Higgins, the undertaker, nudged her sternly, but she simply moved away politely as if she understood that he wanted more room. The priest turned uneasily on the altar. Luella, noticing none of these things, was not aware of the rage and contempt they were all feeling for her. The undertaker went on turning page after page of his prayer book, and then finally he leaned over and whispered, "Would you please stop humming and singing? It's impossible for me to concentrate on spiritual things."

"My goodness," Luella whispered. "Has it got so that a poor body can't hum to herself the songs she's been singing for forty years?"

But the priest could stand it no longer and turning on the altar and looking over the heads of everybody, he said firmly, "There must be no noise in the church during mass."

Glaring angrily at the undertaker, Luella tried to say to him with her eyes, "You see, by talking away and making a fuss like a small boy you humiliate both of us in this way. God forgive you," but she really thought the priest was probably referring to small boys at the back of the church whose parents had raised them to be little savages.

Soon no one would sit in the pew with Luella. By herself, she felt free. She sang quite loudly. It was impossible for those around her to pray. It was impossible for any one, including the priest, to think of God when she shouted a high note, so they thought, instead, of Luella and what a stupid, arrogant, shameless woman she was, denying them all. They began to hate her. They wanted to hurt her so she would leave the parish forever. The priest, stalking down from the altar with long strides, looked as if he wanted to keep going right down the aisle, out of the church, and out of the town.

While every man and woman in the parish who had self-respect and a love of the church was standing out on the sidewalk muttering and whispering of her scandalous conduct, Luella Stevens went home meekly. In the priest's house, Father Malone was sending a message to Hector Haines and Henry Barton, two sober, middle-aged, prominent laymen, to come and see him on urgent business.

When the laymen were alone with him in his library, the priest, shrugging his shoulders and throwing up his hands helplessly, said, "I can't go on saying mass if these things keep on. I'm going to rely on you two men. Lord in heaven, it's a perfect scandal." Henry Barton and Hector Haines, two big, substantial men, cleared their throats and expressed a devout indignation. They were flattered to think the priest had come to them for assistance. The three of them talked gravely and bitterly, planning a way to handle Luella Stevens.

In her pew up at the front of the church next Sunday Luella Stevens, almost cheerful now to be there, found herself singing with the choir as she had done for thirty years. As soon as Catherine Hogan sounded the organ note for Luella's old hymn, Luella began to shout as though she had never left the choir.

Up on the altar the priest, kneeling with his hands clasped, lowered his dark head deeper into his shoulders: and then at last he stood up and said clearly, "Will some one please take that woman out of the church."

Hector Haines and Henry Barton, who were ready in the pew across the aisle waiting for this signal, stepped over quickly and grabbed Luella by the shoulders, one on each side of her. The priest had said to them, "Be quick, so there'll be no confusion." Luella looked around, speechless and frightened. The faces of the two huge, prominent laymen were red and severe as they clutched her in their big hands and hustled her down the aisle. They towered over the small woman, grabbing her as though they were burly policemen throwing a thug out of a dance hall, rushing her down the center aisle.

It was odd the way those who stared at her frightened face, as she passed, felt that they were seeing the end of something. Mrs. Todd, the flour-and-feed merchant's wife, ducked her head and suddenly began to weep, and she only looked up to whisper, with her face bursting with indignation, "Oh, dear, this is so shameful." All the others stirred and shifted miserably in their pews: some wanted to jump up and cry out angrily, "This is an outrage. Who is responsible for this?" and they glared their bitter silent protests at each other. "If she were one of mine there'd be trouble about this, I tell you," Mr. J. T. Higgins, the undertaker, muttered, his face red with resentment. But the quieter ones were so humiliated that they could not bear to raise their heads. The priest, who had not counted on the great zeal of his two prominent laymen, thought, "God help us. What have we done?" and he was so distracted he could hardly go on with the prayers.

Loppy Phelan's Double Shoot

IN THOSE DAYS WHEN GRAIN BOATS FROM CHICAGO, Cleveland, and cities at the head of the Lakes came regularly to the Georgian Bay port of Collingwood, and the shipyard there worked overtime, two boys sat on the rotting stumps at the end of the dock dreaming of lives for themselves far beyond the town.

One of the boys, Sam Crowther, whose father owned the flour and feed store on the main street, was fair-haired, had eager blue eyes, a mild manner, and he dreamed of going to the university and then getting a job in the diplomatic service which would give him a chance to live in Brazil or Chile or Mexico.

The other boy, Hal McGibbney, who had straight black hair, wild and restless narrow brown eyes, and a skin that was always tanned a dark brown, had been living in town about two years. He had come from north of the lakes. His mother and father were dead and he lived with his uncle, Henry Bryant, who worked in the shipyard. He dreamed of living with trappers and fishermen, of remaining alone and untouched by the tame life of the shipyard workers and the town storekeepers.

When they sat together on the dock that summer,

looking out beyond the rim of the bay, the two boys talked about baseball. The town had a good team that played against teams made up from the crews of ships loading grain in the harbor. These ships had names like The City of Cleveland, Garden City, Missouri, and these names taken by the crew teams made the games with the town seem important.

On an evening when there was to be a big game at the fairground, Sam Crowther would go down by the railroad station and across the tracks to Henry Bryant's frame cottage, then give a long whistle for Hal McGibbney, who came out wearing his first-baseman's glove. He would pound the pocket of the glove three or four times, spit in it, then pound it again, frown, then smile a little. He never laughed out loud. "Come on, let's go, Sam," he would say, and then walk rapidly, as if he were in a hurry to get far away from the cottage. He didn't get along with his uncle, who wanted to beat him but was afraid of him now that he was fourteen and big-boned.

Getting close to the fairground, they started to talk about baseball, and soon they were talking about the stories of Burt L. Standish, which all the boys read, and about his fabulous pitcher, Frank Merriwell, and his bewildering curve ball.

The two boys had a regular place just back of the third base bag, but they stayed there only about twenty-five minutes. "Let's watch Loppy for a while now," Hal said. "Yeah, let's see what he's got tonight," Sam agreed, and they withdrew to where Loppy Phelan, the town's relief pitcher, was warming up. They had never seen Loppy pitch in a real game, and they used to wonder why the manager of the town team kept him warming up game after game without ever using him.

Loppy worked in the shipyard. He was tall, gangling, and his mouth seemed to hang open with a surprised innocence whenever anybody spoke to him. He had large, sad brown eyes and wore a strange, faded pinkish ball shirt. Word had gone around among the boys that the shirt was part of the uniform of the Cincinnati Reds in the National League.

The two boys stood behind Loppy and watched every pitch he made with a rapt interest, and one night Hal said, "I wonder if Loppy can throw a double shoot."

"I think he's got all kinds of stuff," Sam said. "Maybe he *could* throw a double shoot."

It was the curve ball of their hero, Frank Merriwell, of Yale. Only Merriwell could throw a double shoot, which was a ball that curved out sharply, and then, as it got close to the batter, suddenly curved in at him. It was the greatest curve of all time.

"Hey, Loppy," Hal called eagerly.

"Eh?" Loppy grunted and he hardly paused in his lackadaisical wind-up.

"Can you throw a double shoot, Loppy?"

Looking a little puzzled, Loppy stopped, put his hands on his hips, grinned, then started his wind-up again. As the ball sped to his catcher, the boys, standing behind him, leaned forward expectantly.

"You see it, Hal?" Sam asked. "What was on it?"

"Boy, oh, boy," Hal said softly.

"Did you see it?"

"Sure," Hal said excitedly.

"Maybe it went too fast for me."

"Throw it again, Loppy."

Hardly heeding them, Loppy let go another fast ball.

"There!" Hal said excitedly.

"Sure," Sam said.

"Holy cow," Hal said. "Loppy Phelan's got a double shoot. Imagine a guy in this town having a double shoot."

After that night, Loppy had his own audience whenever the town team played. They brought all the boys to where Loppy warmed up, telling them about the double shoot and making them watch each pitch Loppy made. One by one the kids who lined up behind Loppy agreed they saw the ball take a twist. Loppy became their hero. When the kids trooped over to line up behind him, he scratched his head and grinned happily.

One night, in a game with the City of Cleveland, the town's regular pitcher weakened. Everything he threw was knocked out of the lot, but he stayed on the mound; the manager acted as if he didn't have another pitcher. But Hal McGibbney, rushing to the third base line and followed by all the kids, began to shout, "Put in Loppy. Use Loppy. Let him throw his double shoot."

Loppy stopped warming up and waited, but the players on the town team only looked mystified. They put their hands on their hips, then shrugged and grinned, and the manager, too, smiled a little. Loppy wasn't called to the pitcher's mound. On other occasions the same thing happened. Then, toward the end of the summer, Loppy Phelan got a job on one of the lake boats and sailed away and never returned. It seemed right to Hal McGibbney that Loppy sailed away.

With other kids, Hal lay in the thick grass under the corner light by Johnson's grocery store and talked about the great pitcher who had been among them and who had never been able to show his class. One by one the boys began to doubt that Loppy Phelan could throw the double shoot, but they were too afraid to argue with Hal. He was too bright, too quick, too intelligent for them.

Then, one night when Hal and Sam had gone down to

the dock for a swim and afterward were sitting on the stumps at the end of the pier, Hal said dreamily, "I wonder where Loppy is now?"

"Maybe he's in Cleveland," Sam said. "Maybe he's in Chicago."

"Maybe he's in the big leagues, Sammy, really pitching that double shoot."

"Say," Sam began hesitantly, "I don't think any of the ballplayers around here believed Loppy could throw that old double shoot."

"We know he could."

"Oh, sure."

"He could have been the greatest pitcher this town ever saw. But a guy can't be anything around here," Hal said contemptuously.

With his arms locked around his knees and the last of the twilight touching the side of his lean, brown face, he stared grimly at the glowing surface of the water. He looked lonely, yet proud of his own loneliness. Sam thought he was dreaming of cities where Phelan would be given a chance to pitch, but suddenly Hal laughed. "Well, I know what I should be," he said sharply. "If you do, too, you'll get moving. I hate my uncle's guts. I'm clearing out of here at the end of the week, heading north. I don't know what's going to happen to me, but I like the woods and the rivers. I'll make something out of myself, all by myself. I never belonged around here, Sammy." At the end of the week he went off without saying good-bye to anyone and the town soon forgot Hal McGibbney.

Sam Crowther stayed at home, forced to forget about his ambitious dreams of life in strange countries. He finished high school, but he did not go to the university, for his father died, and Sam's mother wanted him to take over the flour and feed store, which he did. Shortly afterward, he married Louella Chipman, whose father had come to town to manage the new grain elevator. She was an eager little blonde girl, with a timid streak. She liked church work and euchre parties, and she grew plump and pale.

Sam lost most of his hair, wore glasses, wished he had children, and became, by the time he was forty-four, a dignified figure who had run for mayor, been defeated in a close election, and whose store was a center for political gossip.

One summer afternoon, Sam was sitting on the stool behind his counter glancing at the city newspaper while he talked idly with young Tom Stevens, the redheaded, ambitious reporter for the town paper.

"Look at this," Sam said suddenly, as he looked at a story in which a woman who had been married to the celebrated naturalist, Snow Bird, now claimed that he was not an Ojibwa Indian, but a white man, an impostor. The woman said Snow Bird had divorced her ten years ago and had custody of their son, John Snow Bird. Now she claimed to be destitute. Snow Bird had a great audience and had just returned to New York from a triumphal tour of England. His beautifully written books on the wolves and the deer of the north shore of Lake Superior had been highly praised and had had a big sale.

"A phony. Another phony," Tom Stevens said, with the cynical satisfaction of a young newspaperman.

"Just a minute," Sam said slowly, staring at the picture of Snow Bird and his son.

Snow Bird looked like a dignified, superior Mohawk or Ojibwa, with a thin, high-bridged nose and shrewd, narrow eyes. He wore his hair in two braids with a single feather. The son, who looked like his father and was about fourteen, was obviously a proud, confident boy, and he had been sent to a good private school.

"Hey, you read this?" Tom suddenly asked, quickly looking up from his own copy of the paper. "The woman says Snow Bird came from some town around here – maybe Parry Sound or Midland – and that his real name is McKechnie."

"Well, I'll be damned!" Sam said softly, his eyes bright with excitement. He covered the feather in the Snow Bird picture and studied the picture of the boy alone, and he whistled softly. "The woman's got it a little wrong, Tom," he said. "It wasn't Parry Sound or Midland. It was right here. And the name wasn't McKechnie. It was Mc-Gibbney."

"You sure?" Tom asked. "It says here Snow Bird's New York publisher says the woman's story's malicious blackmail. You sure, Sam?"

"I'm not so sure of that picture of Snow Bird," Sam admitted, trembling, "not with the feather and long hair. And thirty years is a long time. But it's the boy. He looks too much like Hal McGibbney."

"But there are no McGibbneys around here, Sam."

"That's right. Hal lived here with his uncle, Henry Bryant, for about three years. Hell, we were both boys together. Bryant's dead now, and his wife is, too, but lots of people around here remember the Bryants."

"If you're right, Sam –"

"Sure, I'm right."

"Look, let's go up to the library," Tom said, "and see what we can find out about Snow Bird."

Telling his wife to look after the store, Sam left with Tom Stevens. They walked along the sunlit main street and around the corner to the red brick library, where the librarian gave them three of Snow Bird's books and a short account of his life written for a popular magazine. They sat down at the big oaken table and began to read together. The account was straightforward enough; he claimed he was born in a village near James Bay and came down to the north shore of Lake Superior when he was a boy. There was no doubt he had lived in a village called The Mission, at the mouth of the Michipicotten River, for half-breed families there remembered him. He still went back to that Algoman hill country. Most of the Indians on the north shore were Ojibwas, and he spoke their language.

"That all ties in," Sam said eagerly. "He showed up in that north country when he was a boy; after he was a kid around here."

Then he picked up a Snow Bird book about the pursuit of deer by a wolf. "Come on, Sam. Let's go," Tom said.

"Imagine a kid from around here writing stuff like this, and having such a life, a philosopher, too," Sam said in a melancholy tone. "I remember when Hal and I used to sit at the end of the dock talking about the kind of lives we were going to lead when we grew up. Yeah, and we always went up to the park together to watch the ball games." He smiled a little. "There was a pitcher around here named Loppy Phelan. We made him our hero. We used to talk about him all the time. I wander if Hal ever thinks about Loppy now?"

"Who knows?"

"Hal always knew what he wanted," Sam said, tapping the book, "and it looks as if he headed right for it." A faraway look came into his eyes. "I had crazy dreams, too. I used to talk to him about going to Brazil or Mexico. Well, here I am, stuck here."

Tom walked as far as the store with Sam, and then he left and began to make inquiries about the Bryant family and a boy named Hal McGibbney. Then he wrote the story, and it appeared next day in the local paper. It was a clever story with pictures of Sam and Snow Bird and an account of the days when the two boys used to follow the fortunes of the ballteam and celebrate Loppy Phelan's greatness as a pitcher. "I wonder if Snow Bird ever thinks of Loppy Phelan now," was the heading for the story, which delighted the town when it appeared. It was picked up by the news services and reprinted all over the continent.

"I don't like all this, Tom. In fact, I wish I hadn't shot my mouth off to you," Sam said when Tom Stevens came into his store three days later. "I've got nothing but admiration for what Hal McGibbney has done with his life."

"Take it easy," Tom said. "I thought you'd like to have a look at these clippings." In New York, Snow Bird's publisher had issued a statement, dismissing Sam Crowther as an obvious exhibitionist seeking local notoriety. Snow Bird's statement was briefer. "I was never in Collingwood," he said. "I never played baseball. I never heard of this man, Sam Crowther."

"What else can the man say?" Sam asked. "He can't say now that I told the truth." But his pride was hurt. "I mean, he might have said I was only mistaken."

His neighbors agreed. "Sam's no liar," they insisted when they read what Snow Bird had said. "If he made a mistake he'll admit it later on. Nobody should laugh at him." But when they came to the store they smiled indulgently. This sympathetic respect exasperated him. His wife's fear of what would happen disgusted him. "You'll get us into terrible trouble," she cried, wringing her hands, her moist and startled blue eyes shining with anger. All her life she had been uneasy about anything that might cause gossip about her. "You'll have us dragged into court, and we'll lose everything."

A week later, an attractive young woman in a brown gabardine suit came into Sam's store at three in the afternoon and said she was Miss James from the *Montreal Star.*

"I'm sorry, Miss James," Sam said gruffly. "I'm through making a fool of myself in the newspaper."

"But you told the truth, didn't you, Mr. Crowther?"

"Of course I did."

"After checking around here, that's the way I figure it," Miss James said. She had a casual manner. "You've got a fine reputation, Mr. Crowther. So we're convinced Snow Bird is a phony."

"Just a minute," Sam said sharply. "The man who wrote the beautiful stuff he wrote is no phony."

"So he's a real Indian?"

"No. Like I said, he's Hal McGibbney."

"Snow Bird," she said, smiling, "is in Montreal next Saturday night."

"Yeah," Sam said.

"Why not come to Montreal, Mr. Crowther? My paper will pay your expenses. It's in the public interest."

"Yeah," Sam said, confused. He felt he had cheapened himself, yet he had a wondering admiration for the man he believed he had known as a boy.

"Look here," he began carefully, "you have to agree to get him off to one side and not say anything more than, 'Mr. Crowther believes he knew you a few years ago.'"

"Okay, swell," Miss James said. "I'll get the tickets."

She fled because Sam's wife, who had been listening, suddenly rushed in, crying, "What kind of a fool are you?"

Sam knew she would never understand or care that he

had dreamed of a different kind of life. "I am going to Montreal, Lou. That's settled," he said quietly.

Sam wore his good blue serge suit. It was a pleasant trip. Miss James was an amusing girl. After cocktails and dinner at the hotel, they took a taxi to the building where Snow Bird was lecturing, and when Snow Bird came on to the stage, Sam put on his glasses and leaned forward, trembling. Snow Bird, thin and frail and suffering from tuberculosis, was wearing a white dinner jacket and braided hair with a single feather. He had a grave, unaffected dignity.

He talked of a journey he had made in the winter to the country around James Bay and a battle he had witnessed between a lynx and a bear in the twilight.

"I'm not fooled by the look of him," Sam thought stubbornly as he leaned forward, trying to see something that would remind him surely of the boy he had known. But gradually he forgot where he was and his resentment disappeared and his feeling of admiration seemed to come out of a pride in his own youth. When Snow Bird finished and the applause died down and some went to the platform to have Snow Bird autograph books, Miss James said, "Come on, Mr. Crowther, we'll speak to him."

"Please remember, Miss James," Sam said while they were waiting, "we'll just mention my name. We'll leave it up to him. If he says I'm mistaken, all right. I think he'll want to have a talk with me."

Then Snow Bird came toward them. "Snow Bird," Miss James said, trying not to sound too eager. "I'm from the *Montreal Star*. This is Sam Crowther, a friend of yours, I believe."

"Really," Snow Bird said gravely. He looked at Sam, and the muscles around his narrow eyes twitched. He looked steadily at Sam for a long time and then he smiled with an unassailable dignity. "I don't know Mr. Crowther," he said.

"He's from Collingwood," Miss James said quickly. Snow Bird's unruffled dignity had upset her; she felt like a flustered young girl being brushed aside. She forgot her promise to Sam: "Mr. Crowther was sure you had been boys together, played baseball, and that you both used to talk a lot about a great pitcher named Loppy Phelan."

"Does he think so?" Snow Bird asked.

"Maybe I was mistaken," Sam said quickly, searching for some little flicker of recognition. "It's easy to make a mistake," Sam said, nodding. "I thought if we could have a little talk . . . ."

People were edging closer, trying to hear every word, including the black-haired boy in the expensive suit who was Snow Bird's son. "Yes, we know about you, Mr. Crowther," he whispered bitterly. "I know you're out to destroy my father. You are just a cheap liar."

"Wait a minute, son," Sam began, but the hatred in the boy's eyes made him feel soiled and ashamed. He turned to Miss James, who was watching, bright-eyed, and then he abruptly fled from the hall and along the street and down the hill to his hotel, where he packed his bag and caught the night train for home.

But the story of his furtive flight was written faithfully by Miss James. In time, it appeared in the town paper, and Sam's wife cried when she read it. "Oh, you fool, Sam," she moaned. "They'll never ask you to run for mayor again around here. Now we're the laughingstock of the town."

Grabbing his hat, he hurried along the main street to the town paper, and he tried to explain it all to Tom Stevens. "It was the boy that upset me," he began. "He had such faith in his father."

When he saw that Tom hardly believed him, his heart

29

filled with bitterness. "Look, Tom. Print this, have it printed all over the world. The man is a phony. A first-rate phony."

He said this again and again to customers who came to his store. At first they listened, but then he became a bore. When he saw that he had lost all dignity, he suddenly stopped talking about Snow Bird. He hid his bitterness but nursed it in his heart. He began to read the New York papers, particularly the book sections. All that autumn and on through the winter, as if he were pursuing the man, when he came across an item about Snow Bird he cut it out and pasted it in a scrapbook he kept in a locked trunk in his cellar.

In the spring, Snow Bird's New York publishers wrote Sam a dignified letter in which they pointed out that his story, told and retold by malicious gossips, had gravely damaged not only a man's reputation but a very valuable publishing property. They had made inquiries about him and were convinced he was a reputable and esteemed citizen in his community, unlike Snow Bird's former wife, who was simply a grasping, disgruntled, vindictive woman. As an honorable citizen would he not, therefore, be generous enough to state formally that he had made a mistake, and in that way undo some of the damage done to a man who had never harmed him?

Smiling to himself, Sam wrote to the publisher, saying that his own reputation had been gravely damaged in his own home town.

Then, in the early summer, Snow Bird collapsed on Madison Avenue in New York, and his picture was in the paper. They said he did not have the temperament of a man who could stand the long confinement of sanatorium treatment for tuberculosis. Sam Crowther read about it in his store in Collingwood with a strange mixture of sadness, excitement, and a feeling that he was being cheated.

A week later, Sam got another letter from the New York publisher. Snow Bird was dying of tubercular pneumonia, the publisher wrote. His nurse had reported that several times during the night fever, he had mumbled the name, "Sam Crowther." The publisher pointed out that the unhappy question of Snow Bird's identity had been revived, and that they believed he wanted to clear his name for the sake of his son, John Snow Bird. Would Mr. Crowther be good enough to come to New York at their expense? . . .

Sam arrived in New York on a Friday morning when it was raining and was met by Mr. Gilbey, a gray, polite man. "We might as well go right to the hospital," he said. "The poor fellow. It's only a matter of days. Maybe hours."

In the taxi, the publisher was fascinated by the grim, stubborn expression on Sam's face, and he began to feel unhappy as they entered the hospital and went along the corridor to Snow Bird's room. A nurse at the door whispered, "We've given him a sedative that eases the cough, Mr. Gilbey. He may fall into a sleep."

Before he had a chance to look at Snow Bird on the bed, Sam saw the black-haired boy get up from a chair by the window.

"Mr. Crowther, I believe you've met Snow Bird's son," the publisher said gently.

"Yes," Sam said, turning away.

"Snow Bird," the publisher called as they moved closer to the bed. "Snow Bird, this is Sam Crowther. We thought you wanted to see him."

"Sam Crowther," Snow Bird repeated in a hoarse whisper. There was the flicker of a smile at the corner of his mouth. "Sam Crowther," he whispered again. Then, with that name on his lips he seemed to drift away to the edge of sleep or dreaming recollection. Sam, shaken, wanted to cry out and compel his recognition. The boy, standing tensely at the foot of the bed, suddenly cried, "Why did you come down on us? Why did you want to persecute us, Mr. Crowther?"

"What?" Sam asked. He saw Snow Bird open his eyes, watching the boy anxiously. "No matter what you say," the boy whispered, "there are things you can't take away from us. My father has the Indian blood. I know he has it. Isn't that right, Dad?"

Snow Bird, his eyes on Sam, whispered so faintly that his words were a blur of sound, "Yes — and Loppy Phelan had the double shoot."

"I couldn't quite make that out," the publisher said. "I heard, 'yes,' but what was the rest?"

"He said 'yes' Mr. Crowther, and you heard him," the boy insisted.

"Yes," Sam agreed. But he was shocked. He saw young Hal McGibbney sitting on the stumps of the dock that evening many years ago, talking about their pitcher, Loppy Phelan, and he heard himself say: "Hal, maybe he didn't really have that double shoot!" Sam turned to the boy as if he were going to explain, but he could not. He rubbed the back of his neck slowly with his right hand. Then he went closer to the bed, to the man who called himself Snow Bird, whose eyes were now closed.

"Mr. Crowther," the publisher said hesitantly, "so little was said — I mean, can you be satisfied in your own mind?"

"Yes, I'm satisfied," Sam said simply. But then the sudden pain of regret about the way his own life had gone bewildered him. Sam shook his head and hurried out of the room, nursing his terrible loneliness.

The Chiseller

OLD POPPA TABB WAS NEVER REALLY CUT OUT TO BE A manager for a fighter. He seemed too short and too fat, although he'd only gotten soft around the waist during the last year as Billy got a lot of work in the small clubs fighting at the flyweight limit. If it hadn't been for his old man, Billy would have been a chesty little bum standing at night on street corners spitting after cops when they passed. The old man and Billy were both the same size – five foot two in their bare feet – only the old man weighed one hundred and thirty-five pounds and Billy one hundred and twelve.

Poppa Tabb had always wanted his son to amount to something and didn't like the stories he heard about his son being chased by policemen. It hurt him when Billy was sent down for three months for tripping a cop and putting the boots to him. So he thought his son might want to be a fighter and he made an arrangement with a man named Smooth Cassidy, who was very experienced with young fighters, to act as Billy's trainer and handler, and he himself held the contract as the manager. After Billy started fighting in the small clubs, Poppa Tabb bought two white sweaters with "Billy Tabb" on the back in black letters, one for himself and one for Smooth Cassidy. It was at this time that

33

Poppa Tabb began to get a little fat around the waist. He used to sit over in the sunlight by the door of the fire hall and tell the firemen about Billy. He used to sit there and talk about "me and Billy," and have a warm glowing feeling down deep inside.

Late at night he used to wait for Billy to come home from drinking parties with fast white women. He waited, walking up and down the narrow hall of their flat, and he shook his head and imagined that Billy had gotten into an accident. When Billy came in and started to take off his shoes, Poppa Tabb, sitting opposite him, was so worried he said: "I don't want you strolling your stuff so late, Billy."

Billy looked at him. Standing up and coming closer, he said to his old man: "You tryin' to get on me?"

"No, only I know what's good for you, son."

"Yeah. Maybe I know what's good for me. Maybe I know you ain't so good for me."

"There some things you got to do, Billy."

Billy raised his fist. "You want something? You want some of this?"

"You don't be hitting me, Billy."

"Say you want some and I smack you. Or get off me."

After that, when Billy came in late Poppa Tabb just looked at his bright sharp eyes and smelled the cologne on his clothes and couldn't say anything to him. He only wished that Billy would tell him everything. He wanted to share the exciting times of his life and have the same feeling, talking to him, that he got when he held up the water pail and handed the sponge to Smooth Cassidy when he was ringside.

Billy did so well in the small clubs that bigger pro-moters offered him work. But they always talked business with Smooth Cassidy, and Poppa Tabb felt they were trying to leave him out. Just before Billy fought Frankie Genaro, the flyweight champion, who was willing to fight almost anyone in our town because the purses for flyweights were so small, Poppa Tabb heard stories that Dick Hallam, who liked owning pieces of fighters, was getting interested in Billy and taking him out to parties. At nights now Billy hardly ever talked to his old man, but still expected him to wait on him like a servant.

Old man Poppa Tabb was thinking about it the afternoon of the Genaro fight and he was so worried he went downtown looking for Billy, asking the newsboys at the corner, old friends of Billy's, if they had seen him. In the afternoon, Billy usually passed by the newsstand and talked with the boys till smaller kids came along and whispered, staring at him. Poppa Tabb found Billy in a diner looking to see if his name had gotten into the papers, thrusting big forkfuls of chocolate cake into his wide mouth. The old man looked at him and wanted to rebuke him for eating the chocolate cake but was afraid, so he said: "What's happening Billy?"

"Uh," Billy said.

The old man said carefully: "I don't like this here talk about you stepping around too much with that Hallam guy."

"You don't?" Billy said, pushing his fine brown felt hat back on his narrow brow and wrinkling his forehead.

"What you going do 'bout it?"

"Well, nothing, I guess, Billy."

"You damn right," Billy said flatly. Without looking up again he went on eating cake and reading the papers intently as if his old man hadn't spoken to him at all.

The Genaro fight was an extraordinary success for Billy. Of course, he didn't win. Genaro, who was in his late thirties, went into a kind of short waltz and then clutched and held on when he was tired, and when he was fresh and strong he used a swift pecking left hand that cut the eyes. But Billy liked a man to come in close and hold on, for he put his head on Genaro's chest and flailed with both hands, and no one could hold his arms. Once he got in close, his arms worked with a beautiful tireless precision, and the crowd, liking a great body-puncher, began to roar, and Old Poppa Tabb put his head down and jumped around, and then he looked up at Billy, whose eye was cut and whose lips were thick and swollen. It didn't matter whether he won the flyweight title, for soon he would be a bantamweight and then a featherweight, the way he was growing.

Everybody was shouting when Billy left the ring, holding his bandaged hands up high over his head, and he rushed up the aisle to the dressing-room, the crowd still roaring as he passed through the seats and the people who tried to touch him with their hands. His gown had fallen off his shoulders. His seconds were running on ahead shouting: "Out of the way! Out of the way!" and Billy, his face puffed, his brown body glistening under the lights, followed, looking straight ahead, his wild eyes bulging. The crowd closed in behind him at the door of the dressing-room.

Poppa Tabb had a hard time getting through the crowd for he couldn't go up the aisle as fast as Billy and the seconds. He was holding his cap tightly in his hands. He had put on a coat over his white "Billy Tabb" sweater. His thin hair was wet as he lurched forward. The neckband of his shirt stuck up from under the sweater and a yellow collar-button shone in the lamplight. "Let me in, let me in," he kept saying, almost hysterical with excitement. "It's my kid, that's my kid." The policeman at the door, who recognized him, said: "Come on in, Pop."

Billy Tabb was stretched out on the rubbing-table and his handlers were gently working over him. The room smelled of liniment. Everybody was talking. Smooth Cassidy was sitting at the end of the table, whispering with Dick Hallam, a tall thin man wearing well-pressed trousers. Old Poppa Tabb stood there blinking and then moved closer to Billy. He didn't like Hallam's gold rings and his pearl-gray felt hat and his sharp nose. Old Poppa Tabb was afraid of Hallam and stood fingering the yellow collar-button.

"What's happening Pop?" Hallam said, smiling expansively.

"Nothing," Pop said, hunching his shoulders and wishing Billy would look at him. They were working on Billy's back muscles and his face was flat against the board. His back rose and fell as he breathed deeply.

"Have a cigar, Pop!" Hallam said.

"No thanks."

"No? My man, I got some good news for you," he said, flicking the end of his nose with his forefinger.

"You got no good news for me," Poppa Tabb said, still wishing Billy would look up at him.

"Sure I do. Billy gonna be big in a few months and I'm gonna take his contract over – most of it, anyway – and have Cassidy look after him. So he won't be needing you no more."

"What you say?" Old Poppa Tabb said to Cassidy.

"It's entirely up to you, Poppa Tabb," Cassidy said, looking down at the floor.

"Yes sir, Billy made good tonight and I'm going to take a piece of him," Hallam said, glancing down at the shiny toes of his shoes. "The boy'll get on when I start looking after him. I'll get stuff for him you couldn't touch. He needs my influence. A guy like you can't expect to go on taking a big cut on Billy."

"So you going to butt in?" Old Poppa Tabb said.

"Me butt in? That's ripe, seeing you never did nothing but butt in on Billy."

"I'm sticking with Billy," Poppa Tabb said. "You ain't taking no piece of him."

"Shut your face," Billy said, looking up suddenly.

"Shut your face is right," Hallam said. "You're through buttin' in."

"You don't fool me none Hallam. You just after a cut on Billy."

"You just another old guy trying to chisel on his son," Hallam said scornfully.

Billy was sitting up listening, his hands held loosely in his lap. The room was hot and smelled of sweat. Old Poppa Tabb, turning, went to put his hand on Billy's shoulder. "Tell him to beat it, Billy," he said.

"Keep your hands off. You know you been butting in all my life."

"Sure I have, Billy. I been there 'cause I'm your pop, Billy. You know how it's always been with me. I don't take nothing from you. I don't take a red cent. I just stick with you, Billy. See? We been big together."

"You never went so big with me," Billy said.

"Ain't nothing bigger with me than you, Billy. Tell this hustler to run." Again, he tried to put his hand on Billy's shoulder.

"You insult my friend, you got no call," Billy said. He swung a short right to his father's chin. Old Poppa Tabb sat down on the floor. He was ready to cry but kept on looking at Billy, who was glaring at him.

"Goddam, he be your old man. Don't hit him again," Hallam said.

"He can get out. I be done with him."

"Sure you are. He'll get out."

They watched Smooth Cassidy help Old Poppa Tabb get up. "What you going to do about this?" Smooth Cassidy was muttering to him. "You ought to be able to do something, Poppa."

Old Poppa Tabb shook his head awkwardly. "No, there's nothing, Smooth."

"But he your boy, and it's up to you."

"Nothing's up to me."

"It all right with you, Poppa, then it all right with me," Cassidy said, stepping back.

Old Poppa Tabb, standing there, seemed to be waiting for something. His jaw began to fall open. He did not move.

"Well, that be that," Hallam said. He took a cigar out of his pocket, looked at it and suddenly thrust it into Old Poppa Tabb's open mouth. "Have a cigar," he said.

Poppa Tabb's teeth closed down on the cigar. It was sticking straight out of his mouth as he went out, without looking back. The crowd had gone and the big building was empty. It was dark down by the ring. He didn't look at anything. The unlighted cigar stuck out of his mouth as he went out the big door to the street.

The Fugitive

AT MIDNIGHT WALLACE WAS IN HIS ROOM IN MRS. Cosentino's house on Walmer Road making himself a cup of coffee when he heard a soft furtive knock on the door. He was startled because he hadn't heard anyone on the stairs. When he opened the door, Anderson came in and closed the door quickly and stood there with his winter coat collar turned up high around his ears, smiling with relief. "Quite a climb up those stairs," he said.

He leaned against the door getting his breath a moment, and then, as his big brown eyes shifted quickly all around the room, he stood lightly on the balls of his feet as if he were apt to disappear as quickly as he had come. But when he saw that Wallace was glad to see him, he grinned warmly and took off his hat. His hair had gone far back on his forehead and was white at the temples.

"Where did you come from, Anderson? I'm terribly glad to see you," Wallace said. He had known Anderson five years ago in Montreal when he was working at commercial art there and Anderson had been in a stock-broker's office.

"I've been around here a little while," Anderson said.

"Have you got a place to stay?"

"No."

"Why don't you stay here with me? I can speak to Mrs. Cosentino."

"Are you sure you want me?"

"Why, I've never been so glad to see anybody," Wallace said, slapping him on the back enthusiastically and hardly noticing his shabby clothes, his peculiar pallor or his nervous movements.

"I thought you'd be glad to see me," he said, and he grinned as he looked around the room, and then he went over to the couch and lay down with his hands behind his head and sighed contentedly.

They had a cup of coffee and Anderson talked about people they used to know and about his rich uncle in Georgia, and Wallace noticed that he talked about them as if they belonged to a time he hardly remembered. He said he was trying to sell insurance now. That started him laughing and he kept it up till he began to cough. Even when they went to bed and turned out the light he kept chuckling away to himself, explaining he had no luck at all. Wallace, who couldn't sleep listening to the man snickering at his own failure, began to realize that Anderson had probably been in town far longer than he had himself; he got the idea Anderson had been following him around. It was so disturbing he got up and turned on the light and went over to the couch and said: "Tell me something. How did you know I was here, Anderson?"

"I saw you on the street tonight and I tried to catch up with you," he said, looking up innocently at Wallace. I thought you might want us to stay together. Was I right?"

"Yeah. You were right," Wallace said, and he went back to bed and couldn't sleep.

Anderson agreed to pay Mrs. Cosentino, the plump

little Italian who ran the house, more money per week, and she put another bed in the room and bit by bit he became a part of Wallace's life. He followed Wallace around everywhere, grinning happily to himself. Times were bad and getting worse but, as things picked up for Wallace, and he got a little more work from the advertising agencies, he made more friends, among them a radio script writer named Higgins who lived in the next block, and a shrewd blonde named Anna Grant, and late at night he used to go over to Higgins's place and have a glass of beer with him and listen to the radio, and on Saturdays he used to go to Anna Grant's for a cocktail. A couple of times Anderson asked if he could come along. After that, as though it had all been arranged, Anderson began to drop into Higgins's place by himself; he went to Anna Grant's place by himself, too, and if he didn't find Wallace there he chuckled good-humoredly and explained he'd sit around and wait for him.

It got so that Wallace sometimes couldn't stand the sight of him. He wanted to get rid of him. He forgot that only two years ago he had been back on his heels himself. If the man had been trying to work it would have been different, but he had no expectation of ever selling a policy. He was only running around the streets with his hands in his pockets and his head down. If he did sell a trifling bit of fire insurance, the whole thing seemed to become a crazy joke. He rushed out and bought a bottle of local wine and came tip-toeing up the stairs with that provoking snicker of his and his big brown eyes bright with surprise, and he sat down and took off his shoes and stockings, and walked around the floor in his bare feet. Maybe his shoes hurt him, but it was upsetting to watch him padding around the room like that on a cold night, looking for a glass. But he soon made himself comfortable on his couch and grinned and sipped the heavy, sweet wine and kept squenching his cigaret butts on the nearest piece of furniture.

"In God's name, man, have some respect for the furniture," Wallace shouted at him one night,

"It's just a habit," he said. "I'm terribly sorry."

"It's a lousy habit. You got too many of them."

"I know it. You're not going to bawl me out, are you?" he asked, looking very scared. "You don't need to bawl me out."

"No, I'm not bawling you out. What's the matter with you? You give me the jitters."

He put his glass down and said: "I think things are going to get a lot better. I've been talking to people. Just wait till the spring. I got about ten great prospects. They're coming in a bunch." Listening to him, one would have actually believed he expected to make a lot of money very quickly and was full of hope. Every time he felt he was apt to be thrown out he burst into this glow of false enthusiasm; it was just a piece of stupid, bad acting.

"Are you trying to dodge anybody?" Wallace asked him one day.

"Me? What made you think of that?" he said, startled. "Nobody's looking for me. You're pretty funny, aren't you?"

"It's the way you go around, I guess."

"Maybe I'm used to it that way now," he said, apologetically. "You get used to doing this in a certain way. Haven't you noticed it?" he asked eagerly as if an intimacy that came from sharing a bewildering secret had been established between them.

Wallace had met a few girls and he used to go out to a show with one and to a restaurant afterwards when he had a little money, yet no matter how happy he felt with the girl

43

he knew that when he got home he would feel worried and unhappy because Anderson would be lying there on his couch rolled up in a blanket, wide awake, a bottle of his wretched local wine at the foot of the bed, waiting for him.

"How did it go?" he would say, sitting up.

"How did what go?" Wallace shouted.

"How did it go with the girl?" he said, as if that had been all he had been thinking about.

"Listen, Anderson, why don't you get yourself a girl?"

"I'll do it as soon as I get a couple of dollars," he said apologetically, pulling the blankets up over his head as if he was never really warm.

Though Anderson hadn't paid Mrs. Cosentino any room rent since he'd come, he couldn't have been more cheerful about it. He simply changed his hours, and it was always one o'clock in the morning when he came tip-toeing up the stairs, and he was out at six in the morning before Mrs. Cosentino got up. She never had a chance to abuse him. He liked having a little laugh out of this game he played with her.

But Mrs. Cosentino said to Wallace one day, "You know, I'm getting no rent from that no-good friend of yours."

"Friend of mine! Don't be silly," he said.

"No friend of yours?" she said, surprised.

He was ashamed and said quickly, "I mean we had a little quarrel. Certainly he's a friend. The truth is he gives me the extra money to give you on account. Here it is." He felt he had betrayed Anderson and it suddenly struck him that Anderson was there in his life to remind him that up until the one year he'd gone broke he had been arrogant and contemptuous of many good and simple things, and could easily become just as impatient and arrogant again.

One day his friend Anna Grant got angry and said,

"You're welcome here at our place, we like you, but hasn't that terrible man Anderson any life of his own?"

"I don't know," Wallace said. "I'll ask him."

"Tell him to stop hanging around here or I will, and if I tell him he'll know I mean it," she said.

That night Wallace waited for Anderson and said, "This is a bit complicated, but I'd like to ask you what happened to your life."

"What life do you mean?" he asked uneasily.

"The life you must have had before you went broke, the people you knew, the fun you must have had, the things you must have wanted to do when you were a kid – that life," Wallace said, impatiently.

Anderson lay on the couch, rubbing his head, and then said almost to himself, "I guess I lost it somewhere." His eyes were furtive as he waited to see how Wallace would take his answer. When he saw that he had only puzzled him, he grinned and got a bag of buns he had brought in from the corner store and sat down to eat the whole half-dozen buns as though he were starving.

"It was pretty dull over at Anna's place this afternoon, didn't you notice?" Wallace began, rather tactfully.

"Dull? What's the matter with you? What do you want?" he said, chuckling over his buns.

"That crowd gets on each other's nerves. They hate each other. Didn't you notice the sour expression on Anna's face?"

"That's right, I did notice it and couldn't figure what in hell was the matter with her. I figure she had a quarrel with her boy friend."

Wallace tried again, "Aw, this is a lousy town," he said. "I'm fed up with it. I think I'll clear out and go back to Montreal."

"Clear out of here?" he said, taking the bun out of his

mouth, he was so surprised. "I think you're crazy. I'm just getting to like it here," and he whistled as he went out to their little kitchen in his bare feet with the light shining on his toes.

He looked dreadfully thin, yet he seemed to be doing nothing but eat and lie around the room wrapped up in his blanket. Wallace often kept a fresh loaf of special rye bread in the place, and he liked having it, particularly on Sunday mornings when he got up late and made some toast and coffee. He noticed one morning that the bread was half gone.

"Where did the bread go?" he shouted at Anderson.

"Don't ask me," Anderson said, and Wallace knew by the frightened look on his face that he was lying.

It was very hard to catch him at first, but he seemed to grow more reckless and great chunks of the bread would disappear. One cold Sunday morning there was no loaf at all for Wallace when he got up, and he rushed at Anderson, who was sleeping on the couch and shouted at him, "Wake up you bum, wake up," and he shook him and watched his thin face rocking from side to side on the pillow. He hated him while he shook him.

"What's the matter?" Anderson said, rubbing his head.

"You took my bread again. You took it all last night and you knew I'd want it Sunday morning."

"I took a little piece."

"You took the whole loaf, crammed it into you like a pig."

"I was a little hungry last night."

"You're always hungry. You're sitting around here like a wolf all the time. That's all you do, wolf everything up and lie about it. I'm fed up with your living on me. You've wormed your way into my life."

Without looking at Wallace, Anderson got up and

walked along the hall to the bathroom in his bare feet, scared like a rabbit that has been smoked out of a hole, and when he returned he said: "Do you think maybe I'd better go?"

"What do you think?" said Wallace, bitterly.

"I think I'd better," he said, quietly, and since he had no packing to do, no bag to carry, he simply put on his coat and hat and made no noise going down the stairs.

Wallace sat there hating him, hating him not just for the loaf of bread, which was nothing, but for grafting himself onto his life and bringing him one humiliation after another. But the thought of parting with him over a loaf of bread began to fill him with such shame he got dressed and rushed out looking for him. He went over to Higgins's place, he went to Anna Grant's, but no one remembered having seen him. He began to hate himself. He got into a panic remembering the time three years ago when he himself had been light-headed from hunger, and he looked in the taverns thinking all the time of Anderson sitting alone somewhere trying to get warm and coughing, or flitting by people so quickly they didn't notice him. That night he sat up for hours longing for him to come sneaking up the stairs and forgive him.

It was two weeks before he heard that soft, furtive knock on the door, but he was waiting and he jumped out of bed and yelled out, overjoyed, "Anderson, Anderson, old pal, come on in." Wallace was filled with such gratitude to him for coming back that he couldn't speak. The sight of Anderson standing at the door with a shy, pleased smile on his face made him terribly happy. "Don't stand there, come in," he cried.

"I thought you'd be glad," Anderson said as he sat down on the couch and took a deep breath and looked around the room.

"Oh, you knew I'd be, and you were good to come. It was a generous thing to do."

"I was sure you'd be glad by this time," he said innocently, as he began to pull off his shoes.

"Don't remind me of it, please. I was ashamed."

"I waited," he said, smiling.

"Please don't go on like that," Wallace said. Then he saw that Anderson was flushed and trembling. He rushed and got him his blanket, and when he saw him pulling it up around his ears, leaving those terrible bare feet of his sticking out at the end, he knew he was sick and he whispered, "What's the matter with you?"

"It's a pain in my back, maybe my lung," he said. "I had pleurisy a couple of years ago."

"I'll get a doctor, we'll fix you up."

"I don't think so," he said. "For God's sake don't go phoning a doctor this late at night."

"Why?"

"He might get sore."

"Let him get sore. To hell with him."

"No, listen, Wallace, I wanted to tell you you were right."

"What about?"

"The bread."

"Please, please don't mention that now. You wouldn't be sick if it weren't for that bread."

"Yes, I would. Thanks. Look, don't tell anyone about the bread, will you, promise?"

Wallace promised and sat at the foot of the couch sharing that old peculiar intimate secret with Anderson who was breathing very heavily. When his eyes were closed, he had a very peaceful smile on his face.

Doctors came who wanted to take Anderson to the

hospital, but he begged Wallace to let him stay there with him. The doctors shrugged and let him stay. In a week's time he was dying of pneumonia. Wallace, watching him a few minutes before he lost consciousness, saw that furtive little smile hovering around his thick lips. Bending down to him he whispered, "Anderson, old boy, I'm here with you."

"I knew you'd be," he replied. His eyes, as he opened them and rolled them around, looked very soft and brown. He tried to take Wallace by the hand. "I want to thank you for the hideout," he said.

"It's your place. You weren't hiding here."

"I don't mind going now," he said, and he closed his eyes, smiled a little, and while he smiled like that Wallace knew Anderson was more deeply imbedded in his own life than he had ever been. He died that night.

Mrs. Cosentino was very angry at him for dying in her place and they got him to an undertaker's parlor as quickly as possible. The funeral was just as private and furtive a gesture as any Anderson had ever made. Wallace was the only one who went to the funeral. It was zero weather and there was a little snow in the wind. The undertaker's assistants looked ridiculous in their wing collars as they shivered, and when they were lowering the casket one of them said, "I think we may dispense with the ceremony of taking our hats off under these difficult conditions."

The Sentimentalists

It was at the scarf counter at noontime that Jack Malone the young law student saw the yellow scarf on the rack and thought he might give it to his girl for her birthday. His plump friend, Fred Webster, bored with wandering around from counter to counter in the department store, had just said, "Sure she'll like it. Take it," when a gray-haired woman in a blue sailor hat came gliding round the corner and bumped into Malone.

"Excuse me, lady," he said, but she was in his way, idly toying with the yellow scarf. "Excuse me, madam," he said firmly. Moving a step away, she said impatiently, "Excuse me," and went on fussing with the scarves without actually looking at them, and when the salesgirl approached she didn't look up. Reddening, the salesgirl retreated quickly, leaving her there peering through the screen of scarves at the silk-stocking counter in the next aisle.

"Why get sore? She's the store detective. You got in her way," Webster said.

"Why shouldn't I? I don't work for her."

"It's someone at the silk-stocking counter," Webster said, brightening. "Let's watch."

Because they were having a sale, silk stockings were

out loose on the counter and sometimes there was a line of women and sometimes the line thinned out.

"If you were a betting man, who would you say it was?" Webster asked. He knew Malone was proud of his judgment of people and of the experience he got from talking to crooks of all kinds in the law office and in the police court. "I'll bet you five bucks," Webster said. "Go ahead, look over the field."

"It's too easy," Malone said. All he had to do was watch the detective behind the scarves and follow the direction of her eyes, watching three women at the end of the silk-stocking counter who had been standing there longer than the others. It was hard to get more than a glimpse of their faces, but one was a stout woman with a silver-fox fur and a dark, heavy, aggressive, and arrogant face. She looked very shrewd and competent. Her lips were heavy and greedy. If she were going to steal anything it would probably be something very valuable, and she wouldn't give it up easily. On the left of her was a lanky schoolgirl with no shape at all, a brainless-looking kid. And there was a young girl in a red felt hat and a fawn-colored loose spring coat.

All the women at the counter seemed to be sliding stockings over the backs of their hands and holding them up to the light. Getting a little closer, his excitement quickening, Malone tried to see into their faces and into their lives, and the first one he counted out was the girl in the fawn coat: she seemed like someone he had met on a train, or someone he had known all his life without ever knowing her name. In a hundred places they might have seen each other, at summer dances or on the streets where he had played when he was a kid. But while he was watching her and feeling sure of her, the schoolgirl sighed and dropped the stocking she was looking at and walked away.

"That leaves only the two," Webster whispered, coming alongside. His plump good-natured face was disturbed, as if he, too, had decided the stout woman was far too sensible looking to be a store thief, and his estimate of the girl in the fawn coat with the dark hair and the brown eyes was the same as Malone's. "I was thinking it would be the school kid doing something crazy," he whispered.

"So was I."

While they stood together, suddenly disturbed, the stout woman made a purchase and walked away slowly, opening her purse. They both turned, watching the bright-colored bank of scarves, and Malone suddenly longed to see the blue sailor hat go gliding behind the scarves, following the stout woman. But the detective was still there, waiting. You could see the motionless rim of her hat.

"Well, it's the girl in the fawn coat she's watching," Webster said.

"And what do you think?"

"I think the detective's crazy."

"Yet she's the one the woman's watching."

"Listen, I'll bet you that five bucks old eagle eye hiding over there is absolutely wrong about her."

"Not on your life. That's no bet. That kid's no thief," Malone said.

It wasn't just that the girl was pretty. But in the slow way she turned her head, swinging the dark hair over her raised collar, in the light of intelligence that shone in her dark eyes when she looked up quickly, and in the warmth that would surely come easily in her face, Malone was reminded that she might be someone like his own sister. Her clothes were not expensive: the fawn coat looked as if it had been worn at least three seasons. But his sister had looked like that the time they were all scrimping and saving to send her to college. Suddenly, Malone and Webster were joined, betting against the judgment of the store detective. They wanted to root for the girl, root her away from the counter. With a passionate eagerness to see the woman detective frustrated, Malone muttered in her direction, "Lady, you're picking on the wrong party. Just stick around a while and watch her walk away."

But the store detective's blue sailor hat was moving slowly, coming around, closing in. Yet the girl stood motionless. A stocking was in her hand, or her hand was on the counter, and her absent-minded stillness, her lowered head – it became apparent – were a furtive awareness of the position of the salesgirl. Malone went to speak to Webster, and then he couldn't: they were both unbelieving and hurt. Yet there still was a chance. It became a desperate necessity that he should be right about the girl. "Go away, kid," he was begging her. "Why do you stand there looking like that? You're no thief. You're a kid. Get moving, why don't you?" But she bent her head, she hunched up her shoulders a little, and her hand on the counter was drawing a pair of silk stockings into the wide sleeve of her coat. As the store detective came slowly around the end of the scarf counter, Webster said, disgusted, "Just another little store thief."

Malone wanted to slap the girl and abuse her. It wasn't just that she had let him down, she seemed to have betrayed so many things that belonged to the most intimate and warmest part of his life. "Let her arrest her, what do we care?" he said as the store detective went slowly down the aisle. But in spite of himself he thought he would cry out if he stood there. He got excited. He walked along the aisle alone, taking out his watch as if he had been waiting a long time for someone. When he was opposite the girl he stopped, staring at her back, at the bunch of black curls under the rim of her hat, and he was sick and hesitant and bewildered. "Why, Helen," he said, reaching out and touching her, "have you been here all this time?" A wide, forced smile was on his face.

"Smile, please smile," he whispered, because he could see the store detective watching them. "Come away," he begged her. "They're watching you."

Before the scared smile came on her face, the silk stockings rolled in a ball in her palm and half up her sleeve were dropped almost naturally on the counter. She made it look like a careless gesture. "Hello," she said, "I was . . ." then her voice was lost. If he had not moved she would have stood gaping and incredulous, but he was scared for himself now, for he might be arrested as an accomplice, and he linked his arm under hers and started to walk down the aisle to the door.

They had to pass the store detective, and maybe it was because Malone instinctively tightened his hold on the girl's arm that he could feel it trembling. But the store detective, frustrated and puzzled, seemed to smile cynically just as they passed; he hated her for being right about the girl.

When they got outside, they stopped a moment under the big clock. It had been raining out, but there was bright sunlight on the wet pavements and the noonday crowd surged by. In that bright light, as he stood hesitating and the girl's head was lowered in humiliation, he noticed that there seemed to be a hundred little spots on her light coat, maybe rain marks or dust and rain. His heart was pounding, but now that he had got her safely out of the store, he wanted to get rid of her, and he didn't want her to offer any of that servile gratitude he got from petty thieves he helped in the police court.

"Thanks," she whispered.

"Forget it," he said, as if the whole thing had been nothing to him and he had understood from the beginning what she was. "I guess you'd better be getting on your way."

"All right."

"Well, there's no use standing here. Aren't you going along?"

"It doesn't matter," she said, standing there staring at him, her face still full of humiliation.

"You better be heading somewhere out of here. Where are you from?" he asked awkwardly.

"Out of town," she said. Then she touched him on the arm. "Listen, what was the idea?" she asked. While she waited for him to answer her face seemed to brighten. She was looking at him, looking right into his eyes. "Why did you do it? What's it to you?" They seemed to be alone on the street while she waited breathlessly because she had been offered some incredible promise, a turn that gave her a wild hope.

"We were standing there watching," he said uneasily, as he nodded to Webster who had followed them out and was now standing by the window trying to hear what she said. "Me and my pal, we saw what was going on," Malone said. Then, remembering their disappointment, he said bluntly, "We were betting on you."

"How do you mean?"

"When we saw the detective watching you—"

"Yes . . ."

"Our money went on you . . . that she was wrong . . . You let us down, that's all; we were wrong. We lose."

"Oh," she said, startled. As Webster came closer, she swung her head in wild resentment at him. Again they were both staring at her, watching her. She looked around the street at the faces of passing people as if everybody had suddenly stopped to watch her and make a little bet. "A buck she will, a buck she won't, eh!" she said as her eyes brightened with a crazy fury. "Get out of my way," she whispered. Swinging her foot she kicked him savagely on the shin.

As he felt the pain he could think only of how she had asked, "Why did you do it?" and waited breathlessly for some gesture from him. At that moment there did not seem to be a single good instinct, a single good thing in his life that he had not betrayed.

And she came walking right at him as if she would walk right through him if he did not step aside, and she had her head up and her fists clenched tight, going down the street, going deeper into the crowd with the sun touching her red hat and her good legs with the runs down her stockings.

Lady in a Green Dress

A YEAR AGO, WHEN HE WAS AT LAW SCHOOL, HENRY Sproule used to walk as far as the city hall square with five or six fellows from the final year. In the first fine days of the early spring, they walked the wet pavements, carrying their brief bags. They all went into the cigar and magazine store at the corner to talk for a few moments with the woman behind the counter before they separated and went to their law offices.

The woman looked to be about thirty-five, plump, smiling, polite and always glad to see the students. Usually, she wore a simple green dress which seemed to be new and distinctive because it set off her thick blonde hair pulled back into a knot on her neck. The proprietor of the store, a thick-necked Greek, over six feet tall, was delighted to have the fellows in his store making small but regular purchases for the sake of a minute of trivial conversation with the woman. Henry, who was red-headed and lanky, resented the way the proprietor stood there smiling and rubbing his hands, trying to make conversation by whispering, "She's a nice woman, ain't she? But it's a shame she's so married, eh?"

Henry began to go into the store alone and he talked

amusingly and wittily with the girl who would suddenly laugh out loud. She admitted reluctantly that her name was Irene Airth. Henry pleaded with her to go out with him and she teased him charmingly as though he were a very young but very nice fellow.

In the morning classes at the law school that were so important because of the approaching final exams, Henry dozed in his chair and occasionally looked out the window at the new green leaves on the chestnut tree and the blue sky. The city streets were clean. He liked the city in the spring. Soon, he would go away to practice law in a country town and suddenly he was aware that he loved this woman with the fair hair and green dress. Several times he left the school in the morning and went over to the store to whisper intimately with Irene who was a little embarrassed and puzzled by his sincerity, and she was very eager to see him in the mornings. "I don't think she knows what to do about me at all, that's the trouble," he thought. But she told him one morning that she would like very much to have a simple friendly feeling for him. She was so gentle in her explanation and yet so lovely that he could hardly find words to answer her and left the store abruptly.

For a week he was too angry to go into the store, but when he was downtown in the evening he sometimes passed just when she was leaving to go home. One night he followed her, remaining a distance behind the neat figure in the light coat with the pretty cape. She walked to the older part of the city where there were many big dilapidated rooming houses. When she was under a street light, he caught up with her and took hold of her by the arm, "Just a minute," he said.

"Oh Red, where did you come from?" she said, quite casually and smiled.

"I've been following you."

"Heavens, what for? What do you want?"

"Nothing at all, just to be with you, Irene," he said.

She was delighted to see him but afraid to encourage him. "I was going into the house," she said.

Arm in arm and laughing cheerfully, they entered one of the houses and went into a large high-ceilinged room on the ground floor. A dressing table and a bed were at one end of the room. She took off her hat and stood in front of the mirror, powdering her nose while Henry fumbled awkwardly with his hat. Then he noticed that she still had on the green dress.

"Is that the only dress you have?" he said suddenly.

"No, I have another good one, but I don't like it so well. Now, I'll talk with you from the kitchen while I make a cup of tea."

Waiting, he wondered how long she had lived in the room, it was furnished so impersonally. Then they sat beside each other to drink the tea, and smoothing her skirt she said suddenly, "You're a really good guy Red, but promise you won't try to kiss and fool around with me if I let you stay."

"But why?"

"Because I'm happy as it is, for one thing. Then again, I might like it and I'd go all up in the air and I couldn't stand it. Besides, you've got such a nice freckled face."

"Oh, I thought you might be worrying about your husband."

"I do worry about him sometimes."

She looked at him vaguely. Her cheeks were flushed. The blood seemed so warm under the clear skin he could hardly keep from putting his arms around her. Cautiously, he said, "Are you much in love with your husband?"

"Am I in love with him? Of course I am," she said abruptly.

"Where is he?"

"I don't know."

She was angry and a little bewildered. He thought she was going to cry. "I'm awfully sorry. You've no idea how sorry I am," he said. "I just meant . . . . I mean – I don't know what I meant."

Smiling calmly, she said, "You've been very friendly, Red, so there's no reason why I shouldn't explain to you. I haven't seen my husband for eight years, what do you think of that?"

"Where in the world is he?"

"I don't know. It sounds a little funny, doesn't it. Yet I love my husband. I love him more than anyone else. I love all my thoughts of him and the clear bright picture I always have of him in my mind."

Her blue eyes were moist, and she began to tell him that her husband had gone away a few months after they married. "I'll show you a picture of him," she said, and got up to look into a bureau drawer. Then she showed him a small picture of a young man with a good forehead, remarkable eyes and a sneering lip. He was in uniform. "We were married when he came back from the war. We only lived together six months," she said.

"He's a nice looking guy all right. You picked a good one," Henry said.

"Look at me, Red. If I tell you something will you promise never to tell . . . . because I like you so much."

"Sure, I promise. Honest to God."

"Weren't you wondering why he went away?"

"I was, but I didn't like to ask."

"He was going to be arrested for embezzlement. He

stole money, quite a bit I think. He left me a note saying that no one would ever bother me about it and some day he'd pay back every cent and come back. Of course he will come back . . . . if he can. That was eight years ago."

"And you haven't heard from him. He never even wrote to you?"

"No. But I believe there's a good reason for it. I prefer to think that," she said, looking at him steadily.

"You won't mind me saying that it sounds just a bit too simple?"

"I don't mind what you say. But that's how I'll go on thinking about it."

They sat on the old fashioned sofa and went on talking about her husband. Her smooth forehead was puckered into a frown, though she smiled confidently as she told him how she had gone once to Detroit and once to Chicago to attempt to identify the body of a man who was reported to have come from this city, and who, from the brief description, might have been her husband. "I really knew before I set out each time that it would not be Jack but I felt I ought to go," she said. A sudden admiration and sympathy prompted Henry to put his arm on her shoulder, and they were silent.

"How old are you?" he said suddenly.

"About forty."

"Honestly, you look about thirty."

"I know. It makes me quite happy to know it. It's sweet of you to remind me. Listen, Red, kiss me. That's it. Now kiss me once again the same way. Now promise me you'll never kiss me except like that and whenever I ask you to, then we can go on being good friends and see a lot of each other."

When he left her, he walked slowly to the house where

he roomed, and felt intensely alive and good humored. It was such a fine clear starlit evening in the late spring. The leaves were much thicker in the chestnut trees. The warm summer nights were coming on.

Often, in the late evening, he walked home with Irene from the store. Sometimes he was irritated when he realized he was so friendly and sympathetic he was losing his determination. She told him she had had many jobs and liked the newsstand because so many people talked to her. The proprietor, a married man with eight children, never bothered her. One evening Henry gave her three bottles of red wine and some Saint André cheese, and they had a happy evening together, though her kisses were guarded and carefully given. That evening, she showed him the short note her husband had left before he went away, written in a round bold hand. By this time it seemed that he had known her husband a long time, that he knew all the marks on his body and the quaint phrases he had learned abroad. Henry was sure he would recognize him if he ever came walking into the room.

His feeling for her had become so complicated that he began to make enquiries about her husband, who had worked in the city eight years ago as a credit manager for a large publishing firm. There was no difficulty about a few simple enquiries at police headquarters, where, as a lawyer, he had access to the records. Then he talked to the manager of the publishing firm who said quite definitely that the man had never stolen anything that he could have gotten arrested for, and they didn't know why he had left so suddenly. The police department hadn't a thing against him either. "Probably restless after the war," the manager said. "Maybe there was another woman, but he wanted to leave it open for himself to come back."

Henry did not tell Irene he had made any enquiries about her husband. In the afternoon, when he had finished the last of the examinations and was feeling free and lighthearted he hurried over to the store to explain the matter, and then, looking at her, knew that he could not tell her.

"What is bothering you now?" she said.

"Nothing at all. Nothing," he said, "I think I'm a bit of a fool."

Henry remained in the city another week. Whenever he could, he kissed her eagerly, and she laughed and was charming, thinking he was becoming more ardent because he was going away. At the end of the week, when he went into the cigar store, Irene was not there. The Greek proprietor, who looked very unhappy, said she had told him to tell Henry to come and see her as soon as he could.

Henry hurried to her home and found her sitting at the front window crying and holding the morning newspaper in her hand. She jumped up quickly, ran to Henry and, trembling nervously, showed him a paragraph about a man who had been killed by an automobile the night before, and who had died on the way to the hospital. The ambulance attendant had heard him mutter that his name was "Ayers," "Airth," "Airus," or a name like that. The man had been drunk but had whispered that he had a wife in the city.

"It's my husband all right. It's Jack," she said. "What will I do? That's a good description of him." She was holding her hands together and shaking her head from side to side.

"We'll go right down to the morgue," Henry said. "I'll get a taxi." They sat very close together as she cried softly, muttering, "After all these years, after all these years."

At the morgue the officials agreed to show her the

body. They asked Henry if he would care to see a notebook found in the dead man's coat. Henry stood beside Irene, looking at the body on the slab, and then he examined the entries in the notebook while he watched Irene furtively. She peered at the dead man's drooping mouth, the hollow cheeks and the partially bald head. Twice she shook her head. She was trembling with excitement and yet dazed; she hardly seemed to see anything as she rubbed her fingers nervously across her eyes, and then she began to cry quietly while Henry lowered his head, looking again at the notebook, and he saw that the entries written in a round bold hand were a record of bets placed on horses.

Suddenly she cried out eagerly, "That's not Jack. That couldn't be Jack. Why, we were about the same age. He's years older than me, this man."

"Do you want to see this notebook? There's no name in it," Henry said.

"Why would I want to see it," she said, moving toward the door. "Don't you think I know my husband? I could tell him any place in the world."

They walked down the stone steps from the morgue as she dabbed her eyes with a handkerchief and tried to laugh happily. "Thank God that wasn't Jack," she said. "Please don't look so sober, Red. I feel grand." But her face was white. He was frowning. "I'm definitely going away at the end of the week, you know," he said.

"I'll miss you terribly, Red," she said. "How will I ever get along. You've been such a sweetheart."

She kissed him quickly. He watched her hurry across the wide pavement. A puff of wind held back her open coat showing a flash of the green dress. It was nearly noon and the sun was shining brilliantly.

The New Kid

WHEN LUKE BALDWIN WAS THE NEW KID IN TOWN HE WAS very lonely and didn't believe he would ever make any sincere friends. The trouble was that he was a city kid. When his father, a doctor, died he had come to live with his uncle at the sawmill two miles beyond the town. Uncle Henry, the manager of the mill, was a confident, important man, whom everybody respected, but he couldn't be expected to make friends for Luke. The only reliable friend Luke had in those days was the old collie dog, Dan, which was blind in one eye, and not much use to anybody around the mill.

The old dog helped Luke get better acquainted with the boys at school and particularly with Elmer Highbottom, the son of the rich merchant, who had Uncle Henry's approval. Luke himself was too reticent and too quiet; he spoke too politely; and so the other boys jeered at him and would not believe he was really one of them. But the dog was always with him when he showed up at the ball field behind Stevenson's orchard. The boys would talk with the dog and play with it and compare it with Elmer's dog, which also was supposed to be a clean-bred.

Elmer was a skinny red-haired kid, two years older

than Luke, who had become the leader of the boys by the power of his abusive voice and his frantic bad temper. In the gang there were six others: Eddie Shore, the dark and muscular son of a grocer; Woody Alliston, the undertaker's son; Jimmie Stewart, the minister's boy; Dave Dalton, the left-handed first baseman, whose father owned the ice-cream parlor; Hank Hennessey, whose father worked in the shipyard; and Norm McLeod, whose father was the superintendent of the grain elevator. They all wanted to be big-league ball-players. If Luke missed a fly ball, Elmer, the potential big leaguer, would scream at him in derision, and Luke secretly hated him. Lying in the grass by the third-base line with Dan, Luke would whisper, "He's a one-armed ballplayer himself. He just swings that glove at the ball, Dan. If the ball sticks in the pocket he's all right, but he might as well be out there swinging a broom."

He was not afraid of Elmer, but he never said these things to him, for he wanted to go on hanging around with the bunch of boys. Elmer had decided that he would become a great left-handed pitcher. One way of being friendly with Elmer was to stand behind him when he was pitching and say, "Gee, did you see that curve? How did you throw it, Elmer?" Luke, who was lonely and wanted to have friends, also would stand behind Elmer, and one day he said enthusiastically, "Gee, what a hook you had on that one, Elmer! I wish you'd show me how to throw it." It made him a little sick at his stomach to say it, for the ball didn't have a curve at all. "Maybe I will sometime," Elmer said, and that day he took Luke home with him to show him his valuable clean-bred dog.

As soon as Luke saw this dog, Thor, which was chained up at a kennel at the back of the big Highbottom house, he doubted that the dog was a clean-bred. Its legs

66

were too long; it didn't have the long-haired coat of a collie; the hair was more like that of an Alsatian; but it was a big, powerful, bad-tempered dog which was always kept on a leash.

"It's a thoroughbred," Elmer said, "and it can lick any dog in this town."

"If that dog's a thoroughbred, then our Dan isn't," Luke said.

"Then your Dan isn't. This is a fighting thoroughbred."

"Aw, go on," Luke said.

"Aw, go on yourself. Nuts to you."

"Nuts to you, Elmer. Why has it got that crazy look in its eyes?"

"Because he doesn't like strangers, see. And he doesn't like other dogs," Elmer said.

But then Mr. Highbottom, a plump, affable, sandy-haired man with rimless glasses and a round pink face, came out. He was a rich man and a good friend of Luke's Uncle Henry. When Elmer went into the house to get his new first-baseman's glove, Mr. Highbottom explained that Thor was kept as a watchdog; he had gotten the dog from some people in the city who had kept him locked up in an apartment; he had been badly treated. The first night he, Mr. Highbottom, had got the dog he had had to hit him on the head with a club to let him know who was master. He was half collie and half Alsatian. Luke said nothing to Elmer about knowing the dog was not a clean-bred, for he wanted to keep Elmer's friendship.

In the evenings they would all go up to the fairgrounds, especially if a team from one of the grain boats in the harbor was playing the town team. Luke was always ill at ease because he didn't even know the members of the town team; he could not stand behind the bench when the home team was batting, and chat and kid with these great players. So he would listen, or wander among the crowd with Dan following him, or he would drift out to left field, where the gang would sprawl in the grass. They would stay there till it was dark, then Elmer would whisper with Eddie Shore, the swarthy and muscular son of the grocer, and they and the others would go off by themselves on some night adventure on the main street of the town. Luke and Dan were left alone. On the way home, with the stars coming out and the night breeze rustling through the leaves of the great elms along the road, Luke would try to imagine that he was following the boys furtively into mysterious places where he had never been.

But on Saturday mornings it was really worth while to be with Elmer's friends, for then they would go down to the old dock by the rusty grain elevator. There they would swim, with the collie swimming with them, and afterward they would lie in the sun, talking and dreaming. When they had gotten dressed they would go along the pier to the place where the Missouri was tied up, and sit there, peering into the darkness of the hold.

A seaman in a torn black sweater, whose face was leathery and whose hair was iron gray, was sitting on the pier smoking his pipe. He smiled as he watched Elmer Highbottom strutting around. "Hey, kid, how old are you?" he called.

"Thirteen. Why?" Elmer asked.

"Oh, nothing," drawled the seaman. "It's just that I remember when I was thirteen around here."

"Are you from around here, mister?"

"Believe it or not," the sailor said, "I was a kid around here. It was a long time ago." Both Luke and Elmer, sitting cross-legged now at the seaman's feet, listened to him telling fabulous stories about his adventures. Maybe he was lying a little, but his voice was soft, his tone full of affection and his eyes were happy, and so Luke believed him. And after a profound silence Luke said suddenly, "I could do that too. I could stow away some night, I could go down the St. Lawrence. I could sail to Siam."

"When are you going to make the break, son?" the sailor asked with a smile.

"One of these nights. I'll pick a night."

"You," Elmer jeered. "Listen to him, mister. He's never been on a ship. He doesn't know one end of a ship from another. He's just a punk around here."

"I was a punk once," the sailor said, in such a way that Luke felt grateful. He couldn't figure out why he endured Elmer's jeering insults. Gradually all the boys had adopted Elmer's tone with him.

One day they were in Johnson's lumberyard on the south side of the tracks, playing around the great pile of sawdust which was heaped at the back of a two-storey brick building. A ladder hooked to the wall of the building ran up to the flat roof. "Come on, everybody up on the roof," Elmer yelled, and they followed him up the ladder. Sitting on the edge of the roof they all looked down at the pile of sawdust, which was about twenty feet below.

"I'll stump you to jump down," Elmer said, and without waiting for them to yell, "Stumpers go first," he jumped.

One by one the boys began to jump, and as each one fell Dan barked excitedly. But the second boy to jump had taken a little longer to make up his mind, and the third one hesitated even longer, the jump becoming longer and more frightening as he kept looking down; and Luke, who was the last one, had had too much time to think about it.

"Come on, Luke," they yelled . . . "What's the matter with you, Luke? What are you scared of?"

"I'm taking my time. What's the matter with taking my time?"

He wanted to jump, he knew he was going to jump, only he couldn't bring himself to do it at the moment. It was really an easy jump, so he laughed and tried to keep on kidding with them, but he had tightened up and every time he got ready to jump a queasy feeling came at the base of his spine.

"I think he's yellow," Elmer shouted. "He's got glue on his pants." Then they all began to jeer.

Luke wanted to close his eyes and jump, but was ashamed to let them see that he was closing his eyes. That all this was happening bewildered him. And then the collie began to bark impatiently. "Okay, Dan," Luke yelled. Waving his arms carelessly as if he had been only kidding with them, he suddenly pushed himself blindly off the roof and fell heavily on the sawdust, where the dog leaped at him joyfully.

"Well, there you are, bigmouth," he said to Elmer as he got up, dusting his clothes.

"Who's a bigmouth?"

"You've got the biggest, loudest mouth in this town, Elmer," Luke said quietly. "You're a blowhard. A great big blowhard."

"Listen, punk, you want something?"

"You don't worry me, bigmouth."

"You want I should smack you, stupid?"

"Go ahead, smack me, Elmer. I'll show you who's stupid."

"Come on!" Elmer yelled.

Then they were circling around each other and Luke now was happy. It was a crazy kind of happiness; it seemed as if Elmer had been pounding him for a long time and now at last he could openly smack him. As they feinted at each other Dan began to growl. Eddie Shore grabbed the dog by the collar. Impressed by the wild glare in Luke's eyes, Elmer feinted cautiously and then suddenly he ducked and charged, swinging his right, and Luke blindly stuck out his left hand like a rod. Elmer walked right into it. The fist got him on the nose, which spurted blood. Screaming like an old woman, he came clawing at Luke and got his arms around him and they rolled in the sawdust. He was heavier and stronger than Luke and had gotten on top of him.

"Let him up. Let him up and go on fighting," the others yelled. But Elmer, frantic now, his freckled face white, with the mouth gaping open and a trickle of blood from his nose running into the corner of his mouth, had grabbed Luke by the hair and kept banging his head on the ground.

The collie had growled; he lay back, growling, then suddenly jerked his head free and leaped at Elmer. He didn't look like a wild dog, but like a dog being workmanlike. He slashed at Elmer's leg, only at the cloth, but the growl and the sound of the ripping cloth seemed to jerk Elmer out of his frenzy. He was scared. Jumping up, he shouted, "I'll kill that dog. I'll brain it. Where's a brick, gimme a brick!"

"Come here, Dan. Come here, quick," Luke cried. As the dog turned to him he grabbed him by the collar. "You're not hurt," he said to Elmer. "It's only your pants torn a little. Dan didn't bite you."

"I'll brain that dog," Elmer shouted. "I've got a right to kill it now."

"If you want to hit somebody, come on, hit me now I'm standing up. Here," he said to Eddie Shore. "You hold Dan's collar – and hold him this time."

"I'll get you when your vicious dog isn't with you,"

Elmer yelled. "I'll get you after my father has that dog destroyed."

"You can get me any time you want, Elmer. I'll fight you any time you're willing to have a fair fight."

"Aw, go on, beat it. Do you hear? Beat it."

As Luke dusted himself off, taking a long time, he waited for one of the other boys to make a friendly remark, or invite him to stay with them. But they had all grown profoundly meditative. So finally Luke said, "Come on, Dan," and he went off by himself.

Luke got home just in time for dinner. At the table his Uncle Henry said, "Is that a scratch on your face, Luke?"

"I was playing up in the lumberyard with Elmer, jumping in the sawdust, Uncle Henry."

"Oh, you and Elmer are becoming great friends, aren't you?" he said approvingly.

Uncle Henry, in his shirt sleeves, big-faced, thin-haired, his great shoulders hunched over the table, looked as if he had the strength of character to protect fearlessly everything that belonged to him. But Uncle Henry and Mr. Highbottom admired each other. Luke seemed to see Mr. Highbottom coming into the room and explaining that the collie had bitten Elmer. Luke could almost hear them talking as one practical man to another, and coming finally to a practical arrangement to destroy Dan. Suddenly Uncle Henry looked up, their eyes met, and Uncle Henry smiled. But no complaint came to Uncle Henry from Mr. Highbottom, and at school Elmer was as nonchalant with him as if nothing had happened.

On Friday afternoon Eddie Shore, Elmer's good friend, said to Luke, "Going to play ball tomorrow, Luke? Guess we'll see you there, eh?"

"Sure, I'll be up there," Luke said with a grateful grin.

That Saturday morning at about ten o'clock he walked up to the ball field with Dan. Only two other kids were there, Eddie and Woody Alliston, the undertaker's son. It was a cloudy day; it had rained a little early in the morning. While Dan lay under the hawthorn tree, Luke and Eddie and Woody played three-cornered catch. Then the sun came out.

"Here comes Elmer now," Eddie Shore said laconically.

"Soon they'll all be here," Luke said. Feeling a little embarrassed about Elmer, he did not turn to watch him coming across the field. But Eddie, who had the ball, held on to it, a big excited grin on his face. With Elmer was the big dog, Thor, on a chain. The powerful dog was dragging Elmer along. "Why has he got that crazy dog?" Luke asked, turning. Then his heartbeat came up high in his throat and he felt weak, for now he knew why Eddie Shore had grinned. "Come here, Dan," he called quickly. As the old dog came to him slowly, he whispered, "You stay right here with me, Dan. No matter what happens, you stay here with me."

The big dog with the wicked, crazy eyes had already growled at Dan. Thor was three inches higher and years younger than Dan.

"I see you've got your dog with you, Luke," Elmer said with a smirk.

"Yeah, Dan's always with me, Elmer."

"That dog of yours is a mighty savage dog," Elmer said softly. "It goes around biting people, doesn't it?"

"Dan's not savage. Dan never bit anybody."

"Of course, I'm nobody. A dog that bites me isn't really a savage dog. That's not the way I heard it, eh, guys?" With a grin he turned to Eddie Shore and Woody Alliston, but they did not grin, for now that they were close to Thor and had heard him growl they were frightened.

"You better take that dog home, Elmer," Luke said placatingly. "I don't think your father would like it if it made trouble for anybody."

"I'm going to see if that dog of yours wants to growl and bite when there's another dog around," Elmer jeered. Slipping the chain off Thor's collar, he pointed to Dan. "Go get him, boy," he yelled. "Sic him."

"Grab him, Elmer. Oh, please," Luke cried.

Thor had growled, his lips trembling and drawing back from the long white teeth; he growled a little as Dan stiffened, then growled again, his mane rising. And Dan, too, growled, his head going down a little, waiting, and showing his teeth, which were blunted and old.

Suddenly Thor leaped at Dan's throat, trying to knock him over with the weight of the charge and sink his teeth in the throat and swing him over. But Dan pivoted, sliding away to the side, and Thor's snapping jaws missed the throat. Then Dan drew on the strength and wisdom of his breed. His strength was all instinct and heart, and it was against that instinct to snap or chew, or grip with his teeth and snarl and roll over, clawing and kicking and cutting until it was over. As Thor missed, Dan did not back away and wait again. Doing what he would have done five years ago, he wheeled, leaping past the big dog and slashing at the flank; then, wheeling again, returned for the slashing rip at the flank again.

These splendid, fearless movements were executed so perfectly that Luke sobbed, "Oh, Dan," but the slashes at Thor's flank had not gone deep.

The sun, which was now bright, was shining in Thor's wild empty eyes. Growling and scraping at the ground with his claws he charged again; it was like the pounce of a great cat. Again the snapping jaws missed Dan's throat, but the weight of the charge, catching him on the hip, spun him around off balance and bewildered him a little.

Luke was watching with both his hands up to his face. It was as if he was prepared to cover his eyes and scream but couldn't; he was frozen to the one spot. The two boys, Eddie Shore and Woody Alliston, were close together, crouching a little and crazy with excitement. Elmer's jaw was moving loosely and he kept blinking his eyes.

The thin clouds overhead broke up, a blue patch of sky appeared. The damp grass glistened. Thor had learned that Dan was vulnerable on the left flank; the blind eye saw nothing, the good eye couldn't shift quickly enough. Whirling quickly, Thor charged in again on that left flank, knocking Dan over, but the weight of his own charge caused Thor to sprawl over Dan. The teeth could only snap at the flank, and though both dogs had rolled in the grass, snarling and clawing, Dan was soon on his feet again.

But Dan knew now that his instinctive style was no good. When this heavy dog came whirling to the left of him he couldn't see him in time, and he was bleeding just behind the shoulder. It was like watching a bewildered old dog suddenly becoming aware of its age, and yet with courage trying to break itself of a style of fighting which was the only one its breed had known for a hundred years. Circling and backing, Dan drew near the trunk of the hawthorn tree. There he stood with the tree on his left, protecting that flank, so that Thor would have to charge toward the good eye. His head dropped and he waited.

"No, oh, no, Elmer," Eddie Shore said weakly.

"Elmer. Have some sense, Elmer," Woody Alliston pleaded.

"Elmer," Luke shrieked suddenly, and he grabbed Elmer by the throat. "I'll kill you. I'll kill you. Call him off or I'll kill you," he shrieked.

But with a low exultant growl Thor had leaped in again

to pin Dan against the tree, and as Dan swerved a little Thor got his teeth in the shoulder, snarling and shaking his head as he rolled Dan over, shaking and stretching his own neck away from Dan's teeth, and holding on tight till he could draw Dan underneath him on his back and then shift his jaws to Dan's throat and kill him.

The agonized growling and snarling was terrible and yet exultant, and Luke screamed, "Elmer, Elmer, oh, please call him off. He'll kill him, Elmer."

And the other two boys, Eddie Shore and Woody Alliston, awed and sick, yelled, "Do something, Elmer. Don't let him kill him, Elmer."

Fascinated by the power and viciousness of his dog, which he believed he couldn't control, Elmer cried, "I can't stop it."

And Luke sobbed, for it was as if Dan was more than a dog. The collie seemed to have come out of that good part of his life which he had shared with his own father. "Dan! Dan!" he screamed. He looked around wildly for help. On the other side of the tree was a thick broken branch. It flashed into his mind that he should use this branch as a club; this was in his mind as he rushed at the snarling dogs. But instead he kicked at Thor's flank; he kicked three times with the good heavy serviceable shoes Uncle Henry had bought for him.

Thor snarled, his head swinging around, his bright eyes now on Luke, the lip curled back from the fangs. Luke backed away toward the club. As he picked up the branch and held it with both hands, he felt numb all over. There was nothing but the paralyzing beat of his own heart – nothing else in the world.

Seeing him there with the club, Thor tried to hold Dan down with his paws. Then he suddenly growled as he let go Dan's shoulder and whirled on Luke.

76

"Luke, come away from him," Elmer screamed.

"Run, Luke," Eddie Shore yelled. "Get someone at Stevenson's, Woody."

Woody Alliston started to run across the field to Stevenson's house as Luke, waiting, watched Thor's trembling lip. The big dog's growl was deep with satisfaction as he came two steps closer, the head going down.

In Luke's mind it was all like a dream. It was like a dream of Mr. Highbottom telling him he had once pounded Thor on the head with a club, and of a story he had once read about Indians pounding the heads of wild dogs with clubs. But it was important that he should not wait, that he should attack the dog and cow him.

Dan, free now, had tried to get up and then had fallen back and was watching him with his glowing eye.

With a deep warning growl Thor crouched, and Luke rushed at him and cracked him on the skull, swinging the club with both hands. The big dog, trying to leap at him, knocked him down, and when he staggered to his feet Thor was there, shaking his head stupidly, but still growling. Not waiting now, Luke rushed at him and whacked him on the head again and again. The crazy dog would not run; he was still trying to jump at him. Suddenly the dog lurched, his legs buckled, he rolled over on his side and was still.

While Elmer and Eddie Shore were looking at him as if they were afraid of him, Luke did a thing he hated himself for doing. He went over and sat down beside Dan and put his hand on Dan's head, and then he started to cry. He couldn't help it; it was just relief; he felt weak and he ground his fists in his eyes.

"Holy cow," Elmer said in relief, "you might have got killed."

"Gee whiz, Luke," Eddie said softly.

"Are you all right, Luke?"

"You better put the chain on that dog of yours, Elmer," Luke said when he could get his breath. "You'd better tie him up to the tree."

"Maybe he's dead. Oh, Luke, what if he's dead?"

"Not that dog. Not that crazy dog. It's Dan that's hurt."

When Elmer was linking the chain to his dog's collar, the animal's legs trembled convulsively. Opening his eyes he tried to get to his feet, but Elmer had no trouble dragging him over to the tree and looping the chain around it.

Across the field at the gate to the Stevenson house, Mr. Stevenson was talking with Woody Alliston. They could see him point and shrug – there seemed to be no trouble over there by the tree – then he turned back to the house and Woody came on alone.

"Let's see your shoulder, Dan," Luke said gently to the collie lying quietly beside him. The collie knew he had been hurt, knew the muscle above the shoulder was torn and bleeding, yet he lay there quietly and patiently, regaining his strength while his flanks heaved.

"Okay, okay," Luke said softly. Taking out his handkerchief he dabbed at the blood already congealing on the fur. The other boys, kneeling down beside Luke, were silent. Sometimes they looked at Luke's white face. When he had mopped up the blood, he began to stroke Dan's head softly, and Dan, wiggling his tail a little, thumped the grass three times.

"Maybe he's not hurt so bad," Elmer said nervously, for Dan, swinging his head around, had begun to lick the wound patiently; the clean pink tongue and the saliva on the tongue were cleaning and soothing the slash, and Luke and the other boys seemed to be waiting for Dan to come to a conclusion about the seriousness of his wound.

"Can you get up, Dan?" Luke whispered. "Come on, try, boy."

Slowly the collie rose and hobbled on three legs in a little circle, the wounded right leg coming down delicately and just touching the ground as it completed the little circle. Coming over to Luke, who was kneeling and waiting anxiously, the old collie rubbed his nose against Luke's neck, then flopped down again.

"I guess he'll be all right, will he?" Elmer asked anxiously.

"Maybe that leg won't be so good again," Luke said mournfully. "Maybe it'll never be good again."

"Sure it will, if nothing is broken, Luke," Elmer insisted, as he got up and thrust his hands into his pockets and walked around aimlessly, his freckled face full of concern. Once he stopped and looked at his own dog, which was crouched by the tree, his eyes following Elmer. Thor was a subdued dog now. Growing more meditative and more unhappy, Elmer finally blurted out, "I guess you'll tell your uncle what happened, eh, Luke?"

"You knew Dan was my uncle's dog," Luke said grimly.

"If you tell your uncle – well, your uncle will tell my father, and then there will be awful trouble, Luke."

"Well, you knew there'd be trouble, Elmer."

"I only wanted to scare you and chase Dan," Elmer insisted. "I thought Dan would run and howl. I didn't know Thor would turn on you. Gee, Luke, I was crazy. I didn't stop to think." With a sudden pathetic hopefulness he muttered, "I could have told my father that your dog slashed at me. Only I didn't, Luke. I didn't say anything, though he asked me how I tore my pants."

"Okay, you didn't say anything, Elmer. So what?"

"Maybe if you don't say anything, eh, Luke?"

"Aw, I can look after myself too," Luke said grandly.

"Well – in that case I'd sure think you were a great guy, Luke," Elmer said.

"Sure, he's a great guy," Eddie Shore agreed firmly.

Eddie and Woody Alliston wanted to make friendly gestures to Luke, and they didn't quite know how to do it. They felt awkward and ashamed. They took turns petting Dan lovingly. They asked Luke if he wouldn't go swimming down at the dock after lunch. "I'll walk home with you, Luke," Eddie said. "I'd like to see if Dan gets home all right."

"I'm not letting him walk all that distance," Luke said, and he knelt down, gathered Dan in his arms and hoisted him up on his shoulder. On the way across the field Luke and Eddie took their time and worried about Dan.

"Let me carry him now," Eddie said.

"No, we'll see if he can walk a little," Luke said.

It was extraordinary how effectively the old dog could travel on three legs. He hopped along briskly. Sometimes he would stop and let the wounded leg come down firmly, as if testing it, then come hopping along until Luke picked him up again.

"We should take it easy," Luke said. "We should rest a little now and then." When they got to the road leading to the mill they sat down in the grass and took turns stroking Dan's head.

Going along that road, and resting every three hundred yards, Luke and Eddie were beginning a new relationship with each other. They both knew it, and so they were a little shy and very respectful to each other. While they were talking about Dan they were really trying to draw closer together. Eddie was offering a sincere admiring friendship, and Luke knew it and accepted it gravely.

"Well, I'll look for you this afternoon," Eddie said.

"At the dock. Sure, Eddie."

"Yeah. At the dock. Well, I'll be seeing you, Luke."

Halfway up the path Luke suddenly dropped on his knees and put his arms around Dan. It was as if the dog had really been struggling not only against the big wild Thor but against the barrier between Luke and the other boys. "You're some dog, Dan," he whispered, rubbing his face against the dog's nose, trying to show his gratitude.

But when he got back to the mill and saw Uncle Henry going toward the house, mounting the veranda steps, opening the screen door, his step decisive, his face so full of sensible determination, Luke longed to be able to tell him what had happened, not only because the dog was Uncle Henry's property – and property ought to be protected – but because he suddenly believed that Uncle Henry would have done just what he himself had done, and would be proud of him. "Why, the sensible thing would have been to pick up a club and smack that crazy dog on the head," he could almost hear Uncle Henry say. "Why, that's just what I did, Uncle Henry," Luke imagined himself explaining as he followed Uncle Henry into the house. But of course he would never be able to see this glow of approval in his uncle's eyes.

Poolroom

HARDLY ANY ONE WAS ON THE STREET, THE AFTERNOON sunlight was shining so steadily on the pavement and the air was so heavy, sticky, and hot. Steve, carrying his coat in one hand and fanning himself with his hat, was going to the rooming-house where Shorty Horne lived, to take a lesson on the banjo. He was going along slowly and lazily, feeling the hot sun burning his neck.

The front porch of the rooming-house was badly in need of paint, and on such a dry afternoon it looked even worse with the blistering flakes of paint curling in the heat. Mrs. Scott, who had many roomers, was very clean and tidy inside the house, though she did not seem to care what her place looked like from the street. Shorty Horne had the small attic room, two flights up, with the small window over the front porch and another window looking out over a flat, gravelled roof.

Steve, who had known Shorty three or four months, had met him one afternoon in Hudson's poolroom over the cafeteria downtown. Shorty was a small, old fellow, about fifty-five, with very heavy veins on his temples and thin hair he hardly ever bothered combing. His straggly mustache was the same color as his hair, only it was much thicker and stiffer, curling down over his lips, and when he had his hat on, the mustache made him look more vigorous and determined than he was. He always wore a hat with a wide brim. He used to come into the poolroom in the afternoon, look carefully at the men around the tables, and then sit down on one of the long benches by the wall, sitting there watching the fellows play while he slowly ate a bag of peanuts. Gradually a small space on the floor at his feet was covered with peanut shells, the sole of his shoe crunching the shells. Yet he was not really untidy, for when he had finished eating he bent down and laboriously scraped the shells into a small pile, got them all into the bag that had been in his pocket and threw it into the waste-paper basket. He used to do that nearly every day. Nuts, it seems, were not hard for his stomach to digest. If he hadn't known J. S. Hudson, the proprietor of the poolroom, a large-framed, casual yet formidable man, who stood around snapping his suspenders, he might not have been so clean, though he did seem to enjoy getting the shells into such a neat little pile on the floor. For years he had known Hudson, not intimately, but just as one man knows another from seeing him often and getting used to him. At times he had done a little work for Hudson at Hudson's private home, and if the poolroom janitor needed temporary assistance they hired Shorty for a few hours.

Once, after playing a game of billiards, Steve had sat down on the bench beside Shorty, who had begun to make friendly conversation, offering polite criticism of certain shots. Though Shorty rarely played billiards he watched all the interesting shots very critically.

Steve found out that Shorty Horne had no money and no prospect of ever getting steady work. There seemed to be nothing for him to do but pass in and out of the poolroom very quietly without speaking to any one. He acted like a man who was hiding from the police in a strange city. There was so little to know about him you couldn't help thinking he was deliberately withholding something. He couldn't work steadily because he suffered from some terrible stomach and kidney trouble. For two or three hours at a time he would be all right and very genial and happy, and then his insides would seem to get into knots as he bent down holding his sides with his elbows and gripping his hands tightly over his body. Around the poolroom they thought most of his time was spent enduring pain. There seemed to be nothing he could do for it. Steve wondered why he did not die, or why he did not long for death. Yet whenever it rained hard in the afternoons and Shorty couldn't walk from his rooming-house to the poolroom where he could sit and talk cheerfully, he was miserable, for this routine seemed to give him happiness; he knew that a few of the steady customers at the poolroom, on the bad days when he did not appear, grinned and took it for granted that he had died or had killed himself. They liked him, but felt sorry when they saw him holding his sides. They knew he couldn't sleep at night.

He had casually asked Steve once if he could play the banjo and when Steve replied that he would like to be able to, Shorty had offered to teach him. Steve was surprised; no one thought of Shorty spending much time playing a banjo, and yet, as Steve found out when he went to visit him, that was the way he spent an hour of the early afternoon. He got up late, for it usually was hard for him to get to sleep, and when he had had some bran flakes, a little orange juice and a piece of dry toast, he sat for an hour by the window slowly strumming the banjo and looking out over the roof covered with gravel. He looked forward eagerly to having some one there with him and was delighted when Steve began to learn rapidly. The two of them took turns playing the banjo. Whatever pleasure they got out of each other's company had to be immediate and spontaneous, for Shorty would not talk about himself.

So, on this afternoon when Steve was going down the street to Shorty's rooming-house, he was looking forward to a drowsy hour or two, sitting with his shirt off, feeling the faint breeze coming over the roof, cooling his bare shoulder while he strummed at the banjo.

Usually he rapped on the front door and spoke to Mrs. Scott, asking if Shorty were in, before he climbed the long flight of stairs, but today no one answered the door. Mrs. Scott had gone out. Steve went up the carpeted stairs, darkened, for there was no window, dark all the way up to the attic to the door of Shorty's room at the end of the hall. Usually Steve pushed open the door and stood there in the light from the window till Shorty told him to enter. But today, when he tried to open the door, it was locked. Irritated, he rapped and called, "Shorty!"

"Who's there?" Shorty answered.

"Steve."

He heard Shorty getting up and fumbling with the lock, then the door opened onto a kind of a twilight, for the blind, a green one, slit in many places and cracked, was down over the window, with the strong sunlight filtering in to the floor. Shorty, after letting Steve in, went back to the chair by the window. The banjo was leaning against the chair. Shorty was crouching down, his arms wrapped around his waist. Steve, merely glancing at him, thought he was having the pains inside him and wanted to rest.

"Do you mind if I pull up the blind, Shorty?"

"No, go ahead."

"Are you going out this afternoon, Shorty?"

"No."

"What's the matter?"

"Nothing, I just been thinking a bit, I guess. I been thinking. I mean I was downtown last night and saw a fellow. I think I'm going to get bumped off."

"Who'd bump a guy like you off?" Steve said, laughing out loud.

"A couple of hoods," Shorty answered.

"What for?"

"Squealing on them."

"When?"

"Oh, quite a while ago."

His lower lip was trembling. "It isn't that I'm afraid," he said apologetically. "Only I just can't stand the thought of really dying."

"If you don't mind me saying, Shorty, I don't think a guy who puts up with as much as you put up with ought to be much afraid of dying, even if you're not kidding me."

"No, I'm not kidding. I just mean that I'd like to go on living for a long time. I'd like to think about it that way." He spoke so casually and honestly Steve felt ashamed of himself.

"Well, who are the guys you're afraid of?"

"I'm really not afraid of them, only I know what's going to happen. I guess it's coming to me."

"Who are they, unless you don't want to say?"

"I don't mind. You didn't use to hang around Hudson's poolroom in the old days about five years ago, did you? I don't remember you, anyway."

"No. Didn't know the place at all."

"I used to hang around there then. I knew most everybody of a certain kind. It was just about the time I got real sick. If you don't mind me telling you, Steve, I used to pick a pocket now and then, and had a little more money. Hudson was slugged one night when he had a lot of money there, a couple of thousand, I think. I had a hunch who did it. And they were going to get caught for sure, and they came to me."

Steve pulled up the shade on the window. The strong light flooded the room, shining on the rug on the bare floor, on the banjo by the chair, on the iron bedstead painted white and chipping, on some dishes, a can and pail on an upturned box covered with a piece of tin used for a table; and it shone on Shorty, crouched down on the chair, his knees curled up a little, the heels caught on a rung. The toes of the shoes were turned far up. One of the shoes was laced with a piece of brown string.

"Maybe you don't want to fool around with the banjo today, Shorty."

"Oh, I'm feeling all right, Steve."

"Aren't the pains getting you?"

"No."

"Well, what's the matter with you, all hunched up?"

"I'll sit up," he said.

He sat up straight and asked Steve to hand him the banjo. Though he smiled a lot, he was obviously trying to be friendly while his thoughts were far away. The banjo did not interest him, though he strummed it idly, looking out over the gravelled roof. At the end of the roof was a short wall of concrete on a brick foundation and behind that a higher wall of brick. The sun shining on the white surface of the concrete made it a heavy white streak against the pinkish light on the brick. In some places on the roof the light gravel had been worn away and the black tar could be seen melting in the heat. Steve, waiting for Shorty to speak, went on looking out the window till he noticed Shorty's eyes blinking. He saw his head perspiring, beads of moisture at the temples and on the heavy blue veins.

"Did your guts bother you as much then?"

"Sure, only it had just started. I couldn't work. That's why these guys came to me. They said they'd arranged to fix it so it would look as if I'd done the job. They knew they were going to get it. They offered me a thousand to go down, to take the rap, and said to a guy like me it would be just the same, and maybe better because they'd look after me in prison, and I said all right. A little later I squealed on them."

"Why did you do that, Shorty?"

"I got to thinking about Hudson. He was always kind of nice to me and I couldn't stand to have him thinking I had done it. I just hated to have him think I had slugged him. But it was mainly because I was sick and couldn't stand the thought of being shut away. So I told the two guys it was all off and I gave them back their money. They wouldn't take it. I tried to tell them money wasn't much good to me, and I wanted to keep on going down to the poolroom. Well, they slapped me a bit and said they had pinned it on me and I had to take the rap after taking the money. The trouble was, when I took the money, I didn't realize how much I liked the poolroom. But I knew all the time that they'd get me in the long run for squealing. I ought to have got out of the city, but what would I do if I left, the way I am? The poolroom was all I wanted. Where could I go?"

"But what's got into you now?"

"Those guys are out. I saw one downtown last night. He had been asking for me in the poolroom. He just smiled at me."

"If I felt like you do, Shorty, I'd tell the cops, and then get on my horse and beat it."

"I got no more chance than a rabbit. I haven't got much use for a squealer myself, I just seem to fit in around the poolroom. See?"

"Sure."

"Well, I figured the way he smiled at me they'd be around some time today. I know they'll come."

"Is that why you had the door locked?"

"I suppose so. I was sitting here playing the banjo a bit, but it got so I just couldn't stand the notion of someone bumping me off, and I couldn't stop thinking about dying. I hate thinking about dying but I can't help it, it kinda fascinates me."

He picked up the banjo again and looked out the window. His head was still sweating. Shorty twanged the strings slowly, three times. "Don't do that," Steve said suddenly, getting up and feeling scared. "I'll stay here with you, Shorty," he said.

"If you don't mind, I'm not gonna give you a lesson today," Shorty said. His blue eyes were wide open.

"Don't you want me to stay?"

"I'd rather be alone."

"I'll come and see you later, then."

"All right."

"There's nothing you want me to do?"

"No, thanks. Nothing."

"I'll get going, then."

Steve went out, leaving Shorty sitting on the chair, the banjo on his knees, his face turned to the window and his teeth biting into his lower lip. The sun was shining full on his small, round, wrinkled face. As Steve went downstairs he heard faintly the twanging of the banjo. He walked along the street as far as the corner, then turned and walked back to the house, looking up at the front window. The blind was down. Then, because he was uneasy in his own mind, he went up to the house and sat down on the veranda. Shorty was upstairs waiting, and Steve, wondering how such a sick man could be so eager to go on living, felt young and a little ashamed. Alert, he looked at every passer-by, expecting always to see men coming down the street to the house and hear them ask for Shorty Horne. The men, he thought, would be well dressed, only they would wear gold bracelets. Steve was trying to think of something very comforting he could say to Shorty. Across the road, down about half a block, was a schoolyard, half the yard cinders and cement, and only a small stretch of green lawn. A bell sounded in the school. Within a few seconds kids came out the wide doors, little girls in light dresses, who did not remain long on the hot cement but ran yelling to the green lawn to play a while before going out the gate.

An automobile stopped opposite the house. A woman was driving the car. Sitting beside her was a young man who talked intimately, leaning toward her, holding her by the arm and refusing to let her get out of the car. Suddenly they both began to laugh out loud, leaning back in the seat.

Though it was late afternoon, hardly any one came down the street, for the sky was still cloudless and the pavement was hot. Steve sat on the veranda for over an hour. He would not go home and leave Shorty alone in the house.

Then he saw Mrs. Scott coming down the street, a large, ample woman wearing a light blouse and a blue skirt, and carrying a heavy shopping-bag. She was leaning forward. From some distance away she began to smile at Steve. He said to her: "I'm going up to see Mr. Horne. He was lying down a while ago resting. I'll go up and see him soon now."

"The poor man!" she said, wiping the moisture off her

large red face. "I don't see how he can go on living in weather like this."

"It's rotten weather for anybody," Steve said.

"I don't know how he can stand it at all," she said, shaking her head and drawing in a deep breath before going into the house. "It just burns me to a frazzle."

Steve remained on the veranda twenty minutes longer. Before going he intended to speak to Shorty and then speak to Mrs. Scott, but the woman herself came to the door, breathing heavily after coming downstairs, and said to him: "Steve, would you do something for me? I rapped on Mr. Horne's door and couldn't get an answer. The door's locked."

"What do you want me to do?"

"Please open the door for me," she said nervously.

Steve went on ahead of her up the stairs. As they got closer to the attic the air seemed to be mustier, as it was in all the old rooming-houses. He tried the door and called out, but Shorty did not answer. Mrs. Scott was standing behind him, her hands up to her face. Finally Steve swung his shoulder against the door, which opened easily. The room was darkened with the blinds down again. The odor of escaping gas made Steve cough and cover his nose with his handkerchief as he hurried to throw up the window and turn off the gas jet.

Shorty was lying on the floor, his knees curled up, his elbows in at his sides, his head toward the window. He had fallen off the bed. A strip of towelling had blocked the open space between the door and the floor. Shorty's hands were cold. The tin can that had been on his table had fallen to the floor beside him. The banjo was at the foot of the bed.

Mrs. Scott, who had run downstairs when she smelled the gas, came into the room slowly, still holding her hands up to her face. "I knew something like this would happen some time," she said. "The poor fellow, he was so sick, I knew he'd do it."

Steve looked at her and shook his head.

"What'll I do?" Mrs. Scott said.

"You'd better tell the police," Steve answered. He was going downstairs. He wanted to get out to the sunlight. He didn't want to be mixed up in the affair at all.

The Thing That Happened
to Uncle Adolphe

WHEN HIS MOTHER DIED, ALBERT CAME FROM THE COUNTRY to his Uncle Adolphe's shoe-repair shop to learn his uncle's trade and go to school. His uncle was squat and broad-shouldered, and powerful, with a glistening bald head and a fringe of gray hair. It was fun working for him. Albert ran messages and delivered shoes and then came back and sat around watching his uncle trim the leather for a pair of soles with his short, sharp knife.

In the evenings, Uncle Adolphe often took Albert to the houses of friends in the neighborhood. On the way, Albert asked questions about anything that came into his head and got an answer that seemed natural and clear, and made the question seem important. His uncle, full of lively information about everything going on around him, also used to sing while he worked at the bench near the window. Standing in his old khaki-colored smock he pounded away with his hammer, singing at the top of his voice. If people passing on the street turned and gaped, Uncle Adolphe swung his hammer in the air and grinned cheerfully at them.

Then one day Albert noticed that his uncle was working very fast and watching the clock. "Albert, come here," he said earnestly. "Are you listening carefully, Albert? I want you to go down to the corner and cross the road and go along to Molsen's grocery store. Then go in and tell Mr. Molsen you are from your Uncle Adolphe and you have come for Mr. Zimmerman. He'll be sitting there in the back room. He's blind, understand, Albert? You take his arm, see? And bring him along here. And be careful. He's my good friend. You bring him here."

"I didn't know you had a blind friend, Uncle Adolphe," Albert said, getting his hat.

"I met him at Molsen's. He promised to come here and talk to me in the afternoon. He's a very important man. Be careful, whatever you do, Albert."

Albert was very shy going into the grocery store. "My uncle sent me for Mr. Zimmerman," he said. Pointing to a back room the grocer said, "He's been waiting. Go on in." And he called out, "Henry, here's the boy that Adolphe sent for you."

In the back room, a thin old man in a neat black suit sat alone in a rocking chair. His hair was long and white. It stuck out from under the wide-brimmed black hat he had just put on. But it was his calm, thin face which Albert noticed. While Albert was gaping at him Mr. Zimmerman said quietly, "Take my arm, boy." Mr. Zimmerman seemed to know Albert was standing beside him. It was startling. But then Albert told himself he didn't need to feel shy, for after all, Mr. Zimmerman couldn't really see him.

So Albert walked him out to the street. Mr. Zimmerman touched Albert's arm very lightly. As they went down the street Albert grew fascinated by the ease and assurance with which Mr. Zimmerman strode along. Once he even said, "Faster, please." Albert wondered if he would notice if he withdrew his arm and let him walk on alone, and he did this, and Mr. Zimmerman kept on going, but then he suddenly stopped, waving his cane fiercely. "Where are you? Are you playing a trick on me?" he snapped. Outraged, he looked as if he were going to strike at Albert.

"I'm here," Albert said.

"Then you mind what you're doing, and no tricks," Mr. Zimmerman warned him.

So they said nothing the rest of the way, and Albert was glad when they got to the shoemaker's shop and he saw his uncle through the window. He was so glad that he ducked away from Mr. Zimmerman as soon as he opened the door.

"Careful, careful, use your head, Albert," his uncle called sharply, for Mr. Zimmerman was standing there groping around with his stick.

"No fuss, no fuss, please," Mr. Zimmerman protested, irritably. "I'm all right."

"It's just that Albert—"

"Albert's all right," Mr. Zimmerman said impatiently as he sat down, "only tell him next time he's not to play games with me and let me go along by myself."

"Why, I'm ashamed. Is that so, Albert?" Uncle Adolphe said. He was so apologetic as he fussed around Mr. Zimmerman that Albert couldn't believe he was looking at his own uncle. He began to feel truly ashamed of himself, as if he had insulted a very great man. He got out of the way, working at little jobs around the shop, and listened furtively while his uncle and Mr. Zimmerman talked.

He couldn't make much out of the conversation. With both hands resting on the head of his stick, Mr. Zimmerman was talking like a man making a speech. He talked about China and Russia, and the march of history and the future of the people of America. The big-sounding, lofty phrases meant nothing to Albert, except that sometimes they sounded mocking, and sometimes eager or triumphant and seemed to fill Uncle Adolphe with restless excitement. He asked questions, and when he got the answer he scratched his head and looked puzzled. Albert noticed that Mr. Zimmerman never asked his uncle a question about anything, and it offended Albert. In a couple of hours, Uncle Adolphe took Mr. Zimmerman home and left Albert minding the shop.

Then one afternoon Uncle Adolphe said, "Now listen, Albert. I want you to go and get Mr. Zimmerman. This time put your mind on it, see? If you embarrass him again I won't like it and I'll certainly give you a smack, see?"

Hesitating, Albert asked, "Uncle Adolphe, why do you like the blind man?"

"Ah, he's a great scholar. You should have heard him last night."

"I'll bet he doesn't know half as much as you do."

"Me?" he said. "Why, I don't know anything. I'm just a poor, ignorant shoemaker. But if I listen to him then maybe I'll get to learn how to see things. Now go along, Albert."

Albert went down the street slowly, dreading the walk with Mr. Zimmerman. At Molsen's, he hung back timidly. Four men from the neighborhood were there, listening reverently to the blind man. When Albert stuck his head into the room he expected Mr. Zimmerman to know he was there and stare at him suspiciously.

Letting Mr. Zimmerman take his arm, they started out. When they had gone only a little piece he found himself staring up at the blind man's impassive face and wondering, "How does he know so much? Why do they ask him questions? He can't see the streets, or people's faces, or anything in the world. You'd think he'd be the one who'd be asking Uncle Adolphe to come and tell him what's going on all over."

"Are you walking along staring at me, boy?" Mr. Zimmerman asked suddenly.

"I wasn't," Albert began, shocked. Then he grew scared. The other day Mr. Zimmerman had known when he was playing a little game. He seemed to have ways of knowing things that were frightening, and it was as if they were walking arm in arm, yet in different worlds.

"I was wondering how you knew so much?" he said.

"Does it surprise you?"

"I was only thinking–"

"You should be a polite boy and not keep on reminding me that I can't see," Mr. Zimmerman said. "So please don't stare at me." He made a sucking sound with his lower lip. He seemed to think Albert was trying to humiliate him. They went to the shop in silence, with Albert frightened by the hostility growing between them.

"It was a nice little trip this time, eh?" Uncle Adolphe asked, hopefully, as they came in.

"Oh, yes, indeed," Mr. Zimmerman said. But then he smiled reproachfully. "Just the same, I don't think the boy likes me. Do you, Albert?"

Albert shook his head helplessly at his uncle, who was scowling at him.

"What's he been doing now?" Uncle Adolphe asked, humiliated again.

"He keeps staring at me and not saying anything, eh, Albert?" Mr. Zimmerman said, his hand groping for Albert's arm, a knowing smile on his face.

"I just don't know what to say and I couldn't help it," Albert protested. His uncle's face was reddening, exasperated that Albert should always be doing some little thing to embarrass a man like Mr. Zimmerman. He knocked Albert spinning against the counter and scowled at him, daring him to make more fuss. "I guess he's a stupid boy," he apologized. "I haven't been paying much attention to him. I haven't noticed him much." Then he swung his arm at Albert. "Go 'way," he said. "Go on, go on, go on."

Albert stayed out of the store till his uncle took Mr. Zimmerman home.

For the next few days Uncle Adolphe paid no attention to him at all. Albert hung around the bench near the window, waiting for his uncle to be friendly. A couple of times he asked a few timid questions. "Don't bother me, Albert," his uncle said. Albert knew his uncle was seeing Mr. Zimmerman in the evenings. He could tell by the way his uncle stood with a shoe in his hand, his face all puckered up, worrying and muttering. He never sang any more.

Then a week later, in the afternoon, Uncle Adolphe said, "Go and get Mr. Zimmerman, Albert. He's waiting. Now mind, no wool-gathering. It's disgusting that a boy your age can't walk a block with Mr. Zimmerman without making trouble. Do you hear me?"

"I hear, Uncle Adolphe."

"Then don't gape at me so stupidly. Go on," he said.

When Albert went down to the grocery store he took the blind man's arm tighter than ever before. Looking straight ahead, thinking only of his uncle's shop, he guided Mr. Zimmerman along the crowded sidewalk.

"You don't need to pull me like that," Mr. Zimmerman complained. "Just walk, just walk, if you please," he said. "I don't want everybody gaping at me."

Though he felt helpless and lost, Albert held on to Mr. Zimmerman's arm.

By the time they got to the shop Albert was trembling. He opened the door for Mr. Zimmerman, and was so eager to get away that he jerked his arm loose. Lurching to the side, the blind man groped for the door. He missed it and swung around, losing his balance and banged his head against the door jamb. A little blue bruise appeared on his pale high forehead.

"Oh, you stupid, careless, clumsy boy." Uncle Adolphe shouted. "Sit here, Mr. Zimmerman. Oh, what can I say? He's a stupid boy if ever there was one. Please wait. I'll get a little hot water in the back room."

He grabbed Albert by the scruff of the neck, dragging him along. Passing the counter, he snatched a long piece of thick, raw leather. He clamped his big hand over Albert's mouth when they got to the back room. He raised his arm, his face full of cold disgust and rage, and he pounded Albert. Then he pushed him on the floor and rushed to get a wet towel and hurried back to Mr. Zimmerman.

Albert lay there trying not to sob, hearing the drone of their voices, remembering how his uncle used to sing and how bright the world had looked to him until he had started listening to the blind man.

Just Like Her Mother

UNCLE ALEC WAS A SHORT SOLID MAN WITH A SMOOTH unsmiling face and a high forehead that reminded sixteen-year-old Georgie Miller of pictures of William Shakespeare. His clothes always looked too tight on him because, as his wife Marge said, he had a slight tendency to obesity. Yet in spite of his clumsy body and awkward gait he had an impressive quiet dignity. He and his wife lived in a flat over his small book and gift shop. He was not a good businessman. He was too intellectual, too independent and stubborn, and he had an annoying way of shrugging and smiling when a customer disregarded his advice on a book. He sold records but showed real interest only in the customers who liked the classical composers, especially Mozart and Bach.

When Georgie's father died Uncle Alec offered to look after her, and her beautiful young mother, who had been separated from her father for two years, came up from Toronto where she worked in television and made the arrangements. She promised to send fifty dollars a month for Georgie's board, and then she returned to Toronto and Georgie moved in with Uncle Alec and Aunt Marge.

At first she found it hard to feel at home at her uncle's

place. She knew she could never grow to love a sedate, methodical and enormously respectable woman like Aunt Marge. Why Uncle Alec had married her she couldn't figure out. For weeks, too, she was afraid Uncle Alec would make some slurring remark about her mother whom she had never stopped loving.

At the end of the month, when a letter came from her mother and no mention was made of the board money, Aunt Marge made a caustic comment, but Uncle Alec didn't complain at all. Georgie was his brother's child, he said, and he was going to look after her anyway. She wanted, then, to help him in the store. Soon she was of real help because the customers who wanted to buy pop records liked her to wait on them and she learned to talk their language. Soon the little cubicle where they kept the record player became her department.

Uncle Alec would sit at his big corner desk by the cash register and watch her moving around and he would rub the side of his face slowly and meditate. Once he said, "You're a bright intelligent girl, Georgie," and another time he said, "A girl like you with a little spark of something, well, she should have some distinction. There shouldn't be anything cheap and common about her. No, that's right." He seemed to be debating with himself, mulling over some plan and gradually finding pleasure in it.

He began to spend all his spare time talking to her about books and music. When they weren't busy in the shop he played classical records and talked about the composers. If she offered an intelligent perception, his face would soften and his eyes shine. He took her to concerts with him. At home, even when they were having dinner, he would recite the poetry of Keats and Shelley and have her repeat it, and then explain that the wisdom of the race was in the language and when good poems were learned by heart a girl could possess that wisdom.

He had her read aloud to him while he leaned back in the big chair in the living room, his eyes closed, and if she slurred over a word, or dropped a G, or sounded nasal he would throw out his arms, jump up and shout, "No, no, no," as he pounded his diaphragm.

"From here. From here, do you understand, Georgie?" It astonished her that he could get so excited and show such intensity and be so concerned. She was never to use slang, she was to speak slowly and with dignity. When he showed that he was growing proud of her she wanted to please him, and then it became good fun and she became proud of herself. Next year, he said, if they could get the money together he wanted her to go to the university.

His gentle patient concern began to touch every part of her life. In that neighborhood she knew few boys, but sometimes a young man who came into the store would notice her grave blue eyes and her high color. Her fair hair was drawn back into a bun on her neck and she dressed rather primly and wore no make-up, but he would take another look at her eyes and her beautiful figure and ask her out for an evening. But she would frighten him off with her tone and her conversation, and then wonder why he didn't come back again. Uncle Alec would be there to console her. "That's all right my dear ... Never hold yourself cheap. Never be easy. Always be out of their reach, a little beyond them, and later on, when the cheap ones have passed through their hands, they'll remember you with respect and come back."

He insisted that she write faithfully to her mother, and she would take great pains with the letter and then read it to Uncle Alec, who would smile happily if she had expressed herself with distinction, and she began to believe they were both sharing a desire to impress her mother. Sometimes she would ask for the money for a dress or a pair of shoes. Her mother would answer and send the money and say that they were not to worry about the board money; one of these days she would come home for a quick visit and pay in full. The letter would be written in a breezy, careless style with little punctuation and a lot of exclamation marks and many commonplace phrases.

Once Uncle Alec, himself, answered one of these letters to reassure Georgie's mother. He was not worrying about the money, he said. He came into Georgie's bedroom to read his letter while she curled up on the bed, and she was grateful that in the way he wrote he showed no hostility whatever to her mother, although he could easily have implied that he still looked down on her for deserting her husband. The whole tone of his letter was dignified and respectful and Georgie loved him for his generosity and for realizing how fond she was of her mother.

That night she asked, "What do you think mother really does in television, Uncle Alec?"

"Do? But why don't you ask her?"

"I have asked her. I ask her all the time."

"And what does she say?"

"She says she works with directors and producers, but what does that mean?"

"She's having her life, Georgie, just as you'll have yours. All lives are different, and they should be completely different, shouldn't they?"

One day they got a letter from her mother in which she said she was coming home for two days to see Georgie. "Well now, imagine," Aunt Marge said with a cynical smile. "I suppose she's worried about owing us money." But

Uncle Alec took his time before saying anything. "Ten months since you've seen your mother, eh, Georgie?" he said finally. "Well, she won't know you. You've come a long way. You're quite a little lady," and he smiled to himself.

In the afternoon, two days later, Georgie's mother telephoned from the hotel where she had registered. She knew they had no room for her in the apartment. She was calling, she said, before she came up to the shop, to warn them she was counting on taking them back to the hotel for dinner.

Georgie put on her new dark-blue dress. It was a severely modest dress with a high neckline, but when she turned slowly under the close inspection of Aunt Marge and Uncle Alec, they told her she had grown three inches and her mother wouldn't know her. For an hour, she waited at the window. It started to rain, it was time to close the store, though two men still browsed around, and Georgie got excited and fearful, and then with the rain falling hard a taxi stopped and her mother, in a huge mauve-colored straw hat and a squirrel cape, got out waving cheerfully to the driver and came running across the pavement to where she waited at the open door. "Why, Georgie, you dear soul, bless you," she cried, and they threw their arms around each other.

As her mother swept into the store the two men who were talking to Uncle Alec couldn't help turning to stare at her. It was her light hair, her stride, her warm laugh sounding loud in the quiet store and her light careless elegant easy movements. She looked much younger than thirty-six and as she walked the length of the store, her arm around Georgie's waist, Georgie was very proud of her. They stopped to shake hands with Uncle Alec. On the way upstairs, Georgie felt a glow come over her whole being, and she enjoyed it when Aunt Marge, who had on her best brown dress, took on an apologetic manner in her mother's presence as if she felt inadequate.

Uncle Alec finally came upstairs and Georgie sat by herself and listened while they talked. It was a very polite and gracious conversation, and Georgie loved it when her mother, looking over at her, smiled. But she noticed things about her mother that she wouldn't have noticed before; she talked carelessly, used a lot of slang and sometimes swore lightheartedly, just for emphasis, and she had a lazy indulgent smile that made profound conversation difficult.

Her hair was lighter than it used to be. She wore too much make-up. These impressions might have disturbed her if Uncle Alec himself hadn't made them seem unimportant. Her mother joked with him and laughed and listened, making what was said between them seem so sympathetically right and intimate that Uncle Alec, very reluctantly at first, yet surely, began to lose his superior aloofness. He began to make graceful speeches, he played up to her and once he laughed boisterously and warmly. When Aunt Marge became silent, Georgie smiled at her shyly.

When they had taken a taxi to the hotel and had had a fine meal in the big dining room, Uncle Alec wanted to pay for the dinner, but Georgie's mother reminded him gently that they were her guests. Everything seemed to be within her mother's reach, Georgie thought. They went up to her room and there she sat down at the desk and wrote a cheque for nine hundred dollars, the amount she owed for ten months' board. "How do you like that, Aunt Marge?" Georgie wanted to say, but it wasn't necessary to say it. Aunt Marge, her eyes shining with vast satisfaction, made a silly embarrassing speech, and Uncle Alec had to say quickly that the money didn't mean anything to him, Georgie had become a valuable part of his life. He so plainly meant it that Georgie smiled at her mother and felt at peace with everybody.

It was arranged that Georgie would come down to the hotel next day and have lunch with her mother, and then they would go shopping. On the way home, Uncle Alec said to her, "I was proud of you, Georgie. Nice manners. A girl of some cultivation. It was showing, my dear, and your mother saw it." Lying in her bed that night, Georgie heard the murmur of voices in the other bedroom and she knew they were talking about her mother, and she wondered if they felt as good as she did about the evening. Her mother did everything wrong, she thought, and yet with her careless ease and her little laugh she could put a glow on the evening.

At noontime next day, Uncle Alec said to her, "We were in the way last night, Georgie. Have a good talk with your mother. Open up with her. Tell her all you've done and learned. Be yourself. Show what you're interested in. A lot of water has gone under the bridge, Georgie."

"I've got so much to talk about," she said. "Last night I just didn't seem to get started, did I?" When she got to her mother's hotel room she intended to have this conversation, but her mother was wearing a gray tailored suit and it looked very elegant and she began to admire it.

"It is nice, isn't it, Georgie. Oh, darling, we just don't look right together do we? That little dress you have on makes you look like a novice in a convent. Do you want to look like that? Why you don't look like my daughter at all. Are you sure Uncle Alec doesn't want you to wear horn-rimmed glasses?"

"My eyes are quite good, Mother."

"I'm kidding you, honey."

"Yes, I suppose you are."

"I mean, you don't have to dress like Aunt Marge, Georgie. Come here and sit down and let me fix your hair." As she sat down, feeling awkward, she began to like the feel of her mother's hand running through her hair as she talked. "Why do they want to make such a sedate little lovely out of you, Georgie? You're actually pretty, darling. You know what I'm going to do after lunch? I'm going to buy you the silliest gay dress, and you see that you wear it, too."

At lunch Georgie tried to find out what her mother was doing in television, but nothing was made very clear to her. She was doing executive work for a Mr. Henderson, a producer. She got away from Mr. Henderson and talked gaily about Toronto and how Georgie would love it, but something was troubling her. "Georgie, you don't know how quickly time passes for a woman," she said finally, her eyes almost sad as she smiled. Her beautiful, generous, smiling mouth and the loneliness in her eyes that vanished in a moment seemed to Georgie to bring them very close together. "In a few years I'll be old, Georgie. That's the way it is. A woman wakes up and realizes she has suddenly fallen to pieces. In a year you'll be older and in a year I'll be so much older, and then we're going to live together, darling." She made Georgie feel a little sad and yet poetic, as she had felt when Uncle Alec had carried her away with his reading of one of Keats's poems.

She began to talk enthusiastically about Uncle Alec. "He's been everything to me, simply everything," she said, and she told how he worked with her and wanted her to have a good mind and about his consideration and patience. It all poured out of her. She used words Alec would have liked her to use, she showed off and laughed and wanted her mother to see she had a fine discriminating mind. Her mother nodded, listening thoughtfully, her elbow on the table, her chin cupped in her hand.

"Tell me something, Georgie," she said. "Is Alec, well, is he ever critical of me? Put me on the pan? Fry me a little?"

"He wouldn't say anything about you. Why, that's beneath him. His mind is too fine and generous."

"Well, maybe I never understood Alec. Maybe you jumped right into his heart. Why not? You're an angel. And who knows, maybe angels talk like you do, darling. Your mother is light-headed and silly and anything very deep goes in one ear and right out the other, but I'll always be willing to listen to you. Come on and we'll do some shopping."

They loafed around the big stores and even the loafing made Georgie feel luxurious. The little things they encountered in idle moments became so diverting and so amusing. They bought a good brown-leather purse for Aunt Marge and an imported English pipe and a pound of tobacco for Uncle Alec. "Now for the dress," her mother said. "It must be something crazy, almost with a touch of high fashion." For an hour, Georgie tried on dresses. They bought one of fluffy organdie in very pale mauve that billowed out like foam, with the skirt about fourteen inches from the ground. It had two thin shoulder straps.

Her mother, who was leaving on the early train, came back to the shop with her to say good-bye to Uncle Alec and Aunt Marge. When they arrived with their parcels, Uncle Alec was just closing the store. He suggested they all have dinner, but Georgie's mother said she would eat on the train. Aunt Marge came down and they had a jolly time giving the presents. Uncle Alec and Aunt Marge were both surprised and touched.

"I've got half an hour, Georgie," her mother said, looking at her wrist watch. "Why don't you put on your dress and show it to them. Go on, dear. Hurry."

"Yes, I'll hurry," Georgie said, wanting to please her mother. She went upstairs and put on the dress, and when she came down she was trembling a little and didn't know why. Her mother was sitting on the edge of Uncle Alec's big desk, one leg crossed over the other, Uncle Alec was leaning against the poetry section of the bookcases, having lighted his new pipe, and Aunt Marge was holding her purse by the strap and swinging it a little.

"Why bless you, Georgie, bless you, darling, a thousand times," her mother cried. "Now just look at her. Isn't she a picture?"

"It looks – it looks very expensive," Aunt Marge said.

"How do you like it, Uncle Alec?" Georgie asked eagerly.

There was surprise in his eyes as he looked at her steadily, then he put down his pipe. "Yes, that's a very pretty dress," he said quietly. But the expression on his face was so unfamiliar it seemed to her that he had trouble recognizing her, and so she didn't know whether or not he liked the dress.

"Georgie dear," her mother said gravely, "you're going to be quite a looker. Yes, sir, quite a gal." Suddenly she laughed happily and threw up her arms as if she had just recognized her own daughter. "Oh, I'd like to see you dancing around and humming, Georgie. You're so young and beautiful I want to go away seeing you dancing and singing. Put on some records. Where are those records, Alec?"

"I'll do it," Georgie said, running to the little music cubicle. She felt that she and her mother were sharing some kind of a new happiness. She fumbled through the records. She came dancing out of the cubicle, dancing around in slow circles, her eyes on her mother who suddenly laughed – it was such a warm rich pleased careless laugh – and got up and put her arm around her and began to dance with her. While her mother held her so lightly and led her so easily, Georgie felt all the stiffness and shyness leaving her limbs; she wanted to whirl as her mother hummed; she started to sing and her mother sang with her while they danced, and they kept it up till they were both out of breath. Then they stopped and started to laugh, not knowing why they laughed so gaily.

"You've got a nice little voice there, Georgie," her mother said when she could get her breath. "Do you sing much?"

"Not much popular stuff. Uncle Alec likes me to sing the concert pieces."

"Oh, nuts, Alec. Let her relax and be charming. Surely you can see she was born to be charming."

"It's quite true," he said.

"Oh, dear. What time is it? If I don't get a taxi right at the door I won't have time to pick up my bag at the hotel and make the train."

"There's a taxi stand just twenty feet away. Come on," Uncle Alec said.

"That's swell. Oh, you're all wonderful. Bless you, bless you," she cried. "Why didn't I plan to stay longer? Why are things always like this – I have to go just when I'm feeling so happy. It's always like this." She was half laughing, half tearful in the excitement of rushing away. At the door, she threw her arms around Georgie and kissed her. Alec was already out on the street beckoning to a taxi. Georgie, standing at the door, watched them shake hands with each other warmly, and she liked seeing them with their hands out to each other, and she wanted to cry.

"Isn't she lovely?" she asked, when Alec had come in.

But he didn't answer. He was breathing hard as if he had been running and he walked back to the desk and sat where her mother had sat. Now he was watching Georgie as she came toward him. His pale steady eyes and the heavy lines in his forehead worried her; he sighed and pondered and did not try to hide his disappointment.

"The dress must have cost a penny," Aunt Marge said. "Just what did it cost, Georgie?"

"I think it was almost a hundred dollars."

"Did she say where she got the money?"

"I didn't ask her," Georgie said, hardly listening to her aunt as she watched Uncle Alec, whose eyes now were hard and bitter as he stared at her.

"What's the matter, Uncle Alec?"

Ignoring her, he said to his wife, "She looked just like her, didn't she? So very much like her."

"She certainly did. Just suddenly – there they are – two peas in a pod."

"But what's the matter?" Georgie asked. "Isn't it all right if–"

"You won't be like her, do you hear?" Uncle Alec said harshly. "Singing with her, looking like her. She's no good." He tried to control himself but couldn't. He blurted out fiercely, "You won't be like her. That strumpet! Never anything else but a strumpet. She killed my brother. She broke his heart, running off with that cheap actor two years ago. Now it's a new one. And there's money there for a while. Georgie, Georgie–" As he came toward her his eyes glittered and his hand, reaching out for her, trembled. "Take off that dress or I'll rip it off." But she screamed and ran up the stairs and pulled the dress off frantically and tossed it in the corner, and she knew Uncle Alec hated her mother.

She lay on the bed and wanted to cry, but couldn't; her loneliness frightened her. A little later she heard Uncle Alec and his wife come upstairs. She heard them sitting down for dinner, but a chair was pushed back, then Alec came along the hall. "Georgie," he called and he opened her door. "Georgie," he said, "I'm very sorry." He sounded so ashamed and apologetic that she looked up at him. "You see, Georgie," he said gently, "I shouldn't have said what I did, but maybe it's better that it was said, because nothing should be hidden between you and me. Later on you'll forgive me. Come on now. We'll have dinner."

He sounded like himself now, calm and patient, and she had the habit of trying to please him, so she got up and went with him to the dinner table. They respected her silence and the fact that she couldn't touch her food. Once she raised her head intending to tell Uncle Alec that she understood why he had made himself her teacher and had worked with her so patiently; it wasn't just loving concern for her; he had wanted to make her into someone so different from her mother that she would feel completely separated from her whenever they were together.

But she couldn't tell it to him; the painful beating of her heart made it all too complicated. Instead she found herself saying gravely, "I wanted to tell you you're wrong about my father. He loved her till the day he died because he couldn't help loving her, no matter what happened, because she's like she is, and maybe that's what you have against her." But Uncle Alec's hurt troubled eyes seemed to force her to stop and she mumbled, "Excuse me," and hurried back to her room.

As she sat down in the chair by the window, knowing she had said the right thing to hurt Uncle Alec, the truth seemed to come tumbling at her, making her strangely happy. What had been true of her own father had been true of Uncle Alec and he knew it; he hadn't been a hypocrite with her mother; in her presence he had to be gracious and warm and available; he couldn't help it; he loved what was beautiful, it was the wisdom he had tried to cultivate in her, too, and when he was with her mother he felt compelled to respond to something beautiful in her nature, even if it left him feeling angry afterward.

She got up, slipped off the dressing gown she had been wearing and picked up the fluffy dress and put it on. With her cheeks burning she watched herself in the mirror as she walked the length of the room trying to look as her mother had looked yesterday when she swept into the shop.

A Boy Grows Older

IN THE BEDROOM MRS. SLOANE SAT DOWN AND FOLDED HER hands tight in her lap and swallowed hard and said to her husband, "I've got something to tell you about Jim."

Holding the shoe he had just taken off in his hand, he said, "Were you talking to him today?"

"He's coming here for money. I've been giving a bit to him from time to time. I know I shouldn't, but he's got me completely distracted."

"He knows we've got no money to lend," he said, and as he got up and walked around excitedly with one shoe on she knew he was thinking of their little bit of money disappearing day by day. "He knows we've only got our bit of a pension," he said. He had worked hard all his life and they had both denied themselves many little comforts and now she could see a look of terror coming into his eyes that she had seen for the first time the day he had to quit work and they had thought they would hardly be able to live. "Why, what'll happen to us?" he said, turning on her suddenly. "Where does he think we get it?"

She only sighed and shook her head, for she had been asking Jim that question for months, yet every time he got behind in his insurance collections he came around, scared, and got a little more money from her.

"There's no use giving me a setting out," she said. "He'll never believe we won't give it to him till you tell him. If he understands we're through helping him maybe he'll get some sense."

As they sat there solemnly looking at each other and waiting for Jim, she had her old dressing gown wrapped around her and he was sitting on the bed with his white hair mussed from rubbing his hands through it. They took turns blurting things out, questions they never tried to answer, questions that worried them more and more and drew them closer together. When they heard Jim come in and call from the living room, she said, "Remember, I'm going to tell him I told you. I've done all I can. It's up to you now."

Jim was waiting for her, walking up and down with his hat on and his white scarf hanging out as if the wind had blown it free from his overcoat while he hurried along the street. He looked very unhappy but he tried to smile at his mother. His face was so good-natured it was almost weak.

"What is it this time?" she asked.

"Oh," he said, sitting down and starting to rub his shoe on the carpet like an embarrassed small boy, "the same thing, I guess."

"More money again, you mean," she said.

"I guess that's it."

"In God's name, what for this time?"

"The same thing – I'm behind in my collections."

She had intended to shrug and say coolly, "Speak to your father," but instead she found herself walking up and down in front of him, wheeling on him and whispering savagely, "You'd take the last cent from us, and then what do you think is going to happen? Who are you going to run to then?" But he got up and took her arm and muttered, "I'll never ask you again – I promise – but I've got to have it. I'll give every cent back to you – I promise. I wouldn't ask you if there was a chance of getting it any place else." He felt sure of her. "I'll lose my job," he said.

"Maybe it would teach you to have some respect for yourself," she said, and then she added calmly, "I've told your father."

"You told him after all," he said, terribly hurt. "You promised not to."

"I'm through," she said.

He started to work himself up into a temper which didn't fool her at all because he always did it when he was trying to abuse her.

"You're mean," he said. "Plain mean." His words had no real anger and she smiled grimly. When he saw her smile he stopped and said helplessly, "Please, mom, please –" But she said firmly, "Speak to your father. It's his money."

"Mom, just this once more," he pleaded, and when she saw how he dreaded facing his father she was puzzled because he had never been afraid of him, they had never shouted at each other. "I've got to do it, I've got to do it," he kept saying to himself as he walked up and down, and then he turned to her, white-faced, and said, "Well, I've got to ask him, I can't help it," and he went into the bedroom with her following.

His father had gotten into bed and was reading and he could just see the crown of his white head rising over the edge of the newspaper. When Jim went into the room he stood over under the light on the wall. That was where he always stood when he was in trouble. Years ago, when he had been caught in a petty theft at school he had stood there; when he had started to work he used to come in late at night and stand under the light and tell them what had happened during the day, and it was where he had stood the night when he was eighteen and had told them he was going to get married. He was tilting back and forth on his heels, waiting for his father to look over at him, but when the paper wasn't lowered, he said at last in a mild, friendly tone, "Dad, could you loan me some money?"

His father put down his paper, folded it, shoved it under his arm and took off his glasses and said, "What do you do with your money, son?"

As his father stared at him steadily, a silly half-ashamed grin was on Jim's face. "I don't know, honestly I don't," he said shaking his head.

"Well, tell me what you think you do with it. You must remember something."

"Salesmen and collectors are all pretty much alike," Jim said. "They hang around together and it just slips through their fingers and then they're short at the end of the week."

"Then a man like you shouldn't have such a job."

"I guess you're right," Jim mumbled.

"Why don't you hunt for another job?"

"I will – I'll try hard," he said eagerly.

"How much do you need this time?"

"It's a lot, I've got to cover a whole week's collections," Jim said, his head down, his voice faint.

"All that?" his father said, and Mrs. Sloane knew by the way he swung his head toward her, startled, that he was thinking of the money he had saved for himself for his personal expenses such as tobacco, newspapers, a trip to the movies and clothes for himself. As he swung the bedclothes off, his face was flushed a vivid red against his white hair and he kept on staring at Jim. Mrs. Sloane knew he had a bad temper and she grew afraid.

Jim, watching his father coming toward him in his bare feet, muttered hastily, "I guess you haven't got it. I guess I'll go."

"Wait, Jim," his father called anxiously, making it clear he was not going to challenge him at all. "I didn't say I didn't have it, did I?" He spoke as if Jim ought to understand they had always been close together. He was going over to his coat hanging on the closet door. When Mrs. Sloane saw how he fumbled in his pocket for his check book and how his hand trembled as he jerked his pen out of his vest pocket she knew he was scared of something. She thought he was scared of Jim: she resented it so much she turned to abuse Jim herself.

But she said nothing to Jim because she had never seen him look so hurt as he did standing there waiting and realizing that his father was scared. He was watching his father as if at last he understood everything his father felt, and he said in a whisper, "What are you scared of?"

"Nothing," his father said.

"What's the matter?"

"Maybe I was thinking it might be worse."

"What do you mean?"

"Supposing I didn't give it to you?" his father said, and while they kept looking at each other Jim felt the fear in his father that came from knowing how weak he was, a fear that tomorrow or in a year something was apt to happen that would break him and jail him. He turned to his mother, begging her with his eyes to tell him what to do or say that would drive that scared look from his father's eyes. For the first time he seemed aware of their feeling for him. She nodded her head: she wanted to tell him she believed in him, but she was puzzled herself.

His father was writing the check on the top of the dresser. He wrote very carefully, and when he was finished he handed the check to Jim, saying only, "Here you are, son."

Looking at the check as if it were very hard for him to take it, Jim said in such a low voice she could hardly hear him, "I guess I've got to take it, but I'll pay you back. I wish you'd believe I'll pay you back. I don't want to take it if you won't believe it."

"All right, son."

"Well, thanks, thanks," he said.

But at the door he stood for a while with his head down, waiting, as if he couldn't bear to leave them till he was sure they had some faith left in him. He was so grave it made him look years older.

When he had gone his father waited a while for her to abuse him scornfully for not being firm with him, and then when she didn't speak, but stood there looking at the door, he got into bed and pulled the covers over him. After a few moments she went over and got into bed too. But she couldn't lie down. She sat up stiffly, staring down at her husband's face. His head rolled away from her and his eyes were closed.

"I'm glad you gave it to him," she said.

He opened his eyes and said simply, "He's getting older. He was a little different. Didn't you notice it? It made me feel we hadn't been wrong helping him this far."

As she lay down beside him and reached to turn out the light, her hand trembled. She lay very still. Then she turned and put her arm around him, and they lay there together in the dark.

A Couple of Million Dollars

THE WELL DRESSED BIG MAN WITH THE PUFFY-EYED FACE turned suddenly on the street and grinned at a shabby man who was buying a newspaper. The big fellow said, "Why, it's my old friend Max Seagram."

"And you're Myers."

"Sure I'm Myers," he said. It was a cold day in the early winter and Max was wearing a threadbare, light spring coat. "Don't tell me you're not doing well," he said, still grinning.

"The truth is I'm flat on my back."

"What were you doing?"

"I was in advertising in Chicago and I thought I might catch on here, but no luck so far," Max said. He was staring at Myers' grinning face. Ten years ago in Chicago, they had worked together till Myers had been left a couple of million dollars by an uncle who had owned a shirt factory. "What are you doing yourself?" Max asked uneasily.

"Nothing, absolutely nothing. Come on over to the Waldorf and have a drink with me." As he slipped his arm under Max's and they walked along the street, he whispered, "How would you like me to put a little money your way?"

"Doing what?" Max asked.

"Keeping an eye on my wife."

"You're kidding."

While Myers hung on to his arm and talked about his wife, Max felt sick with humiliation. "It sounds easy enough," he said, "but I thought you meant a decent job." Something about Myers frightened Max: something that made him let his arm hang heavy at his side till Myers dropped it and pulled his own arm away.

Going into the bar at the Waldorf, Myers said, "All I want you to do is find out who the guy is she's hanging around with, and that'll be easy because she makes no bones about going out by herself in the evening."

"What'll you do if you catch her?"

"It'll make a nice beginning, just to catch her," Myers said.

As they had one old-fashioned, and then another, Max, ashamed of his shabby clothes, could do nothing but listen and stare stupidly at Myers. "I'll show her to you when she's coming out in the evening sometime," Myers said, pulling at his nose with his thumb and forefinger and grinning slyly. Then he took out his wallet, his eyes on Max's frayed threadbare coat cuffs that Max had tried to darken that afternoon with ink, and a bill slipped from Myers' hand and dropped to the floor, underneath the table. Without looking down, Myers beckoned a waiter and pointed to the floor; he kept on grinning and whispering. The waiter picked the bill up and bowed. Myers waved his hand irritably and said, "Don't bother me. Keep it!"

It was a stupid arrogant gesture, an insult to everybody in the place.

"Here's fifty," Myers said. "That'll keep you going, won't it?"

"Listen Myers, how long have you been married?"

"Five years. But only two years to this one."

"So I wouldn't know her at all?"

"You might. She was in a show when I met her."

"When do I start?" Max said, holding the money.

"Why not take a shot at it tonight?" Myers said. "I can tip you off when she's going out."

Around nine, opposite the Myers' apartment house on Park Avenue, Max walked up and down. The cold wind blew against his legs. He tried to get a look through the doors along the black and white tiled hall as people in evening clothes came out. The giant doorman in the blue uniform was intimidating and he ducked his head and mumbled, "Some buddy! He puts me to work but he never thought of asking me around to see him."

Mrs. Myers was a slim woman with a little green hat, a mink coat, and she had a tall show girl's shape and a soft glowing complexion. She looked so rich that Max had a wild longing to brush against her, and it was easy following her. Sometimes she met a woman friend. Sometimes she went alone to the theatre. There were times when he was close enough to touch the soft fur of her coat. Once, he lost her for a while in a crowd and was terrified.

Every evening, he met Myers at the cocktail hour at the Waldorf and had a drink and reported, "Nothing doing, nothing at all."

Myers was disgusted. "You're not slipping, are you? Look here, Max, you're sure I can trust you?"

"Check it yourself."

"Never mind. She's fooling me and I'll get her. I never miss. Just pin that in your hat, Maxie." They sat for an hour, drinking.

Always, after his third or fourth old-fashioned, his

122

voice grew milder, his face softened, and he asked about the troubles Max had been through with a gentle considerate charm; but a drink later, his voice changed, he started tossing money around at the waiters who winked at each other and grinned, and Max got jittery again.

"You're lousy with dough and don't know what to do with it," Max blurted out.

"Wrong, wrong, wrong again. You haven't learnt anything, Max," he jeered. "I do it because it amuses me."

"But the waiters laugh at you and know you're a sucker."

"I'm a sucker?" He chuckled, wrinkling his puffy eyes. "I'll let you in on something, Maxie. They know I'm a sucker, but what do I know about them? I know how to make everybody here get down and rub his nose in the mud. I make suckers out of them every day." His voice rose, men standing at the bar looked over at him, and there was a frantic, frustrated bitterness in him. "Sure, I can turn this place into a mad house damned quick and any time I want to. I know all about them. I know what they want and I've got plenty of it, hee, hee, hee, hee."

"Go ahead, have a big belly laugh," Max said. "It's a mighty nice big feeling, crawling with coin, but listen, I got a brother in Chicago who never made more than you throw away in a week."

"What are you getting sore about?" Myers said, suddenly soft and soothing. "You want me to subsidize your whole family? I can do it."

"I don't want anything like that," Max said, afraid he was going to cry.

"Then what are you sore about?"

"Nothing you'd understand."

"Here, you're doing fine, here's fifty bucks, sooner or

later she's going to make a break and you be on the job," Myers said, tossing some bills across the table to Max, who stared a long time before he picked them up.

One night, when he was following her, Mrs. Myers got out of her taxi on Fifth Avenue at Thirty-Fourth Street and he hurried after her and almost ran into her as she stepped out from a doorway.

"Well, and who are you, anyway?" she said. "And just what do you want?"

"I don't know you, lady, I don't know what you mean," he said.

"You've been following me for a couple of weeks. You're working for my husband, I presume – well, tell him it's no good. Next time, I'll simply have you arrested," and she turned and started to go down the street.

"Just a minute," he called desperately.

"What for?"

"Don't go like that, please, you don't understand. I used to know him years ago."

"You knew him in Chicago?"

"I grew up with him. Nobody knew him better."

"Maybe, if you don't mind ..." she hesitated. "Maybe you could tell me a few things ..."

"Sure. Look, I've been wanting to talk to someone about him," he said. "I used to work in the same office with him, only he worked twice as hard. I used to loan him money, we used to go to the ball games together and when we were kids my mother used to like having him around because he was hard working." He was so excited to be walking with her, feeling her coat brushing against him, and watching the light touching her fine smooth skin that he broke off and began to apologize for following her. "I was broke, I had to do something. Myers knew I'd take the job."

She walked beside him with her head down, troubled by her own thoughts, and when they were as far as Madison Square, she stepped out to the curb, waved her arm suddenly to a passing taxi, wiped away a few flecks of snow from her face with her gloved hand, and said, "Look here! If he's paying you, you'd better let him go on. You need the money."

"But I'll have to keep on following you."

"It won't bother me like it did," she said, "don't worry about it." Her face was lovely in that light in the snow. "You're very nice, you know," she said, and the wheel of the cab spun and sprayed the snow over the sidewalk, some of it catching his pants cuff, and she was gone.

The next time he saw Myers he said, "I'm not going to take any more of your money for this thing. It's no good, so I'm quitting."

"How did it go last night?"

"The same old thing. Nothing happened."

"Then you're missing out, man. She was excited about something when she came in," Myers said. "Listen, you're my old pal, eh, Maxie? Look! Let me loan you some money. Don't figure I'm paying you for the job. You can pay me back when you want to. What do you say?" He grinned. "Let's you and me have dinner tonight."

"With me in these clothes?"

"You don't need to dress if you're with me. I don't," Myers said.

During the dinner in the hotel Max asked Myers what had happened to him since he'd come into the money ten years ago, and Myers said he had stopped working immediately, gone to Paris and had lived there for two years doing everything rich Americans were supposed to do, until he got so bored he pulled out of Paris and settled down in

London, but he had come to hate the English and went to the far east, to Shanghai, and later to Bombay, and then to the golden temple of the Sikhs at Amritsar, and then he had lived for a month in Moscow and grew to hate the Russians.

After dinner, they went to a night club. The hat check girl beamed, the captain fussed, trembling with eagerness, the manager came and asked if he was pleased with his table and lovely girls in the floor show kept smiling at him wistfully. Yet, he didn't give anyone a tip and he didn't pay his check when they went out.

"Do you own a piece of this place, or what's the set up that you don't have to pay?" Max asked.

Myers grinned. "It's more fun this way," he said. "You know what a sucker's game the night club racket is for anybody with a little dough. I figured that out a long time ago."

"Then you do pay?"

"Sure, I pay plenty, but I fixed it with them so I pay for everything at the end of the month. Then I owe them a hell of a lot and keep putting it off a long time and they hop around like cats on a hot brick. I get full value for my money."

One night, Max followed Mrs. Myers to a little Russian place in a cellar on West Twelfth Street, and she came up to him with her hand out, as if they had become old friends since they had walked in the snow. "I've been terribly restless," she said, "I've got to talk to somebody."

"What's the matter, Mrs. Myers?"

"It's not safe, I know, to talk like this. It's crazy."

"Sure it's safe," he said, anxious to soothe her.

It was warm in the little café, there was the smell of wine and food and a Russian girl was playing a guitar and singing, and when they sat down in a corner at the end of one of the long wooden tables and she started making little patterns with her finger on it, he was sure she was very lonely.

"I don't know anybody who knew him years ago when he was different," she began.

"But what's worrying you now?"

"Nothing, nothing. I just go over and over it." Looking at him helplessly, she blurted out, "You don't understand. I'm scared. He does nothing. He works at nothing. He looks and looks and looks for something to amuse him, and I don't know if I amuse him, or bore him, too. I don't know if he wants me, except I'm something he owns."

"Maybe I'm helping make you feel that way," he said. "I'll tell him I won't follow you any more."

"No, that's no solution."

"What do you want me to do?"

"Nothing, nothing. Let's be friends, that's all. You're sweet to listen to me," she said. Her green felt hat was low over one eye, and he could see the smooth sweep of her golden red hair to the curve of her neck, and she was so close to him, so eager for warmth and friendliness that he had to catch his breath.

"Why don't you leave Myers?" he blurted out.

"I'm scared to."

"But I know what you're really like," he said. "You should be bouncing around having some fun."

"Maybe so," she said, shrugging. "Maybe I'm used to things now. You get used to all kinds of comforts. They become a dear part of your life." There was a weary resignation and something hard and cynical in the way she spoke. "Besides, there are times when he seems charming."

"After three or four old-fashioneds?"

"You've noticed it yourself," she said.

Her lovely face, the shape of her breasts had gotten into his sleep. He began to see Myers' face drifting through the streets, grinning his shrewd and calculating grin at hundreds of people, estimating them all. One night he rushed into the Waldorf bar, stood a moment at the door staring at Myers' broad back, and then began to tremble. Myers had turned and was grinning.

"What's the matter?" Myers said, "Come on and sit down."

"There's nothing the matter with me."

"Why did you stand there pop-eyed watching me?"

"Because I want to tell you –"

"That I'm a little too fat, but it's just an alcoholic fatness ... A little too fat," and Max felt a little edge of malice in Myers' laughter.

"I'm getting a job in an advertising agency," Max said. "In a few days. I don't need to take any more of your money, I didn't do anything for you anyway."

"Sure, you've done lots for me," Myers said.

"OK, but I'm through now, and thank God I can quit. I know you've no use for me," he said.

Myers started to laugh. "Aw, come on down off your high horse. You're not working yet, what's the matter?" And he took out his wallet.

"No, it's no good, if I stay I'll quarrel with you," Max said, and he slapped Myers on the shoulder, tried to smile, and rushed out.

At the café on Twelfth Street, he ran down the steps, stopped abruptly, and looked around as though someone were chasing him. Mrs. Myers, sitting in the corner at the end of the long table, waved to him as if she were expecting him, but he was out of breath and could hardly speak.

"You've been running. What's the matter?" she asked. "Let's sit here and talk. Talk about anything."

"No. I just left him. It's not safe," he said.

"How do you know?"

"The way he grinned at me. He's watching me. He can't stand me, I can tell."

"It's not true," she said. "He let your name drop the other night, and he felt warmly for you. I'm sure he did."

"He let me drop?"

"Yes." Her eyes widened with excitement. "Oh, you're so sweet," she said, "You're a darling," and then he saw the bones whiten in her hands as she gripped at the edge of the table, and then she stood up. "You're right," she whispered. "He's followed you."

Myers came toward them looking like a contented and vindicated man enjoying a secret happiness. In a sprawling manner, he sat down with them and grinned into their faces.

"Aren't you glad to see me?" he asked. "And me thinking it was time we had this little get together."

"Stop your stupid grinning," Max said.

"I must get out of here," Myers' wife said.

She hesitated, and then got up and went as far as the counter. White-faced and watching, she waited there.

"Well, you couldn't resist horning in on what didn't belong to you, eh?" Myers jeered at Max.

"Nothing's gone on, Myers."

"Why'd you drop my arm walking along the street the day we met?"

"I didn't."

"Sure you did, I knew you didn't like me, and I didn't like you either, even when we were kids."

"No, you're wrong," Max said. "And you're wrong

about everything. You think you found out everybody's cheap. You despise everybody."

Myers' face seemed to grow heavy. In the other corner, the Russian girl playing the guitar began to sing. Myers raised his wife's glass and looked through it at the light. He put it down carefully on the table. He blinked his eyes at Max. "You think you can touch what I want," and he shot out his fists, hitting Max hard on the jaw, smacking his head back against the wall. Myers swung again, tipping over the table to get close to him, pinning Max against the wall; he let him have three hard short smashes and then he stepped back and let him roll under the table. "You touched what I want." People crowding around were frightened by the leering arrogant expression on Myers' face. "Get up, stooge," Myers yelled.

Pushing her way through the crowd, Mrs. Myers knelt down beside Max. He whispered, "I just wanted to help you."

"You have, you have," she whispered.

Max went to reach for her arm, but she had half turned away and was looking at Myers with an expression of grief and tenderness. "Come home, come home," Max heard her say as she stood up, and then she looked back down at Max and shook her head as if she were about to cry, but not for him as he lay there on the floor, tasting the blood in his mouth. Stunned, he wondered if all along they had needed someone like him to hold them together. When Myers turned away and took a few steps with her, holding her arm, and started to go with his head down, someone slyly tripped him and he stumbled, nearly sprawling, and he looked around with a dreadfully surprised look on his face, feeling the contempt everybody had for him, but he straightened himself and hurried out with his wife, and they were arm in arm.

The Lucky Lady

When Charlie Springer lost the third race, he looked so crushed and angry that Harriet, standing beside him at the rail, slipped her arm under his but he scowled and made her feel that everyone was unfairly against him.

"It's the hot day, Charlie," she said. "Everything just drags along."

He muttered at the big fat man who had leaned against him. "I haven't even got room to move my elbows. I can't even see those beetles I bet on."

"Cheer up, Charlie. There's always the right race."

"Oh, sure, sure," and then he said irritably, "Don't you ever wear anything but that white suit, Harriet?"

"Why, you always said you liked this suit, Charlie." And it was true. When she had first met him and had worn the suit, he said that it went so well with her blonde hair and long legs he felt like a rich man walking along the street with her. "Only last night you said the suit still looked good, Charlie."

"What's the matter with wanting you to look different sometimes?"

"Because it's unfair, Charlie."

"It was just a crack. Nothing looks right today," he said impatiently.

"I've got nothing else to wear," she said, and wondered why the sun glinting on the gray in his hair made him look so much older than when he had come into Mr. Striker's office to sell some oil stock, and had met her. "I'm broke and you know it, Charlie," and her mouth trembled, for she was ashamed to remind him again that she was broke, always broke from lending him money.

She was so fond of him because from the beginning he had been able to make her feel valuable and he had come upon her, after years of shopping around as a salesman and small promoter, knowing at once he needed her, and all the borrowing from her had only been their recognition of his need of her. But his irritated glance had also touched a secret fear that all the giving on her part only made him feel she was forever committed to him.

"Do you think I like looking shabby, Charlie?" she said. "I was to have a new dress for today. Remember? You promised to pay me back something so I could get the dress."

"I know I did, Harriet," he said quickly, and he looked ashamed. "I know you are broke. I know it's my fault. I know you have to get a dress. I'm a dog to mention the suit. But I thought that with a couple of sure things for today I could make a killing. I guess I mentioned the suit because the dress is on my mind."

"I know I look shabby. I know it."

"Play along with me, baby. The trouble is you're always on my mind." It was just the right thing to say; it touched all her affection for him. "The first little windfall goes to you, Harriet," he said, and he slipped his arm around her waist and abused the jockeys and the backstretch touts who gave him tips, and he sounded like himself and made her feel again that everything she wanted was within her reach.

"I'm not betting the next race," he said. "But in the fifth it's got to be Black Pirate. I got it straight from Jonesey. The fifty we've got left goes on Black Pirate right on the nose." Suddenly he turned to her, deeply reflective. "Are you feeling lucky, baby?"

"Sure I'm feeling lucky."

"Why not?" He was as serious as he had ever been in his life. "Nearly everything good that's come my way has come through you, Harriet. That's a fact. Right now we need a break. If anybody can do it you can, Harriet. Here, you put the dough down and change our luck." He handed her the bills. "The fifty on Black Pirate. Right on the nose. Then you'll get yourself a whole new outfit."

"But if Black Pirate should miss?"

"It's not my day, baby, it's yours."

"Yes. Why not, Charlie?" She laughed, and her hand went out to him affectionately, for his conviction that luck could come to him only through her moved her, made her feel again that he really knew how valuable she was in his life. "I'll get moving now so I won't have to line up."

"Take it easy. There's still the fourth race."

"Here we go," she said, and laughed and kissed the roll of bills in her hand, then pressed the roll to his lips; she had a lovely glow as she left him.

On her way to the wicket, when she was passing the clubhouse gate, she had to circle around a group of men, and then she bumped into a shabbily dressed old woman wearing a long gray out-of-season topcoat and a shapeless black felt hat, who had a newspaper-wrapped parcel under her arm. The little old woman had been standing there, mutely staring at the brilliant sunshine on the infield's green grass, and at the horses and the stable ponies moving up the track to the starting post.

"Oh, excuse me," Harriet said, for in bumping her she had knocked the parcel to the ground, where the newspaper wrapping opened and showed a pair of battered old shoes. "I'm sorry," Harriet said, and as she picked up the parcel she folded the paper carefully around the shoes.

"It's all right, Miss. Thanks," the woman said, taking the parcel, and then as Harriet turned she heard her call, "Oh, Miss..."

"Yes?"

"Maybe you could tell me something," the little old woman said nervously; and then she nodded and seemed to have made up her mind that Harriet had a good face. "It's about this," she said timidly and fumbled in her old handbag. "See," and she handed Harriet a single slip from an office memo pad. "Can you make it out?"

"Bright Star. The fourth race," Harriet read aloud from the writing in a small pinched hand. "Why, it's the fourth race coming up."

"And I was to hand this in at the wicket," the woman said, looking frightened as she took a ten-dollar bill from the old handbag.

"The ten on Bright Star?" Harriet asked dubiously, for it was plain the woman couldn't afford to lose ten dollars. "I've a friend who knows, and on the way to the track I heard him say Bright Star couldn't win a boat race."

"But Mr. Wilkie said—"

"Who's Mr. Wilkie?"

"In the building. The office building where I clean. Mr. Wilkie worked late last night. Often he talks to me. He wrote this down and gave me the ten dollars and said to be sure, and I came here on my way to work."

"Well, never look a gift horse in the mouth, as they say," Harriet said, shrugging. "The wicket is right over there, and I'm on my way there. You can come with me but you'll certainly have to hurry."

"Wouldn't you do it for me, Miss? I feel safer standing right here," she said and she handed Harriet the bill.

"But you shouldn't trust people like that," Harriet said. She was reluctant to take the bill, for the woman's tired wrinkled face told her how much the ten dollars meant to her. "Well, stay right here then. Don't move. Oh, my goodness, the horses are on the track," and she rushed to the wicket and got the money down just before posttime, and then stood there a moment wondering if she shouldn't also put down the fifty Charlie had given her to bet on Black Pirate in the next race, but she was afraid he would abuse her for being a fool.

The crowd roared as the horses broke from the post, but she couldn't follow Bright Star; she didn't know the horse or the number. All she could do was stand there and listen to the voice on the loudspeaker, "It's Shoemaker, Ivy Green and Jackanapes. It's Shoemaker and Ivy Green," and think what a ten-to-one shot, a windfall like that, might do for the little old woman. It could make her feel her life had changed magically. Harriet closed her eyes and began to make a little prayer.

When she opened her eyes the horses were on the far turn. "It's Ivy Green by a half, and Dipsy Dipsy. Ivy Green and Dipsy Dipsy and on the outside, Bright Star." Then, in the crowd's roar as they hit the stretch, she couldn't hear the voice, and the race was over, and she was watching the numbers go up on the tote board, and the man next to her cursed and said, "Goddam Bright Star goes off at ten to one! It was a boat race!" Harriet trembled, then she moved toward the wicket and was the first to hand in her ticket, and she got a hundred dollars.

She made her way toward the clubhouse gate, and as soon as she saw the little old woman, rooted to the spot as if she had been afraid to move an inch, she began to laugh and wave, but the woman, watching blankly, didn't see her until she was only a few feet away. "You won! You won! Imagine!" Harriet cried, waving the bills.

"Did I?" she asked blankly. "How much did I win?"

"A hundred dollars. Look."

"A hundred dollars," she repeated with a frightened smile. "Oh, dear."

"Here. Put it in your purse."

"Yes, Miss," and she did, but the clasp on the old purse was so loose it worried Harriet. "Look," she said, taking the woman's arm, "you can't carry that money in that purse. Where are you going?"

"To work." Harriet's pleasure was mixed with nervous concern; all that mattered now was that the woman should get home safely with her money. Still holding her arm firmly, she walked her out the gate to where taxis were waiting at the curb.

When they stopped by a lamp post she said, "I'll tell you what we'll do. You'll have to take a taxi. Wait. Lean against that post and give me the money." When the little old woman had dutifully handed the money to her she knelt down and pretended to be fixing the lace on the woman's shoe. But she drew the shoe off. Separating one ten-dollar bill from the roll, she made an insole out of the rest, laid it in the shoe and laced it up.

"Remember now," she insisted urgently, "don't change your shoes when you get to work. Don't touch that shoe till you get home. Understand?" and she didn't stand up till the woman nodded like an excited conspirator.

"Now take this ten dollars and pay for the taxi," she

said, handing the bill to her, and then she beckoned to a driver.

"Thank you, Miss. God bless you," the little old woman said when she was in the taxi. They smiled at each other mysteriously. The woman's tired eyes were bright as a young girl's. As the taxi pulled away, Harriet stood there glowing with satisfaction, for the woman's luck seemed to be flowing around her and in her. She felt light-hearted, carefree and young, and could hardly turn away.

Suddenly, she remembered Black Pirate in the fifth and she ran, frightened, through the gate. The race was on, and she knew Charlie would be down there at the rail, all keyed up, thinking the money was on Black Pirate. She couldn't get her breath. She didn't know what had happened to her. Charlie would never understand what had happened.

"It's Golden Arrow, Moonglow and Funny Face," she heard over the loudspeaker, and she closed her eyes and couldn't listen. Then the race was over and it was still Golden Arrow, Moonglow and Funny Face, and she sighed and felt weak.

"Why, I've saved the fifty dollars," she thought, making her way to the rail. "Maybe it's my share of that little old woman's luck." It was a windfall, Charlie would see that it was an incredible windfall. He would laugh, and then wonder, and then he would see that it was intended so she could get the dress. He was waiting by the rail in his expensive light summer suit with the pale blue check, and he was watching her glumly.

"What's the matter? How can you smile?" he asked sourly, while she was still six feet away. "It's your funeral, too."

"Wait a minute, Charlie. Wait a minute. It could be a lot worse."

"Sure. I could have broken my neck. My dough's all gone."

"It isn't gone, Charlie. Look," and she opened her purse.

"What is this?"

"I didn't get on Black Pirate."

"You didn't?"

"No," she said and she laughed and felt breathless. "I was too late. Oh, you'll like this, Charlie. Just as if – well, as if we were being looked after. I got talking to a little old woman and I didn't get to the wicket. So you see, you were right. Luck was with me. If you'd done the betting yourself we'd have blown the fifty, wouldn't we, and now here it is," and again she laughed and wanted to tell him about the little old woman, and she did.

"Well, I'll be damned," he said, grinning. "So here we are right back in the ball game. Let's have the dough."

But she hesitated, waiting for him to remember and say, "No, you really saved this money. I would have thrown it down the drain. I guess it's the money for your dress all right. What a way to get it," and she tried to prompt him a little. "You know I'm broke, Charlie, and I thought..."

"Ah, now, sweetheart," he said, making a big joke of it.

"Charlie, I do need it."

"But you wouldn't be a lovely little burglar, would you?" he asked, laughing. "Let's have it and we'll use it to get some real loot. Why, what's the matter?"

"It was yours all right. Oh, it isn't just the money, Charlie."

"No? What else?"

"Oh, I don't know..." but she couldn't go on. "Here, take it," she said, and she thrust it at him.

But he knew that something was wrong and while he hesitated uneasily she had a moment of wild hope as, half-ashamed, he struggled against being like he was. He took her arm and gave her a little pull to him, and he told her with the pressure of his fingers on her arm that all that was generous and just and affectionate in his nature made him feel unhappy and ashamed; then all his habit of indulging himself with her seemed to weaken his remorse. "Don't you see, darling, this fifty is meant to give us another chance?" This familiar expression of his hopefulness put an ache in her heart because, for so long, she had shared his hopefulness.

As he reached for the money, she knew he couldn't help himself. He was just being himself with her, as he always would, taking a little more every day, taking and taking and putting nothing back in her heart, and worse still, taking away that kind of young light-hearted happiness she had felt standing at the curb, and he always would do this; he would keep on doing it until she was empty and old.

"Yes, sir. This is going to be the fifty that does the trick for us," he said, trying to feel at ease with himself. "Let's see what I've got for the next race. I think our luck has really changed."

"I think it has," she said softly, and as she stood beside him she thought of the little old woman in the taxi, and, staring across the green infield in the sun, she knew that she would be half-way to work. She remembered how she had hoped the woman's life would change, and now, following the taxi in her mind, she suddenly felt herself, too, whirling away from the track, with the incredible good luck that had come just in time to take her out of Charlie's life.

A Pair of Long Pants

FOR A LONG TIME TONY POWERS SAT IN HIS BEDROOM, looking at a pair of long pants his brother had discarded. At last he decided to put them on. They were too long for him, so he turned them up at the cuff. The coat that went with the suit was also far too big, but he knew he could carry it under his arm the way the big fellows in town did on hot days. All he needed now was his father's old felt hat that was hanging on the hall rack. He got the hat, tilted it at a bold angle over his right eye, and went out.

On the way up to the main street in town, the highway along which all traffic passed on the way to the city, Tony felt a little like a stranger, because the long pants made him feel he was walking in a new world; and when he stood in the bright late afternoon sunlight looking at the big red truck parked in front of White's tobacco store, it was easy for him to imagine he had just stepped down from the truck to rest a moment, and soon would be on his way again through the other little towns and the country to the city.

A big fair ruddy-faced fellow in a brown shirt came out of the cigarstore tucking a package of cigarettes in his shirt pocket; and when he saw Tony looking at the truck, he said: "Going my way, Shorty?"

"You going west?" Tony said, making his voice sound brisk.

"Twenty miles, if that'll help. Come on," the truck-driver said.

It had happened so easily that Tony didn't feel shy at all when he got up on the big seat. Taking one of the cigarettes the truck-driver offered him, he began to feel big with excitement. As he looked along the familiar main street, he felt the elation of suddenly being free. With the truck going along a little faster, the big fellow was asking, "How old are you, Shorty?"

"Eighteen," Tony lied.

"They don't grow very big in your neck of the woods, eh?"

"My father was just a little guy. He's no bigger than I am," Tony said. The ease with which he had uttered this bold lie gave him such courage that he was eager to create another life for himself. "Yeah, we're all little guys in our family," he said. "But the trouble is we get fatter later on." As they passed beyond the town and swung round the curve of the highway, and climbed the hill and could see over the rolling country for miles, and see the blue lake to the left and the little town ahead that was a part of the mist at the end of the lake, Tony went on talking eagerly. "My brother's five years older than I am, and he's not as tall as me. And the funny part of it is, our mother's a big woman, maybe nearly five foot ten. What do you make of that?" He was thinking it was such a beautiful country seen like this, the casual glance of an independent and unrestricted man who could stop if he wanted to at any likely-looking spot, or keep on going for miles beyond.

"They call me Mac . . . How about a beer at the next hotel?" the truck-driver said.

"Tony's my name; but I haven't got any money with me."

"If you'd like a beer, I'll stand you one."

"OK. There's nothing I'd like better," Tony said.

But when they were in the next town and crossing the road to the hotel with Tony lagging behind a little, they saw that a group of men, mainly town idlers, were blocking the way to the hotel entrance. Mac simply elbowed his way through, but they closed in behind him, and Tony was left there a little scared, feeling sure if he pushed them, one of them would give him a boot in the pants and tell him to go home, and leave him hovering like a scared kid on the fringe of the crowd. He had a sudden eagerness to retreat to the security of his own boy's world. But he said gruffly in the voice Mac had used: "All right, gang, just a minute." Without even noticing him, they let him pass among them.

He was grinning with delight when he swaggered over to the table where Mac had already ordered two beers, for the way the men at the door had stepped aside had made him feel there was surely something magical in the long pants, and that while he wore them, he would never be pushed around again. Mac raised his glass. "Here's mud in your eye, Tony," he said; and Tony, drinking slowly with him, tasted beer for the first time. It lay fresh and cool in his stomach. Feeling flushed and reckless, he looked around at the others who were drinking there, and it no longer seemed like a mean and gloomy drinking-room. The shaft of sunlight from the window was streaming on what seemed suddenly the most beautiful sight in the world: men sitting together in all contentment while they drank and smoked and laughed, and the room was filled with murmur of their animated voices. Tony wanted to boast, and he began: "You know where I'm going?"

"As far as the city, I thought you said."

"That's right."

"It's too bad I'm only going as far as the next town, because I'd like to have you stick with me."

"There's nothing I'd like better than sticking with you; but I've got to get down to the race-track."

"Say, kid, just a minute, let me guess," Mac said, his face full of delight. "Maybe you're a jock. Is that right?"

"That's about it. My father was a jockey, but he's too heavy now, so he's a trainer. He's taught me nearly all he ever knew."

"Lord, I might have known a little guy like you'd be a jockey. I guess you love it. I'd give my soul to be something like that instead of riding that old red truck."

"Of course I just got started," Tony said, and then he added: "I sort of liked riding that big red truck."

They left the hotel, and when they were crossing the road, the truck-driver did not go on ahead this time, but walked respectfully beside Tony as he talked eagerly about a system he had figured out for beating the bookies. "You know this horse Beau Geste?" he asked.

"It's a mighty good animal," Tony said solemnly.

"A good animal is right, I suppose," Mac said. "But no one can tell what it's going to do. They must be shooting it up to the eyes with dope. Such an animal!" As he used the word "animal," he cocked his head on one side, trying to use it as Tony had used it, so it would have that mysterious professional connotation. "Say, let's have a cup of coffee in this joint down the street a bit, and we'll talk about that animal," he said, pointing to a little restaurant that was freshly painted in green. "I got a dame in there that's nuts about me."

While they sat at the counter in the restaurant, a plump

dark-haired girl of about nineteen years waited on them, and she whispered to the truck-driver: "I was thinking it was time for you to show up, Mac." With a sly smile she looked at Tony, and then she put her elbows down on the counter, leaning close to Mac, and began to whisper in a hesitant, earnest manner. Tony, knowing that she didn't want him to listen, turned his head away. While the mysterious, important, hesitant whispering went on, he felt terribly shy; for he knew that the whispering was becoming a reluctant promise.

Then the soft-skinned girl, straightening up, said suddenly: "Who's the kid with you, Mac?"

"He's a jockey. Didn't you notice his size?"

"Big or small, he's a nice-looking kid, eh?"

"So he is," Mac said, getting up to go back to the men's room.

The dark girl kept staring at Tony and smiling, and when he looked up at her boldly, her gray eyes seemed to grow wise and beyond all his experience in a terrifying way. As she bent over him, bringing her thick black hair, her perfume, the smell of her skin close to him, the strong beating of his heart rose into his throat.

"You come this way often, Mr. Jockey Boy?" she said.

"Not often."

"How old did you say you were?"

"Eighteen," he said, his face burning.

"You don't look no more than fourteen at the most to me. Kind of young for a jockey, I'd say."

"My brother's a jockey down at the track. I exercise the horses. Maybe I'll be in the saddle next year."

"You're a sweet-looking kid. Come in again when you pass this way." When she smiled and whispered, "I kind of wish you were eighteen," he flushed again.

But when he was with Mac and when they were beyond the town and the road was steadily downhill through wooded valleys and farmland with the sky red and the sun going down, he was thinking he was under a spell that scared and exalted him, some magic that made this secret ecstasy free to him.

"Do you know her very well?" he said shyly.

"The dame back in the joint? Didn't I tell you she was crazy about me?"

"She looked pretty hot to me."

"She's a willing kid, but they got to be more than willing to make the grade in my league. She's a little weak on class. She can't hold a candle to the baby I've got in the city," Mac said.

The elation in Tony as he listened to Mac talking about his girl in the city became a restless intoxication; his head was full of whispering and the flash of soft white faces.

"What're you dreaming about, Shorty?" Mac asked.

"I don't know."

"Aren't you feeling good?"

"I feel swell. I don't know why."

"Listen, Shorty: Do you ever get tipped off in advance if anything's going to be pulled off around a track – like a sure thing in a race?"

"Oh, sure. I hear that stuff all the time. My old man's a guy it would be worth a lot of money for you to know." But Tony felt a little scared when he said this, because his father was really a respectable doctor back there in the town.

When they were passing through the next village, which was only a short line of stores, a post office and two service stations, three boys of Tony's age chased after the truck to hang on behind.

"Chase those kids, pal," Mac said. "Can you see them?"

Tony yelled back at the kids, "Go on, beat it," and he enjoyed the scared expressions on their faces as they slowed down and ran over to the curb. Then one who was bolder than the others, a short curly-haired kid, ran after the truck and hung on again, his grinning face full of mockery as Tony shouted back at him: "Get off, you little squirt, or I'll pin your ears back for you." It felt pretty fine to be sitting in the truck in comfort and scaring the kids with stern words. But the boy, who jumped off as Tony yelled, saw that the truck wasn't actually going to stop, and he jumped on again.

"I've the same trouble with kids in nearly all the towns," Mac grumbled. "I haven't got time to be stopping the truck every ten minutes."

"Kids like that get to be pretty much of a nuisance," Tony agreed. "Watch me fix this one."

Opening the door, he put one foot down on the running-board, and just as the kid leaped at the truck, he swung his body out as if he were jumping off, and his face was as fierce and cruel as he could make it. The frightened kid, hesitating as he jumped, missed the back of the truck and screamed and rolled on the road.

They stopped the truck and ran back, and when Mac lifted the kid up, they saw the blood was running from a scrape over his eye, and his body hung limp. They put him down on the grass at the side of the road, and the other kids, running up, huddled around.

"Where's his family?" Mac said.

"They live down the road at the end house, but there's nobody home," a kid answered.

"Hold his head on your knee, Shorty, and I'll get some water," Mac directed.

As Tony held the boy's head on his knees and wiped the blood away from his eye with his handkerchief and thought maybe the kid would die, he looked up in wonder at the faces of the boys and men grouped around him, because not one of the men offered to take his place. He wanted to get up and go away and cry softly and break the magic of the long pants that held him there with the boy's head on his knee.

"Is he hurt bad, Mister?" one of the kids asked timidly.

He was like an older one they expected to reassure them; so he tried to say gruffly: "Take it easy, folks, and give him a little air, and he'll be all right . . . Much obliged, folks." Saying it like that gave him a sense of authority that made him feel much stronger.

Mac came with the water, and soon the boy opened his eyes and said his knee was hurt, and Mac began to knead into the flesh around the knee with his big strong fingers. Whenever the kid groaned, Mac whispered, "It's all right, pal," and there seemed to be a marvelous tenderness in his fingers, and the most comforting smile on his face. Tony began to long to be able to touch the kid with Mac's gentle assurance, and speak to him in that soft comforting way, for the kid was trying to smile at Mac.

Mac gave the kid's knee a couple of hard jerks and worked it up and down; and then he grinned at him and said: "You'll be all right. I'll carry you down to your house for good luck."

With the little crowd following, he carried the kid high on his shoulder down the road to the house and put him down on a couch in the front room; and when he was leaving, the kid, looking up at him with shy admiration, said: "Thanks, Mister, I'll be all right."

Back on the truck, going along the road again, Tony kept looking at the side of Mac's rugged face, wondering how it could be that Mac didn't even seem to realize he had been very gentle with the boy. Tony began to wish that he too, some day, would do the same kind of thing in a way that would be so simple, natural and dignified that any kid who happened to be with him, as he was with Mac, would feel very humble.

But they were coming to the place where the two highways intersected. Mac said: "Well, Shorty, if you're going on to the city, this looks like the place where we part."

Putting out his hand, Tony said shyly: "This is the place, I guess . . . Well – so long, Mac." They shook hands heartily.

"Listen, Shorty: take my name, will you? I got an idea," Mac said. Taking a stub of a pencil from the pocket in his brown shirt, he wrote on a piece of paper he tore from a notebook his name, Thomas McManus, with the address, and he handed the slip to Tony. "Here's what I'm figuring," he said. "Some day you might get wind of a sure thing around a track, and you might want a few dollars to play it with. You get in touch with me, and I'll put up the bucks, and we'll split. What do you say?"

"OK. That's a good idea," Tony said. "I wish you were going with me."

Tony got off the truck, which soon gained speed as it turned and cut along the highway to the right through the fields. Tony stood there sadly, waiting for the truck to get out of sight, because he didn't want Mac to look back and see him turn and start to head back home. The truck was becoming a dark speck against the last of the sunlight.

Sighing, Tony started to walk back the way he had come; but before he had gone very far, he stopped and turned and again looked across the fields. He was hungry, but it was hard for him to pull himself away. Soon it would be dark. The mist was beginning to rise way over there by the woods.

He stood watching the mist rising up like a soft wave from the edge of the woods, and the sky behind the woods was still splashed with red. He began to feel excited, because he saw that the mist seemed to be rolling toward him close to the ground, like puffs of cannon-fire floating among the trees. The sun dropped lower. Soon it would be hard to see; and after the barrage was laid down, the battle would begin that would free him. It was fine to think he was watching a world being won for him, a country over there where Mac still kept going in his truck, a world of horses and men, of soft-skinned girls whispering promises, of a fine bold authority of your own, and of things like the extraordinary gentleness in Mac that had awed him.

With an Air of Dignity

THE LANGLEYS, A HIGHLY RESPECTED, WELL-OFF FAMILY,
lived in a big red brick house on the outskirts of the prairie
town. Old Mr. Langley had been the bank manager until he
suffered the stroke that left him crippled. Living with him
was his housekeeper, a pretty young woman named Rita, a
stranger in town from the east, who was working her way to
the west coast, and the Langley children, Pauline, the town
librarian, and her brother, twenty-two-year-old Steve.

When Steve was eighteen and a little wild, he had
refused to go to school and had hung around the poolroom
and the dance hall with big Kersh and his friends. After
the furniture store had been robbed, Steve, under police
questioning, admitted he had heard Kersh planning to break
into the store. Kersh had been sent to jail for three years.
Steve, changing his life, had gone on to the university in
Saskatoon and was now working in the bank. When Kersh
got out of jail he came back to town and whenever he got
drunk he went looking for Steve and when he found him,
even if it was at the entrance to the bank, he beat him up.

Kersh was a long-nosed truck driver with pale hard
eyes who was over six feet tall. Steve was only five foot
eight and he had small hands. When Kersh came after him

yelling, "All right, pigeon, get out of town," Steve would battle him but he always looked like a slight freckle-faced boy with despair in his eyes. Kersh had beaten him in a restaurant, he had beaten him out on the street, and once in the snow in front of the Langley home. The police had thrown Kersh in jail for a week, but everybody knew Kersh would keep on beating Steve Langley.

On a Saturday afternoon, Rita Whaley, the stranger among the Langleys, saw Kersh's old car turning in from the highway. She was in her attic room standing by the window brushing her hair, letting it hang loose on her shoulders in the long bob she used to wear back east. There was bright sunlight glistening on the banked snow on the Langley drive and from the high window she could see the way the road ran for miles beyond the town into the vast prairie snow. There was sun and mist and dryness in the air, yet it was very cold, twenty below zero.

As the car stopped in the drive, Rita watched Kersh lean back surveying the house. He was wearing a leather jacket and a brown cap. He was not alone. Whitey Breaden, in the front seat with him, was a slow-witted fellow in a moth-eaten coon coat, who worked in a garage and had once dreamed of being a professional boxer. Kersh always brought someone along with him, an audience. Kicking the car door open, he stumbled out and stood staring at the house with all his half-drunken arrogance.

Kersh's big grin made Rita feel sick, for Steve Langley had become important to her. Unlike Pauline, he treated Rita with a gentle respect, as if she were a fine friend of the family and not just a stray girl working her way to the coast. Maybe he understood that in Montreal she had had a bad time, but his courteous respectful manner, filling her with gratitude, seemed to caress and restore her. With Kersh out there now she knew what was going to happen, so she rushed downstairs.

Mr. Langley was there in the wheel chair by the grate fire, and beside him in the rocking chair, Pauline was stitching the hem of a dress. Steve, peeling an orange, was thinner, nervous, and more serious these days. Everything was warm and peaceful. "Kersh," Rita blurted out. "It's Kersh."

"Where?" Steve asked, his face white.

"Out there in the car with a pal."

The orange slipped from his hands and his eyes grew despairing as he watched it roll to the floor. Then, as he looked at his sister, her face seemed to fascinate him. "Steve, what'll you do?" Pauline whispered.

"I don't know," he said helplessly. "Lock the doors, I guess. Yeah, lock the door, Rita." Sitting down, he took a deep breath and closed his eyes. "The drunken lout," his sister cried fiercely. "To come right to our home. All right. I'll have the police out here in ten minutes."

"We've already tried that," Steve said lifelessly. "A fine exhibition."

His father watched him. Old Mr. Langley had lost the power of speech, and he followed everything with his lively eyes. The stroke had caused a curl to his lip and Steve could never be sure if the curl was also contempt.

"Hey, Langley," Kersh yelled. "Come on out. I want to see you."

"Don't say anything," Steve said.

"What if he tries to come in?" Pauline asked. "I'm frightened, Steve."

"If he's good and drunk he'll go away."

But Kersh had begun to pound on the door. "Come on out here, little pigeon," he roared.

"Steve, don't," Pauline cried.

"I'll get him out of here. I've got to."

"No. Please Steve. My God. Not again. This is our house, our home," Pauline pleaded.

"I'm not afraid of him. I'm not," he said doggedly. Then he swung around to his father who sat so motionless in the wheel chair. The crippled man still looked like a dignified figure with his white hair and his neat black coat. Before he had been stricken old Mr. Langley had been a tall powerful man with a commanding presence and Steve had always had great respect for him. His father's eyes were bright and critical.

"I'm not afraid of him, don't you understand?" he said, making an angry apology to his father. "I'm just not big enough. I can smack him again and again. And then what? I can't go on."

When his father turned away, Steve looked at his sister who nodded sympathetically, and then at Rita Whaley, who tried to hide her concern with a nervous shy smile.

"Hey, Langley," Kersh yelled. "I'm right here on your doorstep. Come on out. Or maybe I should come in."

"If he tries to come in," Steve whispered, going slowly to the window, "I'll kill him. Somehow I'll kill him. I've got a right to kill him."

There was heavy frost on the windowpane and Steve breathed on it and began to rub away the frost so he could look out. Then he saw Whitey Breaden's face at the lowered window of the car. Whitey was waiting with a big derisive grin. Kersh was over to the right of the path, scowling, blinking because the sun on the snow dazzled him, and then he lurched suddenly in the snow, going down on one knee, cursing. In the cold bright sunlight his heavy red face shone with so much mean drunk brutal contempt that Steve's right leg began to shimmy and he couldn't control it. He turned with a crazy smile and left the others and hurried upstairs to his room. He got the twenty-two he used to hunt rabbits with and came down to the window again.

"You big fool, Steve," his sister cried out. "Oh you big fool."

"Get away," he said as she came close to him.

"It'll only make it worse for you, Steve," she said.

"I'd shoot him like a rabbit," he said, "if that's all there was to it."

"Hold on to yourself, Steve," she said.

"Maybe I could talk to him," Rita said.

"Keep out of this, Rita," he said.

"No, listen, Steve," she said, "a girl can do things with a guy like that." She touched his arm gently. She had an apologetic smile, as if she felt her confidence in her ability to handle Kersh revealed an aspect of her life she had tried to hide from them.

"I know how you feel, Steve," she said. "I can get him to go away."

"Forget it," Steve said.

"I know Kersh," she said.

"Yes," Pauline said. "Rita knows Kersh. Kersh knows her."

"What're you talking about. I said no," he said.

"Steve," Pauline said. "This is nothing to her."

"Pauline," he shouted.

"It's all right, Steve," Rita said, fussing with her hair. She got her muskrat coat from the peg in the hall and went out.

Steve peered through the spot on the window pane that he had rubbed clear of frost. He waited until she came into the sunlight. She was holding the collar of her coat tight across her throat and taking slow delicate steps in the snow because she had on low shoes. A bright sun glowed against a shimmering prairie mist.

While Kersh waited with a grin, Whitey Breaden got out of the car and stood beside Kersh as she came to them with an easy smile. Then, the three were talking and she looked like a little girl beside Kersh in his leather jacket. Kersh pointed at the house, laughed and patted Whitey on the back, and then he took Rita's arm in a confidential gesture. She shrugged, hesitated, and looked back at the house. Suddenly she left them and came in quickly.

"I knew he wouldn't go," Steve said to her.

"They'll go all right," she said.

"No, they're not going."

"Well," she said awkwardly. "Kersh wants me to go into town and have some dinner with them. I don't know. What do you think?"

"If it's just a matter of going to town," Pauline said quickly, "then why not?"

"Maybe I can talk some sense into Kersh," Rita said.

"You're crazy," said Steve.

"No, go ahead, Rita," Pauline said.

"I'll change my dress," Rita said and hurried upstairs.

Steve and his sister, silent with their father watching, were suddenly embarrassed. But Pauline, a severe proud girl, said irritably, "I'm not worried, Steve. A girl like Rita can always handle a man like Kersh."

"A girl like Rita?"

"Yes, a girl like Rita can look after herself. She won't stay with us long. It's not as if she belongs here with us."

Rita was coming downstairs in a green dress and she had a lot of lipstick on. Hurrying to the hall, she got her overshoes on, but as she knotted the lace on the right shoe, she looked up and paused as if she suddenly understood what they were saying about her.

"If you're worrying about me it's a mistake," she said. "It's nothing. I'll be back in an hour or two."

Steve and Pauline watched her get into the car with Kersh. When the car turned out to the road, Steve, wherever he moved, was sure his father's eyes were on him. An hour passed, and then it was dinnertime. He could not eat, nor could he read after dinner. He found himself saying, "It was mighty good of her. She knows Kersh. Rita's been around." He went up to his own room and stood by the window watching the road in the long lonely prairie twilight. His hurt bewildered him.

Finally, he began to get dressed and in a slow methodical fashion he shaved carefully, put on a clean white shirt and his best blue suit. He wanted to look like an important man who didn't belong in Kersh's world. When he went downstairs where his father was dozing by the fire, he saw how the hot coals were throwing a fiery reflection on his father's broad calm forehead, and he frowned. He put on his overcoat and the expensive fur cap they had given him at Christmas and went out and along the road to town, walking slowly.

In the night air, there was a shining winter brightness and great height to the darkness, with a sweep of yellow-green and red northern lights across the sky. His feet crunched on the frozen snow. It sounded as if he had on squeaky new shoes. A freight train moaned in the long night. Down the road, the cluster of lights in the center of the town shone and then the houses were closer together and he began to walk faster, as if he had made a plan. But he had no plan at all.

The quiet street led to the park in front of the big white hotel and a row of stores was across from the park, all closed, with no lights except in one narrow window, Mike's restaurant. When he got to the window, he peered in: Mike was at the counter with his pointed bald head and his mustache, sitting on one of the row of counter stools with the torn leather seats, and back in the corner by the kitchen, at the end table, Kersh, Breaden and Rita and a barber named Henry Clay were joking and laughing. Kersh was the first to see Steve come in and he frowned and scowled and stood up slowly. "Mike," he called. "You were closing up, weren't you?"

"I want no trouble, Kersh," Mike said.

"You said you were closing up."

"I'm closing."

"Go ahead, then."

"What's the game, Steve?" Rita said, her face flushed. She was ashamed that Steve had found her laughing. "I thought you wanted to keep away, Steve," she cried. "So, why don't you?"

"I was passing by," he said. "I thought you might want to come along with me." In his good clothes, he looked like a serious young man.

"Listen, pigeon, beat it," Kersh said, grinning at Whitey Breaden who smirked and took out a nail file and began to clean his nails. "Or maybe I don't make myself clear, Mr. Langley?" he added.

"I'll go in my own good time, when Rita's ready," Steve said.

"I try to make you understand I feel lousy about my whole life when I see you pigeon," Kersh said. He had had a lot to drink and his pale blue eyes were half shut. "Okay," he grunted, "it's always a pleasure." He slapped Steve viciously on the mouth and then he waited. "Come on, hit me," he said. "Come on. Come on."

"No, I'm not going to hit you, Kersh."

"So what's this?" Kersh asked, and when Steve saw the confusion in the pale blue eyes his heart leaped. "So now the punker's yellow," Kersh said. "See, now he's yellow."

"He was yellow three years ago," Whitey said. "A yellow pigeon."

But Kersh didn't like Steve's tight superior smile as he held his hands straight at his sides.

"Superior little punk, eh," Kersh yelled and grabbed Steve by the collar, choked him, slapped his face, and kept on slapping in a frantic eagerness to make Steve raise his hands and resist, but his hands didn't come up, and Kersh, slamming him against the wall, grunted, "Grin at me you bastard, grin."

"You're making a big mistake, Kersh," Steve whispered.

"How can a guy take it?" the barber said, and Rita stared at Steve.

"Here," Kersh coaxed, thrusting out his own jaw eagerly. "Hit me here."

"I don't need to," Steve gasped.

"Hit me right here, baby," Kersh pleaded, tapping his jaw delicately with his forefinger.

"I don't need to. No."

"So what's this?" Kersh blurted out. Blinking his eyes, he looked at the others to see if they felt he was being mocked. He was enraged. Then he smashed Steve on the jaw; he smashed him again and waited, but the crazy smile remained on Steve's face, and he would not back away. His fine fur hat had been knocked off, his white shirt was flecked with blood from his mouth, and there was a silence, a silence that embarrassed them all, and then Steve touched his swelling eye with his hand, swaying a little as he tried to smile. Rita put her hands over her face. She started to cry.

"It's a gag," Kersh whispered, feeling the others

withdraw from him. Bewildered, he cracked Steve on the jaw and watched him slump to the floor.

"It's not right, Kersh," Mike protested. "That's not right."

The barber, who had got up, leaned over the table and looked down at Steve. "It's wild," he said softly. "Very wild."

"Shut up," Kersh yelled as Steve, raising himself on one knee, wiped the blood from his mouth. "What's the matter with you, Kersh?" Steve whispered.

"Me?" Kersh yelled. "What the hell is this?" and went to hit him again, but stopped suddenly. A sick look came into his eyes. "The guy ain't right in the head, I sucker myself hitting him," he said slowly, turning his back on Steve and appealing to the others. "Did I go after him? He came after me. The broad wanted to come along. All I want is that the guy should keep away from me."

"I'll tell him," the barber said.

"Come on, let's blow this joint," Kersh said. He wanted to swagger but he was afraid the others weren't going to come with him. "So what about it?" he asked.

"Yeah," the barber agreed. "I think we should go. Come on, Whitey."

As they went out, Mike said, "I kinda think that guy won't bother you again, Steve."

"I don't know," Steve said, sitting down and straightening his collar.

"A guy like Kersh ain't used to feeling like a punk," Mike said.

Going to the counter, Mike poured a cup of coffee and brought it to Steve. Rita had dipped a handkerchief in a glass of water and was wiping his face. "You don't look so bad, Steve," Mike said. "Are you all right?"

"It's nothing," Steve said, grinning a little, gulping down the coffee. Neither he nor Rita spoke. When he had put on his fur hat he said, "Come on, Rita," and he smiled at Mike and they went out.

The cold air stung the cuts on his face. He noticed Rita had forgotten to put on her gloves. "Put on your gloves, Rita," he said.

Walking in step, she kept her head down. It was a long time before he realized she was crying.

"Hey, what's the matter, Rita?"

"Nothing." Stopping, she took out her handkerchief and wiped his mouth. "That blood is drying in the cold," she said. "Look, I know I can't stay around your place any more."

"You can stay as long as you want, Rita."

"No. Not in that house with your sister. She thinks she knows what I was. She's sure she knows what I am. Well I don't want it. I won't have it. Anyway, I was going to the coast, wasn't I, so – now I'm on my way."

Then, as they walked along in silence, her grip on his arm tightened.

"I still can't figure out why you came after me," she said.

"Well, I got thinking."

"You've got your good suit on. You got all dressed up to come after me."

"What else could I do?"

"But to stand there and be beaten."

"Beaten? Who was beaten? Not me!" As they walked in step, their shoes squeaked in the hard snow. The street was long. It ran into the prairie, and the prairie into the cold sky. They were both watching the ribbons of light on the rim of the prairie sky.

The Fiddler on Twenty-Third Street

THE BASEMENT HAND LAUNDRY ON TWENTY-THIRD STREET
was closed for the night, so Joseph Loney got his fiddle and
sat down at the end of the long table littered with shirts and
aprons waiting to be ironed and began to play. He played
his fiddle every night before he went down to the corner to
have a drink with his friend, Jimmie Leonard.

His wife Mary, stooped a little and thin, was at the
window on a level with the street, and she felt sullen and
resentful as she waited for her husband to put on his hat and
coat and go off for the night. He would spend his money
drinking, and sleep late in the morning, and then would
have the same old sheepish grin as he scratched his head and
tried to joke with customers who grew irritable when the
laundry they had been promised wasn't ready.

Looking out the window Mary saw a little girl in a
leather jacket leaning against the lamppost, smiling and
still and listening to the fiddle music, and as Mrs. Loney
watched, a boy came along and stood beside the girl and
grinned and listened too.

Mrs. Loney, who had no children of her own, watched
the boy and girl with a troubled longing that puzzled her.
Turning, she glanced at her husband, whose hairless head
shone more brightly under the light than any white stiffened

garments hanging on the wall, and she felt she could hardly blame him for going out night after night seeking places where there was laughter and companionship.

Outside another little girl, holding by the hand a small boy in a red sweater and a red woollen hat, had joined the other children, their faces turned to the laundry window, listening eagerly.

Mrs. Loney called out suddenly, "Play harder, Joseph; make it sound louder."

Joseph, smiling brightly, scraped away on his fiddle. Mary, pressing her face against the window, saw the little girl who had been holding the boy by the hand start to dance, raising one hand over her head and putting the other on her hip, going around and around in a circle.

"The children on the sidewalk are listening, Joseph," Mrs. Loney called. "Maybe they'd love it if we asked them to come in and listen."

"Sure, ask them in," he said.

Mrs. Loney called to the children, "How would you like to come in and listen, children? Maybe you could have a concert in here."

They looked at her shyly; the girl who had been dancing took hold of her little brother's hand and the bigger boy began to shuffle away.

Yet Mrs. Loney was smiling and still coaxing them. "Don't be shy, children, maybe you'll be having a lot of fun."

At last the girl with the straight hair and the short skirt, the one who had first heard the sound of the fiddle, came forward boldly, and then the others, not so timid, followed her down the steps. They huddled together at the end of the long table, smelling the steam and the irons that were still hot, staring at the pile of freshly ironed shirts.

As soon as Joseph started to play again the children, fascinated at the way he puckered up his face and grinned and winked one eye and kept pounding his foot up and down in time with his music, began to smile. Suddenly he jumped up, still playing the fiddle, and danced around the table, grinning over his shoulder as he passed them, encouraging them to follow. He lifted his knees high. The children began to laugh. Mrs. Loney was delighted to see the bolder girl, whose name was Emily, get up and start to follow Joseph, and the boy, Phil, was grinning shyly, and the polite little girl, Margot, who never let go her small brother's hand, was tense and wide-eyed with excitement. Mrs. Loney called to her husband, "Maybe you could play something, Joseph, they all could dance to, or maybe they'd all like to take turns doing something."

Wiping his red face with his handkerchief, Joseph said, "What one of you is any good with his feet?"

"Margot can do a jig, Margot can do a jig," Phil shouted. The sedate little girl glared at him angrily, muttering, "You keep quiet, Phil Thompson."

"Yes, she can," Emily cried.

"I can't, I really can't," Margot said.

But they pushed her out on the floor, so she took a deep breath, nodded to Joseph Loney to play something for her, raised her hand, and with a gravely solemn face began to dance a jig.

Mrs. Loney coaxed the children to perform, and she praised their talents lavishly. The bold girl, Emily, was a Catholic, and when it was her turn she told how her aunt had been dying for months and how she had got to like saying the prayers for the sick at the aunt's house, and she asked them if it would be all right if she knelt down and said the prayers that she liked best.

Soon they were all laughing and praying and singing, and Mary Loney realized her husband had forgotten about going out for a drink. With the fiddle and bow clutched in his left hand, he sat on the edge of his chair leaning over the children who were on the floor at his feet, his voice rising and falling, and his face glowed. Mary Loney felt such a sudden contentment that she was afraid to speak for fear of distracting them. She was full of thankfulness that she had some little biscuits left from dinner.

That night she lay awake a long time, listening to her husband breathing steadily beside her, marvelling at the look of pleasure on his face all evening.

Hardly a night passed after that when she did not say to her husband as soon as he had finished his dinner, "Aren't you going to play a tune on the fiddle to-night, Joseph?"

He lit his pipe, then got his fiddle, and she watched at the window for the children to come. Sometimes they all came together, sometimes one by one, all fond of Emily's prayers, and they loved to kneel down on the floor with her and repeat the prayers while Joseph plucked at the fiddle with his thumb in a kind of accompaniment.

The children grew to love Joseph Loney and often seemed to forget that his wife was there with them. Knowing this made the delight she got from their company seem like a precious secret. She hadn't felt so contented in years. She was ready to feed them when they grew tired and were thinking of going home.

But one night when the children came Joseph Loney was not there with his fiddle. His old friend, Jimmie Leonard, had come looking for him, and they had gone out together.

The children came at the same time the next night. When Mary Loney let them in they saw she had been crying. "He didn't come home last night and he hasn't come home yet," she said to them.

"Oh, something terrible's happened," they said.

"I don't know what to do," she said.

Instead of going home, the children, fascinated by Mary Loney's despair, sat down on the floor as they did nearly every other night and stared at her. It was silent while she worked her lips and swallowed hard, and then her eyes suddenly filled with tears, her lips trembled and she began to cry.

Growing frightened, the children felt that Joseph Loney was close to death wherever he was. Suddenly Margot asked, "Was he wearing a brown coat? I saw a man that looked like him wearing a brown coat and he was getting into a car near Madison Square."

The rest of the children looked at Margot in envy, and then Emily cried, "Oh, now I remember. I saw a crowd down at the corner last night and I was sure I saw Mr. Loney..."

Mrs. Loney, realizing the bright imaginations of the children were making them remember and believe in things that had never happened, cried angrily, "Please be quiet, and don't tell lies."

Emily said, "Oh, now is the time when we ought to pray for him. Let's all kneel and say a little prayer." She knelt on the floor, and the others knelt too, with their faces full of excitement.

"Look! Over there," Emily said, pointing at a little table against the wall that had a bowl of artificial flowers on a clean white cloth. "That will be the altar." She clasped her hands against her breast and bowed her head and had them repeat after her, "Oh, dear Lord, let nothing happen to him, and bring him home safe and sound."

This prayer that had such a simple beginning turned out to be long and rambling, with Emily pausing from time to time to hear her words repeated, and Mary Loney, listening to their childish whispers and watching their earnest faces, began to feel that somehow her life had reached a turning point.

Then they all heard the sound of a trumpet, a beautiful soothing sound, and then the sweet harmony of a cornet and a stringed instrument. The children got up off their knees, sure their prayers had been answered. For a moment they were too scared to move, and they looked at Mrs. Loney whose own heart began to beat unevenly and she, too, was frightened.

Crowding around and looking out of the window, they saw two men with horns and one with a mandolin, each with a little framed and printed sign hanging from a button on his coat, shuffling slowly along the sidewalk in the way blind men do, while they made their music, and a small boy walked a little ahead carrying a tin cup.

Still startled, Margot said, "Just the same, it was funny."

"Aw, I could have told you it was something like that," Phil scoffed, but his tone showed how serious and disappointed he was.

"Children, children," Mrs. Loney cried, but the simplicity of their belief had upset her. She began to wail, "Oh, you're so young. You don't know what I've had to endure. It's terrible to have had to put up with the things I've put up with in my life."

She knew by their silence and staring eyes that they would be unyielding in their resentment if she should try and make them feel her bitterness, yet she did not know why she wanted their sympathy, why she wanted them to feel close to her; and, with nothing to do but sit there and feel separated while they stared at her, she began to feel helpless.

Then Joseph Loney's sister, whom Mary had 'phoned, came in and sat down and sighed and tried to smile pleasantly. Joseph's sister, who looked like him and was as thin, was usually comforting but today her patient, understanding smile irritated Mary, who remembered suddenly that this woman had sobered Joseph up on the nights years ago when he came courting her.

"I know you're not worried at all," Mary blurted out. "But that's because from the beginning you never expected anything better of him . . . It's different with me. Year after year I've never stopped hoping."

"Did you hear from him?"

"Not a word since he went out with Jimmie Leonard."

"That Jimmie Leonard is a no-account man if ever there was one. I wouldn't worry if something put a blight on his life."

"But Joseph staying out all night when I was sure he was straightening up. Why, I let myself feel so hopeful for the first time in years. I was feeling contented. I was a fool."

Trying to smile soothingly, the sister said, "Joseph was picked up last night and taken to the station. He 'phoned me and asked me to break it to you. He's on his way home."

"Oh, my Lord!" Mary Loney wailed. "What will I do? Wait till I set eyes on him. A night in jail at his time in life! And me wasting my life trying to make him decent!"

"Don't be too sure you've made his life any too easy for him," the sister-in-law shouted angrily. "If you weren't dogging him for one thing it was another till he had to turn to something to feel he was alive."

"Have you no shame, woman, to be talking before these children?"

"Why don't you send them home?"

The children were standing stiffly against the wall, and when Mrs. Loney looked at their white, frightened faces she saw they were staring at her resentfully. "Go home, children," she cried angrily. "You should have gone home long ago."

"I'll be the first to go," the sister-in-law said, and held her head high and walked out.

One by one with lowered heads, the children backed toward the door, keeping their eyes on Mrs. Loney as though sure she would jump at them. But they did not go far. Mrs. Loney, sitting at the window, saw them standing outside and she could hear their chatter. Their excitement made her frantic, but then she heard them shout. They came leaping down the steps, pushing open the door and shouting, "Here he comes, Mrs. Loney. Hurray, hurray, hurray! Here he comes," and then they rushed out again to welcome him.

Through the window she could see him coming down the street, his head lowered and body bent so he wouldn't have to look in the neighbors' windows, stooped and shuffling in his familiar, beaten way, and it was like watching years of her married life flow by, and the happiness and security of the last few months became like something held out to tease her.

The children were still shouting, "Hurray, hurray." Then they came through the door. "Here he comes, Mrs. Loney." She saw them grabbing his arms and hanging on to his coat, and then when they were at the door they pushed him into the room.

Her body rigid with anger, she tried to make him look directly into her eyes, but he succeeded in sitting down without appearing to see her. While the children gathered around him, he let his head droop, clenched his hands between his knees and waited.

His shame and silence were almost too terrible for the children to bear, and in bewilderment they looked at Mrs. Loney, unable to understand why she showed no gladness when she had worried and waited so long.

Then Joseph looked up and sighed, and spoke in a way he had not spoken for years. "I'm sorry, Mary," he said. "I didn't want it to happen again like this. I'm very sorry."

When Mary only shook her head bitterly, he shrugged and in shy apology smiled into the faces of the children. As Mary saw their faces light up with gladness and sympathy, the injustice of their childish disregard of her filled her with resentment.

Joseph got up slowly and went into the kitchen and came back with his fiddle, still moving in the same slow way, and sat down and twanged the strings with his thumb. Too bewildered and indignant to know what to say, she could only watch him.

He started to play one of the old songs. He broke off, took the fiddle from under his chin and seemed to look at it in disappointment. Then he started to play another song and tried two or three more old songs of his youth, and as each failed, he seemed puzzled. Mary, clenching her fists, shouted, "So that's all there is to it, eh? It's just going to be like that, eh, and you're going to sit there and have nothing to say? I'll show you." She rushed at her husband, grabbed the fiddle out of his hands and tossed it across the room. As the fiddle fell they heard one of the strings snap. The fiddle lay upside down near the little table with the flower-pot on it.

The children, with horror and fear of Mrs. Loney in their faces, began to edge to the door. Phil was the first to dart out to the street, and Margot, pulling her little brother after her, followed, and Emily bumped into Margot going up the steps. Frightened, Mrs. Loney whispered to her husband, "Joseph . . . the children."

But when he did nothing but smile at her in that puzzled, wondering way, she cried out helplessly, "Children, children," and rushed out after them, urgent and eager as she stood on the street crying out, "Come back, children, come back."

The children, who had retreated along the sidewalk, only backed away a little farther when they heard her calling. Realizing they would not return even if she ran along the street after them, she rushed through the door and pleaded desperately, "Joseph, oh, Joseph, do something! Don't let them go like that."

Joseph, picking up his fiddle, looked at his wife's frightened, pleading face and said, "What'll I do?"

"Call them. Call them. They won't come back for me," she said.

Joseph hurried out and she heard him calling, "Hey, kids, hey, kids." She saw him take a few steps after them, holding his fiddle over his head, and she waited, looking out into the street, feeling old and frightened.

Then Joseph came in and sat down at the end of the long table and began to play a fiery tune on his fiddle with the broken string. He smiled and nodded to his wife, who still watched out the open door.

"They'll come," Joseph said confidently, as he went on scraping with his bow. She nodded humbly, and as the solemn faces of the children came closer a fearful eagerness kept growing in her.

All Right, Flatfoot

AT MIDNIGHT KARL CAME INTO THE HOTEL LOBBY AND approached the desk with a self-conscious air, asking for Mr. Bristow, the boxing promoter. He was only nineteen and in his first year university and not accustomed to being in hotel lobbies at that hour. "Mr. Bristow?" said the neat, cool night clerk. "Why, there's Mr. Bristow right over there," and he pointed to a group of men standing by one of the marble pillars about ten feet away. "Mr. Bristow," he called softly.

A big-shouldered, heavy man about forty-five, who was wearing a dark brown suit and a snap-brimmed brown hat on the back of his head, left the group and came toward the desk. He was good-looking with bold regular features and cold blue eyes and a face which in repose was like a piece of gray stone, but when he grinned as he came closer his expression changed and he seemed to have an engaging jolly self-assurance.

The clerk had merely nodded at Karl, and Mr. Bristow, without waiting for Karl to speak, put out his big hand. "You're Karl, aren't you?" he said. "How are you, Karl? So your uncle's laid up, eh?"

"He had a touch of pleurisy, Mr. Bristow."

"He sounded all right on the phone, Karl."

"He's all right, only he has to stay in bed."

"Well, it was nice of you wanting to come down and meet me, Karl."

"I've always wanted to meet you, Mr. Bristow," Karl said shyly. "I've heard so much about you from my uncle."

"It's nice having you want to sit around with us. You look just right to me, Karl," Mr. Bristow said warmly as he took him by the arm and led him toward the two friends. Karl grinned. He liked Mr. Bristow immediately, felt at ease with him and decided quickly that he was even more impressive than he had expected him to be.

Ever since Karl had been a kid he had heard his Uncle John talk about his old friend, Willie Bristow, who had had such an exciting, successful life in the biggest cities on the continent. Willie had made money out of fighters and he had kept it. If Willie hadn't liked the easy careless sporting life he could have been a great politician or an industrialist, according to Uncle John, for he had a very remarkable quality: he had great instinctive knowledge of a man's weakness; he knew how to handle people.

They had only walked across the lobby, but Willie had already made Karl feel like an old friend and the two men to whom he was introduced seemed to accept him as someone who was important in Willie's life. Both these men were smoking fine cigars and they wore good clothes and they shared the same mellow nonchalance. The thin one with the tired eyes and the intellectual stoop was Pierre Ouiment, a fight manager from Montreal whose boy, a lightweight, had been knocked out two hours ago in the Garden.

The other was Solly Stone, who had been a fighter himself ten years ago, and now had an unmarked, bland, moonlike face and the soft chuckling assurance of a man with a rapidly growing bank account. They went on talking about the fight, teasing each other because they had all lost money. Then Willie said, "Just a moment," and he went back to the desk and Karl, who was more interested in watching Willie than in listening to his friends, saw what his uncle had meant.

Approaching the desk, Willie called, "Hey, you . . ." and the neat polite clerk, who had jerked his head around in indignation, quickly smiled. With his big hands flat on the desk, Willie gave the clerk some instructions about delivering a parcel the next day, and then he looked at his watch, returned to his friends, hardly listened to them and finally said impatiently, "Oh, come on up to the room and have a drink. That dame can come up to the room."

It was a big double room on the fifth floor and the window was open with the curtains bellying in the warm night wind and the sound of tugboat whistling coming from the harbor. "Take off your coat, Karl," Willie said. The others, and Willie too, had quickly taken off their coats.

"I'm all right like this," Karl said.

"Come on, take it off, be one of us," Willie said and he took the coat from Karl. Then he opened a box of cigars and took a bottle from his bag. For his friends, he poured generous drinks, but for Karl he poured a very small one which hardly colored the water with which he filled the glass and he whispered sympathetically, "Nurse it along, Karl, as a favor to me. I don't want your uncle bending my ear about getting you into bad habits."

Advice of this kind might have offended Karl if Willie hadn't offered it so intimately, or if he hadn't had such a comradely touch which made Karl want to please him. Willie hadn't poured himself a drink: in fact he drank nothing until the girl he had been waiting for, a girl with thick shining hair in a black dress, who had a good-natured smile and a beautiful figure, came in with a bottle of special imported Scotch, which was Willie's favorite drink. The girl was the secretary of one of the directors of the Garden and she knew a lot about fight managers and promoters.

For ten minutes Willie was wonderfully considerate of her, and his friends smiled and winked at each other and watched him intently.

"You know," said Pierre, "I still figure Willie was right in betting on my boy. It was a sucker punch that got the kid."

"It was a sucker punch from where I was sitting," Karl said, and they argued about the fight.

"What business are you in, Mr. Stone?" Karl asked suddenly.

"Mr. Stone. What's this Mr. Stone stuff, Karl?"

"Well . . . Solly."

"That's better," Willie said. "And as for Solly, he's got a hundred and fifty thousand salted away."

"How did you make it, Solly?"

"That's easy," Solly said softly with a bland grin. "You see, Karl, when I was twenty I was a fighter. And in New York I won sixteen straight fights."

"For which he got three dollars and twenty cents apiece," Willie jeered.

"No, four dollars and eighty cents," Solly chuckled. They were all laughing heartily and didn't hear the knock on the door. At the second knock, Solly said, "The house dick for sure."

"Let me handle this," Willie said with real enjoyment.

When he opened the door, they could see the two tall, gray-haired detectives peering into the room. Blocking the door with his huge body, Willie said quietly, "Why, you're my boys, come on in and have a quick one."

"No thanks, no thanks, Mr. Bristow." The detectives answered with false smiles and deprecating gestures. "You're making a little too much noise. Other people on the floor complain when they want to sleep and well, you know . . ."

"Sure," Willie said and he walked out to the hall with them. When he returned he said with a shrug, "Flatfeet are all right only you got to take a little interest in them. What were we saying, guys?"

Then they began a conversation about who was the most stylish fighter they had ever seen. It was the kind of conversation Karl wanted to hear, wise and salty, and his young face was full of eagerness. He felt happy. His one drink had warmed him: he began to dream of being in faraway cities with Willie Bristow and having a share of his exciting life.

He found himself talking positively about fighters he had never seen and his opinion was respected because he was a friend of Willie's. First they talked about Benny Leonard, then about Kid Chocolate. "Chocolate, yeah, Chocolate, the nicest piece of fighting machinery I ever saw," Willie said. Solly and Pierre each longed to tell about the last time they had seen Chocolate in the ring, and their voices rose and they laughed happily, throwing their arms around each other's shoulders, each one trying to offer some splendid illumination about the perfection of the great black fighter's style.

"This is wonderful – wonderful," Karl thought, grinning gratefully at Willie, who was sitting on the edge of his chair, the collar of his expensive sport shirt pulled open, his bright expensive silk tie sliding across the shirt every time he jerked his head back and laughed hilariously.

Karl forgot all about the time until someone knocked on the door, then he looked at his wrist watch. It was two-thirty. "The house dick again, I suppose," Willie said and he chuckled to himself. On his way to the door he switched off the light, then he opened the door and there was the tall, hollow-cheeked, gray-haired detective standing in the lighted hall, blinking his eyes in surprise.

Willie stepped out and closed the door quickly, leaving them in darkness. Before anyone could get up and turn on the light, he had opened the door again, turned the light on himself and was leading the thin detective into the room. "Karl," he said, "pour this guy a real hooker. I can tell a man with an awful thirst."

"Okay, boys," the detective whispered, a guilty, apologetic smile on his face. "Only keep the noise down, eh? Let's keep it quiet."

"Here you are, colonel," Willie said affably as he handed him the drink Karl had poured. "Get this into that parched gullet, then take your coat off."

"Well, just one," the house detective said, sitting down on the edge of the bed.

"A guy like you, an old-timer, looks as if he might have an opinion on a great fighter," Willie said.

"Now that's a funny thing, Mr. Bristow," the detective said. "I was a battalion champion in the war."

"Drink to the battalion champion, gentlemen," Willie commanded. As they all raised their glasses he went on, "These boys think Kid Chocolate was the nicest-looking fighter they ever saw. Did you ever see him?"

"That I did," the battalion champion said enthusiastically, "and right here in this town about fifteen years ago." With a quick smile he added in a pleading tone, "Keep the voices down, OK, boys?"

"We want to know what you thought of Chocolate," Willie said in a whisper.

"For my money," the detective said with a solemn glance at the glass which he had emptied in one splendid gulp, "Chocolate was the real fancy dan. A great artist."

"I knew it, he's one of us," Willie cried in admiration. "Fill up his glass, Karl."

Again they began to talk eagerly about Chocolate's great fights, about his ability to deliver a straight punch from any angle, and the detective's eyes began to glow. He felt happy and free. His opinions were being treated with respect and when he made a joke there was a burst of hearty laughter. Soon they were making more noise than they had made all evening.

"There's just one thing I can't understand," Willie said suddenly as he sat down on the bed beside the detective and put his arm on his shoulder. "How did a fine guy like you ever become a snooper?"

"Well, you know how it is," the detective began awkwardly.

"Go on, tell me why."

"I don't know," he said, fumbling for words. In his deep, apologetic embarrassment he looked almost innocent. "It's a living, see. I've been at it ten years. I've got a wife and two kids. A married man has to have steady work, eh? It's something you get used to. Some guys look for trouble. I mean, well, it's not so bad."

The fumbling apology had moved Karl, who suddenly felt happy when he saw Willie, Pierre and Solly nod gravely to each other. The flushed face of the detective suddenly lit up. He relaxed again, took another drink, his eyes shone and he started to sing softly, "By Killarney's lakes and dells . . ."

"The man's got a voice too," Willie cried.

"A real baritone," Solly said enthusiastically.

"If only there was a tenor here," the detective sighed.

"I'll be the tenor," Karl said. So they sang "Killarney" with dignity and restraint, then swung easily into "Annie Laurie." In the happiness of the song and the noisy enthusiasm of the applause the detective forgot where he was; he forgot about his job and the lateness of the hour.

Karl, turning, looked at Willie Bristow with wondering admiration, for it was Willie who, with his magical assurance, had touched this man and drawn him in among them. Someone irritable who didn't know how to get along with people would have been intimidated by the detective's knock on the door and would have let him spoil the evening.

The detective, liking Karl's happy smile, had backed him into a corner and was telling how his father had taught him to use his fists and how he had dreamed in his youth of being the world's light heavyweight champion. The detective had a very good memory of his youth and his eyes had softened.

Over by the window Willie and Solly Stone were having a serious conversation, keeping their voices low. A puff of wind from the open window blew the light curtain across Willie's face and he frowned and twisted his head and brushed it away and leaned closer to Solly. Pierre, who had been talking casually to the girl, turned away and stood behind the detective, listening and puffing methodically on his cigar. Suddenly, he blew a great cloud of smoke at the back of the detective's neck and grinned in derision when the detective began to cough.

Some little memory of his youth had struck the detective as being so good, so amusing, that he wanted Willie to hear it, and he went over to him and tapped him on the shoulder. "Listen to this, Willie," he said with a strange innocent smile. Willie frowned and waved him away impatiently. "This is good, Willie," the detective pleaded. "You'll like this. I want you to hear it," and again he rested his hand on Willie's shoulder.

"I'm talking myself," Willie said abruptly.

"Sure. Go ahead," the detective said, drawing up a chair. The intrusion annoyed Willie, who looked at the smiling detective steadily for a moment.

"You've finished that drink, soldier?" he said calmly.

"That I have," the detective agreed with a deprecating chuckle as he held out the glass, thinking Willie was going to fill it again. "And it's first-class stuff too."

"All right, then, flatfoot," Willie said crisply. "You've had a couple of drinks. That's your pay-off. Now get out of here and don't bother us any more."

"What?" the detective whispered in a bewildered tone. He seemed to be trying to believe they were kidding him. Then he looked stricken, for Willie was waiting with an assured, hard smile and the detective's eyes shifted and he looked around as if he wanted to hide himself, but there was no place to hide, and he became obsequious and muttered, "Yes, sir," and walked quickly to the door. "Thanks, gentlemen, for the drinks," he said in a tone of comic dignity, but he did not look back.

"Nice work, Willie," Solly said, grinning in admiration. "I wondered how long you were going to put up with that crumb."

"Yes, Willie," Pierre agreed with a meditative air. "Easing him out might have been difficult."

"Him. Don't worry," Willie said contemptuously. "I know how to handle those flatfeet. He knows when his ears have been pinned back."

"But . . ." Karl began.

"But what, Karl?"

"I don't know," Karl said unhappily. He was struggling against a terrible disappointment in Willie. "He was letting himself go and feeling happy . . ." He could still see the detective's hurt eyes. "I guess I got to like the guy a little," he said awkwardly as he looked from one face to another.

"You'll get wise to those guys later on, Karl," Willie said casually. "I've handled dozens of them. I know how to handcuff them."

"Yes, I guess you do."

"I'm going to take you out with us now, Karl, and buy you some first-class Chinese food. I know the place to get it. I want to have a real talk with you, Karl."

"It's getting late," Karl said and he stood up slowly.

"Oh, nonsense, Karl. This is your night."

"No. I have to go," Karl said with surprising firmness, for as he dwelt on Willie's big, red, friendly, smiling face he felt himself pulling away in sudden fear, knowing that just as Willie had handled the detective and Solly and Pierre, he was now ready to handle him, too.

A Little Beaded Bag

When young Mrs. Evans came in at dinner time and noticed that the little white beaded bag she had tossed on the chair in the bedroom that afternoon was gone, she was sure Eva, the maid, had taken it. The girl, helping her clean out the chest of drawers in the bedroom, had found the bag she'd put aside a year ago because the little white beads had come loose around the metal clasp. Mrs. Evans had hesitated, remembering the night she'd carried it to a party after returning from Europe, and then she'd sighed, knowing she would never get it fixed, and tossed it at the rubbish on the paper spread out on the floor.

"My, it's pretty, isn't it?" Eva said as she picked it up. Mrs. Evans took it from her, looked at it, wondering if she ought to keep it after all, and undecided, tossed it onto the bedroom chair.

When her husband who was a young lawyer came home she might never have mentioned the bag if he hadn't sat down sullenly and refused to speak to her. They had quarreled the night before. They had been married only a year, but in the last few months there seemed to be some tension and strain between them that puzzled her and made them sometimes want to hurt each other terribly. When she saw him hiding gloomily behind the newspaper, she was touched and regretted the quarrel: she wanted to tell him that he was wrong about last night, that he was crazy if he thought she really expected him to drop all his old friends, and that she understood he could still be in love with her and yet want to have some freedom of his own.

"David," she said, a little timidly, "David, I was thinking –"

"I'm tired," he said in a surly voice, and when he didn't even look at her, she suddenly remembered that he liked Eva and used to ask her questions about her family on the farm, so she said, casually, "You may be interested to know Eva stole that beaded bag of mine."

"What's that? What bag?" he exclaimed.

"You know the one, the one I had a year ago."

"Why, the kid wouldn't touch it," he said sharply. "You know that as well as I do. She's a fine kid. You've been trying for weeks to find some little flaw in her, and you've had to admit, yourself, you couldn't. Don't start picking away at her."

It seemed so unjust that he should challenge her, and as they faced each other, she said bitterly, "I'm not picking at her or you. I'm telling you a fact. The bag was there this morning and it's gone."

"I don't think she's taken it, that's all," he said.

"We can soon find out if you doubt it," she said.

"Well, I certainly doubt it."

"Of course you do," she replied, "of course you do. You mean you doubt my judgment about everything. Well, I'll show you," she said, and she smiled very brightly at him.

She went into the kitchen where Eva was getting the dinner ready. She sat down and watched the girl's soft hair, and her plump young shape as she moved around. The girl grew nervous and began to smooth her apron and look scared. Mrs. Evans kept watching her, never smiling, never speaking, and when Eva reddened and half turned, she offered no explanation. Eva could no longer stand the shrewd, calm, knowing expression in Mrs. Evans's eyes, and she turned nervously. "Is there anything wrong, ma'am?" she asked.

"Do you remember that purse this morning?"

"Yes, ma'am. Weren't you going to throw it out?"

"You know I wasn't throwing it out, Eva."

"Well –"

"Somebody took it."

"Maybe I threw it out in the trash barrel," she said, and she looked at Mrs. Evans, as if pleading with her to make some friendly little remark about it being unimportant and that she was sure the bag would turn up.

But Mrs. Evans, seeing how disturbed the girl was, said easily, "Eva, would you run down to the drug store and get me some cigarettes?" and she smiled.

"Right now?" the girl asked, reluctantly.

"Yes, right now, please."

Eva was frightened and sullen, trying to make some kind of plan as she stood there. Then she turned to go back to her room, but Mrs. Evans called sharply, "You don't need your coat, Eva. Just go as you are." They faced each other, and for just a moment Eva resisted an antagonism she did not understand. In the last month she had hardly spoken to either Mr. or Mrs. Evans. When she heard them quarreling at night she was afraid they would call her to bring them a drink and her hand would tremble and Mrs. Evans would be impatient, and then Eva would hear Mr. Evans defending her good-naturedly. But now she nodded obediently and went out in a wild rush, for she was scared of losing her job.

Mrs. Evans went straight to the girl's bedroom and David followed, scowling at her. She trembled with excitement going through Eva's dresser drawer, pushing aside little boxes of cheap powder, an old photograph of Eva's father, who was a big, poorly dressed man, a few letters which she held in her hand wondering if Eva had talked about her; and then with her heart pounding with excitement as she listened for the sound of the girl's footsteps, and feeling strangely like a thief herself, she went to the cupboard and pulled out the girl's club bag and fished through the nightdress, the old tattered prayer-book, the love story magazine. At the bottom was the damaged white beaded bag. She stood up triumphantly and smiled at her husband who turned away as if he was sick. As she followed him into the living-room the door slammed and the girl came rushing in, flushed, her eyes full of apprehension, and she handed Mrs. Evans the cigarettes.

"Thanks, Eva," she said, a little coldly, and the girl reddened and wheeled around and went into her bedroom.

"Well, now, was I right? Am I right about something?" she said to David.

"No, you weren't right," he said quietly.

"It was in her bag, you saw it yourself," she said. "Don't you believe your own eyes?" But it bothered her terribly that he only stared at her. She whispered, "Haven't I got a perfect right to find out if I've got a thief in the house? What are you staring at me for, wasn't I right?" He sat there as if she were a stranger who puzzled him.

Then they heard Eva calling, "Mrs. Evans, could I speak to you a moment, please?" and she came in, holding out the dainty little white purse, trying to smile innocently. But her eyes showed how completely helpless she felt with the little white purse, as if something bright and elusive had betrayed her.

"You found it," Mrs. Evans said uneasily.

"Yes, I found it, don't you see," she whispered, nodding her head eagerly, begging Mrs. Evans to just take the purse and not make her a liar.

"Where did you find it?" Mrs. Evans asked.

"In the trash barrel," Eva said, never taking her eyes off Mrs. Evans's face. "I must have picked it up with some papers and things. I remembered I put all those things you wanted thrown out in one pile, and I thought I might have picked it up, too, and I went and looked. I'm very sorry, Mrs. Evans."

"Why, thanks, Eva, thanks," Mrs. Evans said, hesitating, and when the girl hesitated, too, and then went, she hoped it was all over, but when she turned to David he was more distressed than ever. She grew ashamed, yet she fought against this shame and said, indignantly, "What's the matter with you? She took it and she knows I caught her."

"Maybe you're satisfied," he whispered.

"I don't know what you mean," she said.

"You know she didn't intend to take it. You know you made her a thief. You humiliated the kid, you took away her self-respect," he said, coming close to her as if he was going to shake her. "My Lord, if you knew what you looked like going through the kid's things."

"I didn't, I didn't," she whispered.

"You're ruthless when you get started – just like I told you last night, utterly ruthless."

"It's got nothing to do with us," she said angrily.

"Yes, it has. You're still at me, and it doesn't matter about the kid," he said. "Keep it up, keep getting everything tighter till it snaps and then we'll hate each other."

He looked so disappointed that she put out her hand

and touched him on the arm. "I didn't mean it like that. I knew I was right, that's all."

"Sure, you were right. You're right about so many things," he said, shaken a little because she looked frightened, and he muttered, "I don't know what's the matter with you," and he swung away from her and she heard him going out.

She sat down with her hands up to her face. As she looked down at the little beaded bag, so small and unimportant, it seemed that day after day with her doubts and discontent she did a whole succession of little things that were right but they only cheapened her life and David's, as she had just cheapened Eva's.

She got up and hurried to Eva's bedroom and called anxiously, "Eva, may I come in?"

Eva was sitting on the bed, sullen and fearful, waiting.

"Eva – this purse," Mrs. Evans said, holding it up and trying to smile. Eva looked away, her face red. "I only wanted to see if it could be fixed," Mrs. Evans said. "There are a few beads loose. You're good with a needle, aren't you? Couldn't you fix it up for yourself?"

"I don't know. It's awfully pretty, isn't it?" Eva said, taking it in her two hands and fingering it shyly, "It's terribly pretty."

"Take it, please take it," Mrs. Evans whispered, and Eva looked up astonished because Mrs. Evans had one hand up to her lips and though her voice was eager her eyes were brimming with tears as if she were begging Eva to help her.

Big Jules

THEY WERE HAVING A LOT OF FUN IN THE NEIGHBORHOOD
with Big Jules Casson. Word had soon gone around that he
had promised his old man he would never get into trouble
again after he had been sent to reform school for stealing
from Spagnola's fruit market. The boys whose leader he had
once been, and who had been afraid of him for years, found
that he wouldn't fight back; they mocked him on those
winter nights when he came hurrying home from the job at
the printing shop his father had got him. A big, rawboned
seventeen-year-old who seemed to have realized suddenly
that he would soon be a man, he started running the minute
he got off the bus. He trotted along with his head down and
his hands deep in his overcoat pockets. When he passed the
cigar store where the boys were playing the slot machines,
and they saw him through the open door and yelled – "Hey,
when did they let you out?" – he never turned his big serious
face.

But one night in the middle of the winter, when it had
been raining and half snowing for hours and he came
trotting past the cigar store, someone called out, "Hey,
Jules, what are you doing tonight?"

This time the voice seemed to be soft, friendly, and

casual. So Jules stopped and turned. As he came into the light, his face showed how eager he was for companionship if only they wouldn't kid him. Near the cigar-store door were three fellows whom he had grown up with. There was Phil Harris in a new overcoat, tight at the waist, with a pearl-gray felt hat, lighting a cigarette for Alf Maguire in the same old dirty overcoat he had worn the last five years. But the one who had called to him was leaning against the window, in a leather jacket and a peak cap – Stuffy Meuller, whom Big Jules hadn't seen for three months. It was hard to see the expressions on their faces through the light stream of snow. So Jules went toward them slowly.

"What's on your mind?" he asked eagerly.

"Well, if it isn't my old friend, Big Jules," Stuffy Meuller said enthusiastically. As he reached up and slapped him on the shoulder, Jules grinned warmly. "Maybe we could go to the fights, eh, guys," he said eagerly. "I haven't been to the fights for months."

But Stuffy Meuller, a little guy that Jules could have smacked down with one swing, kept up the elaborate enthusiasm. "Wait a minute, give me a chance to get used to you. I didn't know they had let you out."

When he saw that they were smirking at each other, Big Jules wanted to plead with Meuller to shut up. But Meuller, enjoying himself, went on, "If you weren't doing anything I thought we might take a little trip over to Spagnola's fruit market. What do you say, Jules?"

Jules was peering at their grinning faces that looked so red and shining and mocking in the light and the snow. Then he shook his head, as if puzzled. "Lay off, can't you lay off a guy?" he muttered. He was leaning close to them, holding himself taut, as if he had just had an insight into what he would always be. His face suddenly frightened them.

Scared, they backed away. But this only seemed to hurt him more. "What's the matter?" he pleaded, taking a step after them. Shooting out his hand, he grabbed Meuller by the shoulder. "I'm not going to hurt you," he pleaded, for now they were looking as frightened as if he had been going to pull a knife on them.

"Beat it, Stuffy," Phil Harris whispered, shoving Meuller away. "Get going. He's taking the plug out."

As they went up the street he stood there, helpless, for now it seemed that in some way, after digging at him for months, they had found out that he was still what he had always been. After a little while, he started to go home, thinking desperately that maybe they were right, that if his life belonged to the lanes around Spagnola's fruit market, if he had been pinned there forever the night the police caught him and the others rifling the till – even if he was just a kid when it happened – then the dream he had been carrying around in him for months of working hard and making something out of his life was all gone.

Then he suddenly began to walk faster, feeling a great longing to look into the faces of his own family and see if they, too, were really only waiting for him to get into trouble again; maybe they, too, were always thinking of the fruit market and the years when he was growing up near it. So when he went into the house, he hung back near the door of the living room, his hat still on his head, the melted snow dripping off the brim, and he looked around suspiciously. His father, who had been sitting in the armchair at the head of the table, his arms spread out over the evening paper on the table, did not look up. Nor did his mother. She was fixing the collar of his sister Alice's dress, and Alice kept saying, "Please hurry, or I'll be late." But as Jules still stood there staring at them, they turned one by one. He looked so excited and suspicious that his mother's hand began to tremble. Her face showed that she was alarmed. Then his father, opening his mouth blankly, suddenly looked very grave and folded up the paper.

To Jules it seemed that they were just as frightened as the fellows at the corner, and he cried, "Why are you all gaping at me?"

"Why, son," his mother said, "what happened?"

"I ran into Meuller and some of the guys down at the corner," he blurted out, "and I didn't smack them. See, I didn't smack them."

Then Jules's father got up and began to walk up and down the room. Jules could see how worried he was. His head hung down a little and the patch of white hair at the back stuck up in the light; it was as if something he had been dreading for months were coming at last to a head: the anguish he felt, which he could not conceal now, gave Jules a painful but deep satisfaction. "I was right. This is how they've been feeling all along," he thought.

"What's Meuller to you, son?" his father said, stopping in front of Jules with his hands out appealingly. "You're a good boy, see," he said, taking a step closer, his worried face full of gentle concern. It was as if he wanted to put his arm around Jules but was too shy. "You're working and doing well, isn't it so? And we're proud of you." His voice broke a little, but he went on, "We're proud of the way you handled yourself, son."

"Aw, cut it out," Jules said harshly. "That isn't what you're thinking."

"It's the way I've been feeling, Jules."

"Meuller's a bum, Jules," his mother said, taking him by the arm and trying to get him to sit down. "Sure you should smack him, but he's no good. Why should you put your hands on trash? Me and your father only want that you shouldn't let such things bother you, son, see?" When he didn't seem to be listening, she said desperately, "You don't need to worry, you don't need to worry about anything anybody says. We're sure of you, son."

But Jules was looking at his sister Alice, who had sat down with her hat on and her hands clasped tight in her lap. She was two years older than Jules. She had never gotten into trouble, she was very pretty, and she had always seemed beyond the reach of any of the neighborhood boys. It was the way she carried herself. But now there was an angry flush on her face. In that flush, and in her silence, Jules thought he saw at last the true picture of the humiliation he would always bring to his family.

When Alice got up grimly and started to go along the hall, Jules followed her and grabbed her arm.

"Go on," he whispered, "say it."

"Say what?"

"I never give you a chance to stop being ashamed of me, eh!"

"Jules – "

"That boy friend of yours – why don't you ever bring him around here?"

"You're going crazy, Jules. He was around here last night."

"Sure," he said. "When I wasn't here."

Then her eyes blazed, but she looked as if she were going to cry. "Why don't you get some sense?" she whispered. "What's the use of hitting Meuller? Nobody's going around watching you, can't you see? Jules, can't you see?"

As she tried to take his arm comfortingly, he knocked it away. "Damn it all, stop sympathizing with me," he said. He didn't want to hear anything more. All he wanted to do was go out and find Meuller – or any other guy who would dare open his trap – and beat his brains out.

Going along the street, looking for Meuller, he kept gripping his hands tight, exulting in the release and freedom such violence would bring to him. But when he got to the corner and looked around, there was no one standing near the cigar store. There were no marks even in the snow, nothing to show that they, or he, had ever stood there. Then, as he looked up and down the street vaguely, wondering which way he should go, he felt an immense longing to have everything that had ever happened to him up to a few months ago wiped clean, just as the white falling snow had covered up and wiped out his footprints and Meuller's.

He turned to look into the store through the window, but he couldn't see in because of the way the snow, swept against the panes, melted and streamed down. Then it got so that he couldn't even see the window. Spagnola's fruit market kept coming into his head; he could see nothing but the old shed with the baskets of fruit, the little store, the lane behind. Turning away, he started to walk fast, trying hard to think of other things, like the little soft-eyed girl who had come into the shop where he worked. But it was no good. He couldn't get the fruit market out of his head. It began to grow feverishly bright.

It was there blocking him every time he tried to move away from it, and while it was there, he could have no big dreams, no great eagerness, no future to work for. Then the magnitude of this one spot in his life began to awe him. He felt he had to see it and look at it again.

He was four blocks away from home, going down the street where the fruit market was, and he knew within himself that he had been deliberately heading over that way.

Keeping on the other side of the road, he walked slowly past the lighted fruit-store window. Through the glistening glass he could see the pyramids of oranges and lemons and purple plums and red apples; and then he saw old Spagnola himself waddle into the light. "There it is. Just like it'll always be," he thought.

To get closer, he crossed the road to the lane that ran past the side of the store, the lane where the kids used to meet at night. Out of the store came a shabby woman carrying a big paper bag, and Jules ducked furtively into the lane. As he went along by the fence, he looked back once at the trail of his footprints in the snow. Again he felt the longing to have this place and that couple of years in the reform school dumped magically out of his life.

Then he was at the old gate that led into the yard behind Spagnola's place. Hundreds of times he had hopped over it when it was locked, at first just to steal an apple or a peach with the other boys – and then go running madly along the lane with Spagnola shouting after them. The gate was open now. Slow, wondering, disbelieving, he went into the yard. There was the shed, the roof a white slope of snow. At the back of the store, on the stoop, was a big pile of empty baskets.

As he got closer to the place his wonder, his unbelief, kept growing. The place suddenly seemed shabby and unimportant. He wanted to cry out bitterly that it was a terrible thing that such a tumbling down blot of a place should always be in his head, should always be there in the eyes of his father and mother when they were worried about him, and in the eyes of everybody who knew him when they looked at him.

On the ground beside him was an empty basket. Swinging his foot savagely, he sent it crashing against the stoop.

At the sound of the crash, a shadow filled the lighted window; then the back door was thrown open, and the beam of light fell on Big Jules, who stood there, bewildered and motionless.

Rushing out old Spagnola yelled, "Hey, you, hey!" He came rushing at Jules, his arms wide, his white apron flapping like a sail.

Jules turned to run, but slipped in the mud and the snow, and when he looked up and saw Spagnola close to him, the man's short little arms opened wide to grab him, he felt crazy. It seemed that not only Spagnola but the years around the place when he was growing up, and Meuller and all the other guys, were trying to hold him tight, hold him there forever. He had to break the grip it had on him. He had to destroy it. So he took a leap at Spagnola, like a flying tackle, his head getting him in the chest, bunting him sprawling on the snow. Instead of running, Big Jules looked around wildly. Then he started kicking at the pile of baskets. Yelling "Help! Help!" Spagnola got up and jumped on Jules's back, but he couldn't hold him. So he went on shouting while Jules crashed against the piled-up baskets and kicked at them and sent the splinters flying in the snow as if he had to keep it up till he smashed the whole place and Spagnola's fruit market was wiped forever from the earth.

But Spagnola's weight on his shoulders was pulling him down and exhausting him. At last he crashed on the stoop with Spagnola on top. "I got you, I got you," Spagnola grunted. But Jules wasn't even trying to move.

Then Mrs. Spagnola came waddling down the path of light. "Hold him, hold him!" she yelled. "I'll get the police."

"He's crazy. But I got him," Spagnola said.

Jules lay there dazed, hardly hearing anything, but

when Mrs. Spagnola, bending down, cried, "Look, look would you! It's Jules Casson!" he began to tremble.

"So it is," Spagnola said.

"What was he trying to steal?" she asked.

"But there's nothing out here to steal in the winter," he said, astonished.

Hoisting himself up on one elbow, Jules sobbed, "Don't get the cops. Please don't get the cops. Can't you see? I only wanted to get a look at the place – because – because I couldn't get it out of my head."

He looked so stricken and bewildered that the Spagnolas shook their heads at each other and shrugged in wonder.

"Only yesterday his father was talking to me about his Jules, saying such good things," Spagnola said to his wife. Then he said to Jules, "What is this? You should tell us."

As Jules looked up at their wondering faces, he saw that there was nothing to fear from them. They were wanting to take him in and help him as if he were some trapped animal they had found when they opened the door. "I . . . " he stammered, and couldn't go on. But he kept nodding and nodding his head gratefully, as if in their friendly worried faces he had found a release from a bad violent dream about himself.

This Man, My Father

THE WEEK I WAS GIVEN A GOOD POSITION IN THE BROKER'S office, I moved into a fine new apartment and wrote to my father and mother in Windsor. I hadn't seen them in five years, and I asked them to come to New York.

At the station, they came up the iron stairs from the trains very slowly. When my mother looked up and saw me waiting, her round worried face suddenly wrinkled in smiles. By the slow steps she took and the way her hand kept gripping at the rail, I knew her bad leg and her heart must have gotten worse.

For twenty-five years my father had been a letter carrier in Windsor and he had just been retired on a small pension. While I was kissing my mother, whose arm as she held me trembled, my father, now a stout, white-haired man in a blue serge suit, stood to one side fumbling shyly with his heavy gold watch chain. I had never felt close to my father. When I was a kid, he got excited easily and often shouted at everyone in the family. Even now while we stood together in Pennsylvania Station, I wondered why I had been so delighted to see his face and I tried to figure out why he had looked so glad to see me.

Afraid he might say something affectionate, I said

quickly, "Is Thelma getting along any better with her husband?"

"Oh, son, son, the way that turned out," my mother said, taking me by the arm on the way to the taxi. "Your sister has had to come to our house for things like vegetables and canned food. That man never was any good."

"That business will stop right now," my father said firmly. "We'll have a hard enough time ourselves living on my miserable pension."

When we were going into my apartment house on lower Fifth Avenue, the uniformed doorman opened the door for us, and my father, making a low bow to him, said, "Thank you very much."

At once I remembered that my father, all his life, had made such humble gestures to strangers. Yet the doorman did not seem to be startled; he even smiled in a new bright way. But when we got into the elevator and my father made the same deep bow to the attendant, I was annoyed at his humility. My mother nudged him. Knowing she had more pride, he looked at her anxiously, and she tried to tell him by her fierce expression that he wasn't to shame us. In those few moments in the elevator while I was annoyed and my father, rebuked, grew irritable, we quickly re-established the old relationship among us.

Before my father got his letter-carrying job we had been very poor, and when I was a kid I used to long for a time such as this when I'd be making money and they'd be coming to see me, so I sat down in the apartment grinning with contentment while they looked around eagerly. My father started examining the woodwork and the way the walls were finished. My mother looked at the material in the window drapes. When they started calling to each other and pointing at things like children, I felt a little like crying.

"I guess it costs an awful lot to live here, son. Are you sure you can afford it?" my mother asked.

"I'll be able to from now on. It took a long time waiting, but I was sure it was coming," I said.

With her arms folded across her chest and a worried expression on her face, my mother looked around and said, "I hope you didn't move into this place just because we were coming." Then, she took a deep breath and turned suddenly and looked at me, and it was as though all the hope she had ever had for me, her son, while I was growing and while I was away from her, was justified in that moment while we smiled at each other.

My father, making clucking noises with his tongue as he rubbed his hands on the woodwork of the mantel, turned and said, "How much are you paying here?"

"A few hundred a month. It's a small place," I said.

He straightened up, glared at me with his face flushed with indignation and burst out, "You must be crazy, man. I hope you're using your head and know what you're doing with your money. I hope you've got more sense than you used to have and you're not making a fool of yourself." While he wagged his finger at me, I felt that old hostile resentment rising in me.

"Joe, Joe, have you no sense," my mother said to him sharply. "Why should you talk to him like that? Be quiet. He knows what he'll be able to afford." While my father, flustered and ashamed, tried to smile at me, I began to laugh out loud. The thread of a sudden, silly, familiar passionate quarrel among us had made me feel I was at home again.

"Come on, let's go out. I've been waiting to show you the town," I said.

My mother looked down at her ankles, but she got up willingly. Then she sighed and sat down, saying, "I'd love to go, but couldn't I have a little rest first? Couldn't you and your father go?"

My father said rapidly, "He doesn't want to go just with me, isn't that right?" and when I nodded he was even more agitated. "Come on, Helen, come on," he pleaded. "I'll walk as slow as you want. We'll come back as soon as you start to get tired."

Feeling the shyness between us, my mother laughed and said, "Oh, go on. It'll do you both good to have a walk before dinner."

My father looked at us with his blue eyes, seeing us both together and close to each other, then he said quietly, "All right, I'm ready," and he buttoned up his coat and put his hat on the back of his head.

I felt cheated as we went out together. I had looked forward to hearing my mother's burst of enthusiasm as I showed her the town. But my father was following me a few steps behind and in a way that only annoyed me. He didn't make his low bow to the doorman either. Maybe what really annoyed me was that the elevator attendant and the doorman had smiled at my father and said, "Good day, sir," more respectfully and cheerfully than they had ever done to me.

My father was looking up the avenue at the way the line of buildings cut like a cavern into the horizon. Certain it was making him feel humble, I said lightly, "Quite a city, eh? Makes you feel a little strange?"

He seemed to be puzzled about something, then he said quietly, "No, it isn't that it seems strange. It doesn't seem half as strange as I thought it would."

I had counted on him being wide-eyed and wondering, and I said a bit tartly, "Well, I got a big kick out of it the first time I looked around."

"I mean it reminds me of London," my father said. "It's different of course, but it gives me some of the same feeling, maybe it's just the big-city feeling London had."

I had forgotten that my father had been born in England and had come to Canada when he was twelve years old. Again, I felt cheated and didn't know what to say to him.

"I'd love to see Wall Street. Could we go there?" he asked.

We took the subway downtown, and as we walked through the narrow streets of the financial district my father's growing wonder and complete childish acceptance of everything I told him made me forgive him for not being so surprised in the first place. He began grabbing at my arm and pointing at things. Once he asked me the name of a big new building, and when I couldn't tell him, he darted across the street, peered at the brass plate near the door, and came bouncing back through the traffic, with me standing there sure he'd be killed, to report briskly and make me feel helpless.

But it was when we were down at the waterfront, looking across the river at the tugboats and the sunlight on Brooklyn, that we really began to feel closer together. My father had been sniffing the air, smiling to himself and peering in seamen's taverns we passed as we walked along. Suddenly, he took an extra sniff, his face wrinkled up in a wide grin, and he stood still, crying out, "It smells like a fish market!" We were at Fulton Street and the smell of fish was very strong now. On the road, there were little bonfires of refuse. Grim, old, slow-moving seamen passed us on the sidewalk. "Yes, sir, it's a fish market," my father repeated.

"Sure it's a fish market, but what about it?"

"I haven't smelt anything like it in years."

"It's just a stench to me. Let's move along."

"Isn't it lovely? It reminds me of Billingsgate in London," he said. "When I was a boy I often used to go down to the fish market." Turning, he got the smell of the fish market again, looked across the river, took a deep breath and was delighted.

"Why didn't you ever mention being a kid in London before?" I asked.

"I must have forgotten it. It seems such a long time ago," he said.

I felt suddenly that I knew little or nothing about my father as we cut up through the lower East Side. But we began to share in the discovery of broken-down poolrooms, we liked the swarm of Italian, Chinese and Jewish faces that passed us. And it was not nearly as strange for my father, the man walking beside me in the good, freshly pressed blue serge suit and the hat on the back of his head, the postman from Windsor, as it was for me – foreign faces, bright colors, dirty streets, the odors of a seaport he had long ago forgotten, all had come alive for him down there by the waterfront. Again and again he said, "When I was a boy," and the softness and innocence of his voice made me full of wonder, because I had grown up thinking him irritable and loud with excitement. "This is what he was like when he was a kid?" I was thinking. "Maybe he's always had an easy, mild way with him like this, and we haven't known it. When he was a kid I would have liked him." Feeling years older than my father I took his arm, but when we crossed the road I knew I was restless about something.

"Are you tired?" I asked.

"Me tired? I could walk miles," he said.

"How about going into the lunch wagon there for a cup of coffee?"

"Whatever you say," he said, and we went into the lunch wagon that was on a corner near a garage.

My father always ordered raisin pie with a cup of coffee, and I remembered how fond he had always been of it. While I watched him eat with his head down and his hat almost slipping off the back of his head, there remained in me that mixed-up feeling of being with a kid yet being with my own father.

He was so hungry I knew he hadn't had anything to eat on the train, but he looked up suddenly and said, "When I get back home I wish I could get some little thing to do."

Surprised, I said, "Why, you'll be all right. You'll have your pension and I'll be able to help some now. It's going to be different now because I'm in the money."

"But I'd like it better if I didn't have to be a drag on somebody else. Why shouldn't I be able to look after myself?"

"All right. Maybe I'll be able to set you up in something soon."

My father was looking at the man behind the counter, a little runt of a man whose face was half hidden behind the steam from the coffee boilers, and he whispered, "I'll bet a dollar I'm twice as active as your friend there. Why couldn't I open a place like this back home?"

While my father went on watching the withered-faced man behind the counter rubbing a few cups with a towel, I began thinking again of his childhood in that other city, London, so far away from the lunch wagon. Then I heard him say quietly, "As long as I could make enough to give me the feeling I was working. It's terrible to feel there's nothing for you to do." The way he spoke, the stillness I felt in him when he had finished, made me realize how frightened he had been growing day after day. While I had been sitting there dreaming of the beginning of my father's life, he had been sitting beside me dreading the end of it. It made me unhappy. We went out and started to walk again.

The street lights were lit when we got to Washington Square. My feet were tired, yet I did not want to get home because I knew I was not satisfied. I could not understand my restlessness. Before we went in we stood together looking up the avenue at the glow of lights in the twilight, and my father said, "It's certainly nice here. It's hard to imagine a nicer place."

It was dark in the apartment and we thought there was nobody there, but when we listened we heard the sound of heavy breathing. I turned on the light, and my mother, who had been sound asleep, sat up, startled, crying, "Joe, Joe," feeling around on the bed for my father. "Where am I?" Then she stared at us, swallowing hard as she tried to smile. "I was frightened," she said.

We were both grinning at her, and maybe she felt we were sharing some secret, for she rubbed her eyes and said, "Look at the two of you. What have you been doing?"

"Just walking," I said.

"I was down on Wall Street," my father said eagerly. "I looked across the river and saw Brooklyn, and it was beautiful in the sunlight."

She felt something between us that aroused her and she said, "What were you talking about?"

"Nothing, nothing at all," I laughed.

She was a terribly curious woman and she pleaded, "Please tell me," but when I only laughed she turned to my father and brightened and said, "I had such a good feeling before I fell asleep. I was thinking of the way we worried about the children, and all the times I tried to give Harry here a little good advice. It felt so good to be here with him and see how he was getting on."

"That's right," my father said energetically. "He can't say we both didn't give him good advice."

"Both of us?" she jeered at him. "Why, Thelma was always your pet. You were scared to open your mouth to Harry for fear he'd leave home, and it was only when you got mad that you shouted at him."

My father's neck reddened in the old way as he prepared to become desperately apologetic, and my mother went on, laughing at him. "Son, can you ever remember your father quietly insisting that you pay attention to what he had to say?"

I laughed and shook my head and said, "No, I can't." But when I saw my father looking over at me with that baffled, helpless expression I cried out, "For heaven's sake, mother, leave him alone. Let's not start running him into the ground while he's here."

The loose skin around my mother's throat was working up and down, and her eyes grew desolate. "I'm not trying to take the credit for your success," she said. "You never used to speak to me like that. I guess you've grown away from me a little," and she got up slowly to put on her hat and go out with us.

"It's nothing, I was tired," I said, trying to soothe her, but my father, who had been sitting still, suddenly smiled at me.

While he smiled like that I felt him walking beside me; I felt that mystery of having been close to the boyhood of a man who was now old and who was sitting beside me smiling at me. I had seen the innocence of his childhood restored to him for a little while. As I kept looking at him the restless excitement and wonder were growing in me. I had a great hunger to know of the things that had delighted him, the things he had hoped for when he was a kid far away in London and happy, before he ever thought of Canada or heard of Windsor – this man, my father, whom I had found walking down near the Fulton Street fish market.

The Way It Ended

As they sat around the table in the little room the detectives used in the neighborhood police station, Hilda Scranton told the detective who had found her working as a waitress in Detroit, and Miss Schenley, the social worker, that they were wasting their time; her mother wouldn't dream of complaining that she was incorrigible.

She was a big girl for her age, sixteen, not really pretty, yet with a wide, attractive mouth, good eyes and thick black hair. She was sure that in her yellow summer dress she looked like a full grown woman and she tried to act like one, but it was a hot night, and as the little beads of moisture appeared on her forehead and upper lip and her make-up wore off she became just a defiant, worried girl. "If you were my daughter," the solemn, graying detective said, "and you ran off like that I'd spank you until you couldn't sit down." But Hilda knew he had decided that she was just another wayward girl, and she knew too that he watched the way her dress tightened across her breasts when she moved, so she lowered her eyes and smiled demurely, embarrassing him.

She didn't want them to see that she was really listening for the sound of her mother and dreading it, for she was afraid her mother would stand there grimly and say, "This is the end. I've tried everything – everything, and I can't do anything with her," and then she didn't know what would happen to her. So, as they waited she tried to make a friend out of Miss Schenley, the neat, thin, social worker with the funny little green straw hat. Miss Schenley was a trained psychologist and she said she wanted to be helpful and understanding. Turning to her with a graceful little motion of her hand, Hilda opened her eyes wide and in good, soft, polite language and with an air of troubled, intelligent reluctance tried to explain the difficulty she had had with her mother, and why she had run away, and in a little while she was sure she could use Miss Schenley as a protection against her mother.

There was nothing she wasn't ready to tell Miss Schenley, and she did, though, of course, not exactly everything, because Miss Schenley really wanted to know only why she didn't get on with her mother. She had to get it all in before her mother came, for Miss Schenley understood there were certain things her mother couldn't believe; her mother still thought of her as a child. It had gotten worse in the last year, since her father had died. She felt smothered by her mother's concern and she had no chance to have any life of her own.

Then, the desk sergeant in the outer room called to the detective who got up and went out, and Hilda heard her mother's voice, and Miss Schenley frowned and meditated. "Well, here she is, Mrs. Scranton," said the detective. Hilda wanted to meet her mother with a bold, unyielding look, but her mother had on the old blue two-piece dress with the white bow at the throat, the dress Hilda had discarded. And she looked so much older than she had looked just a week ago. Hollow-eyed and tired, her hair untidy, she showed in her face everything she had been doing the last week and the last year; the waiting at the window, the telephoning, the little prayers, the restless nights and the anger. She seemed to stand there with her jaw trembling, heaping it all on Hilda.

"Hilda, are you all right?"

"Of course I'm all right, Mother," she said, but she turned away, feeling angry and humiliated.

"Sit down, Mrs. Scranton," the detective said, pulling a chair out for her.

"Hilda and I have had a fine long talk," Miss Schenley said cheerfully. "You know, Mrs. Scranton, I like your Hilda."

"Yes, she's quite a likeable girl."

"And I don't think there's anything basically wrong with her."

"Of course there isn't, Miss Schenley. Hilda's a little reckless and careless, but she's not a bad girl, and I'm sure she'll settle down."

Hilda didn't like the way they were talking about her as if she weren't there, but then Miss Schenley said, "However, the fact is Hilda doesn't want to go to school and she doesn't want to live at home."

"All that has happened only in the last year," her mother said, but she sounded too anxious, as if Hilda had been misunderstood and she wanted only to protect her. "She'll grow out of it, Miss Schenley."

"Mother, please," Hilda said resentfully, "don't talk about me as if I were a little child."

"Well, in many ways you still are a child," she said calmly.

"But in other ways Hilda is quite a big girl," Miss Schenley said patiently, "and it makes it hard for her," and she smiled at Hilda. It proved she was on her side and Hilda could hardly conceal her satisfaction. "I've got quite a bit of Hilda's history from her," Miss Schenley went on, "and I'm wondering if the whole trouble may not be that you worry too much about her."

"Of course I worry about Hilda, I'm her mother."

"But I mean about every little thing, her clothes, her parties, her music, her friends, her language."

"But I'm the only one there is to be concerned," Mrs. Scranton said with a patient smile as if she had just perceived that Miss Schenley was hard of understanding. It irritated Miss Schenley and Hilda said quickly, "Oh, Mother. Miss Schenley is a psychologist," and her mother nodded apologetically.

"And those boys in the park," Miss Schenley said. "Why don't you trust Hilda with them? Try it, why don't you?"

"Those boys. You don't know those boys. Trust my daughter with them in the park at two in the morning? Why, that would be shameless."

"Well, the boys won't come to the house if they're going to find Hilda sitting in your lap, Mrs. Scranton. Naturally she prefers the freedom of the park, don't you see?"

It was just what Hilda wanted Miss Schenley to say, but the tone in which she said it and her patient smile made Hilda feel cheap, and she had to avoid her mother's eyes as Miss Schenley went on. "It may be that Hilda expects to find you living in her pocket, eating her life up. If I were you I'd try and stop worrying about her. I'd say, 'All right, don't go to school: get a job,' and see how it works out."

"But you don't know Hilda. You don't know her at all." Her voice broke for she was outraged and ready to lose control of herself. "Why, she'd stay out all night."

"Not if she had to go to work in the morning. Once you make up your mind you're not going to do any more worrying..."

"Not worry about Hilda? Why, till the day I die–" But she faltered and looked bewildered, and Hilda wanted to speak to her but there was nothing to say.

"You see, Mrs. Scranton," Miss Schenley said easily, "it's just possible you may be a little too possessive about Hilda."

"Possessive?"

"Oh, thousands of mothers are possessive about their daughters, just because they love them. And they give them no chance to feel responsible. Maybe you like worrying..."

"Like worrying?" The hurt surprise in her voice worried Hilda. Her mother seemed to be wondering if she had some flaw in her nature that would make any daughter feel smothered, and her eyes filled with tears and she blurted out, "In heaven's name, Hilda, what have you been saying about me?"

"Nothing that isn't true," Hilda muttered, as her mother stared at her blankly. She wanted to say more but she couldn't get her breath and she concentrated on the detective's cigar butt on the ash tray, then hated him for sitting there listening, and for some reason she thought of the fine clothes her mother used to wear, and how she used to get her hair done once a week. "You know you do like to worry about me," she whispered.

"Well, the point is," Miss Schenley said soothingly, "Hilda's nature is what it is, and your nature, Mrs. Scranton, is what it is. Maybe you're hard on each other. But Hilda's young. She can change." Miss Schenley paused, and Hilda, out of the corner of her eye, saw her glance at her mother, pale and tired in the shabby dress. "Nobody's going to change you, Mrs. Scranton. It's too late for that. But maybe we can do something for Hilda."

"The main thing is," the detective said, standing up impatiently, "I can see Mrs. Scranton doesn't want to charge Hilda with being incorrigible."

"Of course I don't. Of course not."

"Well, she's your daughter. You might as well take her home now."

"Come on, Hilda," Mrs. Scranton said stiffly. As she stood up she lifted her head with dignity and put out her hand to Miss Schenley. "Thank you for trying to be of some help."

"Sometimes it's good to talk these things out," Miss Schenley said, and then, as her eyes met Mrs. Scranton's, for the first time she looked embarrassed. "Hilda, for heaven's sake, from now on, try and be responsible."

"Yes, Miss Schenley," she said meekly.

Outside on the street that led through the little park to their home, they fell in step and Hilda waited for her mother to turn on her and abuse her fiercely. But she didn't turn on her, she hurried along, her mouth in a thin line, her head bent with her troubles. Hilda knew all that she was thinking; she was worrying about what she might have done in Detroit, and wondering what there was to say to her now.

They reached the little park and went along the cinder path by the fountain. In the shadows of the bushes in the corner were the benches and they could hear laughter and giggling and then a raucous voice coming out of the shadows. As they walked along, grim and silent, it was all familiar to Hilda. It was just like one of those other nights when her mother, after waiting at the window, had come out to wander around for hours. And if she herself had been with one of the fellows in somebody's house until very late she would come out and hurry along the street, knowing she would encounter her mother, and usually she would see her standing at the corner where she could watch both streets. Her mother would be so relieved to see her that there would be a few moments of silence and in those moments Hilda would talk quickly, "Why are you waiting around? Everybody knows what you're like. Why do you make such a baby out of me?" Then her mother would get control of herself and scold her bitterly. They would walk along, trying to keep their voices down so they wouldn't wake the neighbors. And now, again, her mother was walking her home, ready to call her shameless and ungrateful and a terrible heartbreak.

The sound of their footsteps in her mother's silence became unbearable for she knew how her mother was berating her in her thoughts, and it was unfair that she was giving her no chance to defend herself. "Well, why don't you say something?" she blurted out.

"Say something, Hilda? Why?" she asked lifelessly. "People don't know how I feel. I don't seem to matter."

"I don't know what you mean," Hilda said awkwardly. But everything suddenly became strangely unfamiliar. At first she didn't know what was wrong, and then she realized that her mother, as they walked along, hadn't been brooding over what might have happened to her in Detroit; she hadn't really been thinking of her at all; she had been thinking of herself and her own life. Hilda felt off by herself, and then lonely.

"I must have looked an awful fright back there with those people," her mother said as if trying to explain something to herself. "Imagine. Too late. Too late. Why, I'm only forty, Hilda."

"Yes, that's right," Hilda said uneasily.

"Only six months ago Sam Ingram asked me to marry him."

"You didn't say anything about it."

"I thought I should wait until you were a little older. Maybe it's too late now."

"I didn't know," Hilda said, and she was afraid to turn and look at her, afraid she would see that she had never really known what she thought about anything, and now it was like walking with some one entirely apart from herself, another woman with a life of her own.

"I should have fixed myself up a little before I ran out," her mother said, stopping by the light and fumbling in her bag for her mirror. "I shouldn't look like this on the street," and she patted back loose strands of hair.

"Put on a little lipstick, mother."

"Yes, I'd better."

"Here, use mine," Hilda said, opening her purse. With a shy gesture she offered her lipstick like a woman offering it to another woman whom she doesn't know very well. Her mother's hand trembled as she marked her lips and Hilda watched the lips come together and then part, moistened and brightened, and in the anxious face she seemed to see everything that had been happening in her own life, all lined there on her mother's face, and a heavy weight seemed to come against her own heart. Then she was angry and impatient with herself, and angry at everything that had been said in the police station.

"That's better. You look fine now," she said, and as they walked on home she felt years older, and knew that something was ended.

The Consuming Fire

ALL THE LITTLE QUARRELS THAT JULIA WATSON, THE GIFT-shop owner, had with her husband she blamed on his lovable childish impulsiveness and the fact he had got drunk and lost his job. She thought she understood how he felt because she was more worried about his job than he was, and his problems had become her problems. But when she heard he was seeing a little floozy named Eva Smith, she was sick for three days. Then, when he left her and wrote that he wanted a divorce, she felt like a dead woman.

She wrote and said, "Alec, please don't be stubborn. You don't need to feel ashamed. That little girl is only playing with your vanity. I know you do crazy impulsive things, but don't let that little powder puff ruin your life." But he wrote and told her he was neither ashamed nor stubborn and didn't want to be forgiven. Unbelieving and bewildered, she tried to realize that he had put his life outside her love.

Yet she had such a loving nature that she began to reach out furtively to touch Alec's life. People said he was no longer seeing any of the old crowd or drinking at the old places. "The poor darling," she said, feeling sure he was ashamed. Her heart ached for him more than ever. She

asked old friends to invite him to dinner. When she found
out he was broke, it gave her joy to find a friend who would
loan him money. She set out to find a job for him. Day after
day she went from friend to friend till she was tired out, but
at night, lying awake, it seemed like when they were first
married and very poor and Alec was looking for work.
Then, one day she met a publisher she had gone to school
with. She pleaded with him for Alec, warm and glowing
with love, a handsome woman of thirty-five, her mouth
open a little in expectation. "You're such a darling, Julia,"
he laughed. "What chance have I got against you?"

The sweetest satisfaction touched her again. But that
night, as she closed up her shop, the publisher phoned her.

"Alec won't take the job," he said.

"Oh, he must. He needs it terribly."

"He knows that."

"Then why?"

"He thinks you got it for him, and he says to tell you
no – absolutely no. And that's final."

She wanted to cry out that it was stupid and unworthy
of him. With all her love she wanted to protest that she was
only trying to help as she would help one of her salesgirls.

As she hurried along Grove Street, she was bursting
with an eagerness to explain that she counted for nothing,
that he should think only of his own good. But when she
was opposite the house, looking up at the lighted windows,
her courage failed. If the girl smirked at her, or watched her
with sullen hatred, she knew she couldn't bear it.

She went up to the door and looked along the narrow
hall and up the narrow stair with its broken tiles. It seemed
incredible that he would want to live there. When she
rapped on the door her face was glowing with good feeling
and concern for him. But when he stood there, white-faced,

tired and thin, and with no friendly smile, her mouth opened and she faltered and said timidly, "Well, you aren't that upset just to see me, are you, Alec?"

"I'm not upset at all," he said.

"I only want to talk to you for a minute."

"Why did you come here?" he asked uneasily.

"It's about that job ..." she began, but her voice trailed away, for though he was listening, he did not seem to be paying attention to her words.

Then, distressed, he shook his head and said in a worried, impatient voice. "This is no place to come. I live here and I don't live alone, as you know. What's the use?" He blocked the door, his arms folded, yet not looking at her, as if he were afraid that the warmth of her generous nature would suddenly touch him and draw him close to her. "There's nothing to say about the job. I don't want it. That's final. Don't you see?"

"But you were going to take it," she pleaded.

"Sure."

"And when you found out I had something to do with it – oh, Alec, you must hate me. Why, why? If it were just for a friend, if it were just for one of my customers, they wouldn't slap at me like that." Then she was suddenly short of breath, because he said nothing to help her. "Alec, you should take that job. I'm not trying to get you to come back to me. But I believe in your talent like I might believe in the talent of someone I hardly knew. Forget there was ever any love between us," she said. "I could still believe you had talent, couldn't I?"

When the stubborn, boyish, unyielding expression that she had seen a thousand times on his face after they had begun one of these little struggles came into his eyes, she brightened and felt a sudden mad eagerness to persuade him as she had so often done. For the girl she felt only restless impatience.

"Let me come in and talk to you, Alec."

"All right, all right," he said, stepping aside.

The room, with its old red-covered plush furniture, its little kitchen cabinet with the figured curtain drawn across it, and the faint but pervading smell of gas, gave her fresh confidence. All she had to do, she thought eagerly as she sat down, was to keep on talking reasonably with him and she could suddenly lift him right out of the squalid place. His generous nature would open up to her, she would hear again the shy laughing apology.

"I don't think you'll go till you've said your piece, so go ahead," he said sighing.

"It's not just what your life is now," she began, looking around the room. "Even if I'm dead you'll want something better than this."

"I'm not taking that job," he said calmly.

"But why? Alec, tell me why."

"It's a free country," he said stubbornly. "A job comes my way and I don't choose to take it. What's the matter with that?"

"Why, nothing at all," she said. Then she couldn't help it, she burst out indignantly, "That's not you talking, Alec."

"No?"

"No, indeed. You're not a petty man," she said. "It's the – well, it's Eva, isn't it? Oh, why can't you both see that I'm not plotting anything? You've listened to her, haven't you? If you love her you should. But she shouldn't make you do a thing that will hurt you just for the sake of taking a crack at me."

"Eva," he called out suddenly.

"All right," the girl called from the bedroom. "I'm coming."

While they waited, and Julia trembled with eagerness to face the girl, every gesture Alec made seemed harsh and unyielding and yet a little desperate: she felt a tug between them and it gave her joy.

Eva came out of the bedroom powdering her nose laconically. She had her hat on and was dressed to go out. "I heard you talking, Mrs. Watson," she said carelessly. As Eva took a last look at herself in her little hand mirror, rubbed her lips together, and then put the mirror in her purse, Julia was shocked. There was going to be no struggle between them. Eva was like a soft feathery little milk-white doll, and as she crossed the room she seemed confident that her soft shapeliness would be looked after by someone no matter what happened. Julia couldn't understand why he did not see the sluttishness in the girl.

"I knew you'd be around sooner or later, Mrs. Watson," Eva said. "I'm sorry I'm on my way out."

"Then you knew more than I did," Julia said, reddening.

"Maybe I do."

"I wish you wouldn't misunderstand why I'm here," Julia said quickly. "I'm not trying to . . ."

"You're here about that job, aren't you?"

"Yes."

"That's what I meant."

"I mean you're not – I mean I'm not trying to get in your way," Julia insisted.

"You're not getting in my way, lady," Eva said.

"You don't resent my interest?"

"Not that. I wanted Alec to take the job." Then, while Julia waited, feeling dreadfully insecure, as if she were touching something in Alec she had never known, Eva turned to him and said impatiently, "For Heaven's sake, why don't you take the job? It sounds like a decent job to me. What do you care where it came from?"

To Julia, it seemed the girl was pleading her case for her and she was sure Alec, looking at Eva's soft shapeliness, would give her anything she wanted, and she couldn't bear it: she lowered her head and scraped her foot on the carpet, she was so ashamed to be there. But Alec said harshly, "You keep out of this, Eva."

"Suit yourself," Eva said. She smiled at Alec. There was acquiescence in her full red mouth. Julia could see she always yielded. Then, looking shrewdly at Julia, and finding nothing dangerously seductive in her aggressive eagerness, she said, "You won't mind if I run along, will you?" She went out.

Humiliated, Julia stared timidly at Alec, and when he only waited, unmoved, she whispered, "Can't you see she's indifferent to you?"

"Maybe she is," he said, shrugging.

"But she doesn't love you."

"I like it that way. Just that way," he said.

"All right," she said. "Only you should take the job unless you hate even the thought of me." She was pleading with him not to destroy all she had left, the memory of the years when they had loved each other. "I'm mixed up," she said. "I don't know why you have this terrible feeling about me."

"Julia, I don't hate you," he said, looking miserable. "I'm not trying to hurt you." Then he seemed to lose his breath. All the love she had given for so long seemed to touch him suddenly and make him mute. But he shook his head, pulling away resolutely. Looking around the mean room with the old furniture and the long faded window drapes as if it were a new life that he had to guard desperately against her, he whispered, "Sure, I've treated you terribly. But, my God, Julia, you've run my life for years. I was smothered. I'm not a child. And even now when I leave you, you keep coming in and out of my life arranging it for me. You can't stop. This job – it's nothing. But it gives me a chance to say no to you." Then he shouted, "I'm saying no, no, no. Stop."

"No to what?" she asked, bewildered.

"Your care for me. Your love," he said.

"My love."

"Look, Julia, there's hardly anything left of me."

"I only wanted you to be happy," she whispered. But she looked so powerless and frightened that he cried out, "There hasn't been anything that's me for years. It's been all you. Every little thing, day after day."

He came close to her and she went to put her arms around him and cry out that he should tell her everything he hoped for and she would share it, but with his eyes he seemed to be begging her to keep away, so she drew back, scared to touch him. She was suddenly frightened by her own eagerness, and her whole life seemed to be full of people she had pushed around because they liked her. She was terrified because she saw she consumed them. She put her trembling hands over her face.

"Julia, don't cry," he said. When she didn't answer he went closer and bent over her.

"Don't touch me," she begged him. "Keep away from me."

"If you think I'm refusing the job just to hurt you –" he began.

"Oh, no. Don't take it, don't let it touch you," she

cried, so self-effacing and so suddenly humble that he stared at her. "I didn't understand," she whispered, but he was shy with her, bending over her, touching her as if she were still the eager Julia, yet a woman he had never known.

On the Edge of a World

ON OUR STREET, THE BEST HOUSES WERE LARGE AND ALWAYS well-painted, and in each house there was only one family. The corner house belonged to a wealthy man named Dirk Henders, who lived there with his young wife and thirteen-year-old son, Paul.

Farther up the street, the houses were smaller, and some were broken into flats. These houses were always in need of paint, and grass never grew on their front lawns. On the third floor of one, Johnny Roberts lived with his father and mother and three older sisters. Johnny's father was a bus driver and the family had a hard time getting along. Johnny was the same age as Paul Henders, but he was small for his age, and Paul was three inches taller. The two boys did not like each other. In fact, none of the neighborhood children liked Paul, who was a clumsy, awkward, pale-faced boy.

In the evenings, Johnny would sometimes watch Paul and his father and mother coming along the street together. Mr. Henders was a tall, solemn, fine-looking man. Paul's mother, who was years younger than her husband, wore expensive clothes; she was a pretty woman and had a superior air. Johnny believed that Paul felt superior too, because of his fine parents.

When Johnny was going along the street with his own father and mother and they met the Henders family, he wished he were more friendly with Paul because Paul's father bowed and spoke with such distinction and his wife had a cheerful smile. Their voices were soft and polite. Johnny's people were blunt-spoken and excitable, and Johnny couldn't help wishing that his father wouldn't go out in the evenings in his bus driver's leather jacket. He wished his father and mother spoke slowly and politely to each other, as he was sure Paul's parents did. He blamed Paul for these things he was wishing and the way he was feeling.

In the summer evenings, Johnny and Fred Stewart, a tall thin boy, used to box with each other in the lane. One hot evening, Johnny was trying out a punch he would not have used against a good boxer. He waited till the taller boy came at him, crouched, then suddenly leaped in the air, snapping out his left; he got Fred on the nose every time. But as a punch it was no good, because a smart boxer could duck and get him with a counterpunch when he was off the ground and helpless. As they mauled each other and laughed, Fred said, "Look who's here."

Paul Henders was watching them with an earnest scowl on his face. "How's it going?" Paul said, looking at Fred Stewart, who was his own size. "Why do you let him keep his glove in your face? Why don't you stick your arm out?"

"You don't think I do so good?" Fred pulled off his gloves. "Here, Paul, old pal, you show me. Come on, Johnny; he wants to show me."

"I don't know what I can show you," Paul said. He suddenly looked lonely.

"Sure you can," Fred said. "Here. Let me tie your gloves on."

When Paul faced Johnny Roberts, he did not show much confidence. Crouching a little and losing the advantage of his height, he thrust his left arm out. Grinning, Johnny moved around him warily, for he had never seen him fight and there was a chance he might be good. Paul pawed at him and Johnny jabbed at his eyes, then did it again and again, liking the way Paul blinked stupidly. He saw that Paul was simply a big, clumsy, strong fellow with no talent, so he began to clown and amuse himself. He tried out the fancy sucker punch. Crouching, he waited till Paul came at him; then he leaped, shooting his left over Paul's arm and smacking him on the face every time, and every time he seemed to become taller than Paul. Blood began to trickle from Paul's nose.

"Okay, Paul," Fred said. "You've had enough."

"I guess it looks easier than it is," Paul said apologetically. He was sucking in his breath. When they had taken his gloves off, he sat down and held his handkerchief over his nose. He did not seem to be ashamed, just interested.

It began to get dark, and Fred and Johnny quit boxing. That was the part of the night, or the beginning of the part, that Johnny liked best for, after pummeling each other and sweating, there was a warm friendly feeling which lasted for hours between him and Fred. He was disappointed when Fred said he had to go home.

"Say, Johnny," Paul began awkwardly, when Fred had left, "you know that punch of yours – the one where you leap up and it doesn't do a fellow any good to be a lot taller than you?"

"That punch? That's amateur stuff."

"I'd like to learn to do it, Johnny."

"It only looks good against a big, slow guy."

"How about letting me practice with you?"

"It's too dark," Johnny said flatly.

"Come on down to my place," Paul pleaded. "We can practice in the cellar."

It was embarrassing, because they had never liked each other, yet Paul was making it seem important. Johnny had never been in the Henders' house. "Okay," he said. "Just for a while."

At the big house they went down the cellar steps. "Is that you, Paul?" his mother called. It was a low, warm, easy voice, and Johnny liked it. "It's me, mother," Paul answered.

"Let's see now," Paul said grimly, when they had the gloves on. Crouching low, he jumped up in the air about a foot, lashing out with his left. Johnny grinned. It looked awful. "Maybe only a little guy should try a punch like that," Johnny said doubtfully. "It looks all right if you can leap like a dancer. You just don't look like a guy who ever danced, Paul."

"Show me again," Paul said earnestly. He was so desperately serious that Johnny tried hard to give him a picture of the punch. He had him leaping all over the cellar – crouching, then leaping. Gradually, Paul began to look a little better. But Johnny couldn't imagine him really hitting anybody with that kind of punch.

"Look, Paul," Johnny said, "I don't think a tall fellow like you should try to use such a punch. You'd only use it against somebody taller and slower. You're pretty tall."

"That's the way I figured it," Paul said. "If it was someone big and strong and tall, too tall for me, but someone who couldn't box, it might work – mightn't it?"

"It might at that. Who've you got in mind?"

"I've had a couple of fights . . ." he started to say. Then his voice went very low. "I've had a couple of fights with my father."

"I see," Johnny said.

"It's not easy," Paul said quietly. "And it isn't just me." He looked at Johnny. "He starts in on my mother. I try to stop him. See?"

"I see," Johnny said, but he was listening to the sound of quick, eager footsteps overhead, the footsteps moving in a circle. Then there was a heavier step at the front of the house – a long, firm step going along the hall, turning into the room overhead, stopping, then turning away and going on upstairs. Johnny stood up. "I guess I'll be going," he said.

Paul accompanied him to the street. It was dark, and the moon was rising. "It's always there," Paul said slowly. "My mother keeps saying she has a right to some life of her own. And then he . . . Could we box again soon?"

"Oh, sure," Johnny said. "So long, Paul."

Going up the street, he could hardly think clearly. The Henders were the last people he would expect to be cruel to each other. He went into the living room of his own home, where his father was reading the newspaper and his mother was sewing. They hardly looked up. Johnny seemed to be still listening for the sound of footsteps moving overhead, while he stared raptly at the faces of his parents. They often quarreled and there were sharp words, but he never had wondered why they sometimes seemed to pull wildly away from each other.

"Going out again, Johnny?" his mother asked.

"No. There's nothing to do," he said. It was peaceful there in the living room, and neither his mother nor his father was bothering about whether they had lives of their own. Maybe they didn't know it was what they wanted. Maybe that was why his father and mother never broke openly with each other as Paul's parents did. It was not hard to imagine either one saying angrily, "I've got a right to some life of my own." It could happen easily. But it did not happen.

He went out to the back porch and looked over the back-yard fences at the long rows of lighted windows. On other nights those lights had seemed like the lights in the windows of peaceful homes. Suddenly, he felt that he had no idea what was going on behind the drawn shades against which shadows sometimes moved. All kinds of wild things could be going on, but he would never be able to know anything about it just from meeting people politely on the street; and so, standing there at the porch rail was like standing at the edge of a frightening, complicated, exciting world, which he might someday have to try to understand.

The Novice

THE NOVICES USED TO WALK BY THE HIGH BRICK WALL dividing Dr. Stanton's property from the convent garden and whisper that soon the Mother Superior's prayers would be answered and the doctor would sell his house to her. For five years the Mother Superior had been trying to buy it from the bigoted old man, to use it as a residence.

The Mistress of novices had asked them to pray that the doctor, who had declared his old home would never be part of such an institution, might be persuaded to change his mind. The Mistress pointed out that God was often more willing to grant favors when the prayers came from fresh eager young souls. Sister Mary Rose, who had been a novice for four weeks, and who was determined to endure all the hardships till she one day became a nun, listened to the Mistress telling how she might help the convent. Sister Mary Rose was a well built slender girl with a round smooth face who looked charming in the habit with the little black cape. She was suffering none of the pains and troubles of some of the novices; the plain food was almost tasteless at first but she ate hungrily; she got to like immensely the well-buttered slice of bread they had at collation hour in the morning; her body ached at first from the hard bed but, to herself, she insisted she did not feel the pains, enduring this small discomfort much more readily than Sister Perpetua, who secretly stretched her pillow out lengthwise every night so her shoulder blades and hips would be well protected. Already two or three of the novices who had sharp pains in the back, or who had lost all appetite, were taking it as a sign that they really did not have a vocation and were wondering how much longer they would stay at the convent. Because she had such very good health, Sister Mary Rose hoped she might be an instrument of great blessing to the convent.

In her nightly prayers she made it a secret between herself and God that she was the one novice who was most anxious that Doctor Stanton might sell his fine house to the convent. She prayed for almost an hour, kneeling on the floor in her long nightgown, her bare heels just touching, her eyes turned toward the long narrow window looking out over the brick wall into Doctor Stanton's garden while the moonlight slanted down over her shoulders. At this time, she was convinced that her prayers would be heeded more readily if she followed the precepts of St. Theresa and tried to live the life the Little Flower lived when she had been a novice. But she didn't ask that a shower of roses fall from heaven; she asked only that Doctor Stanton might sell his house to the convent.

For many days, she prayed and fasted and was as much as possible like a little child and nearly always in a state of grace. When one of her relatives sent her a box of candies she at once gave it to the Mistress of the novices and would not take one for herself. But she got a little thinner. She was pale and her eyes were too big for her face, which was hardly round now. Then at midnight, when she was sitting in her stall in the choir, she fell forward on the floor, fainting.

The Mistress, an elderly, severely kind, practical woman with a finely wrinkled face said, as she rubbed her wrists, "Sister Mary Rose, you haven't been eating."

"I'm sorry," she said, still feeling dizzy, "I've been fasting to receive a favor." She sat awkwardly in her straight-backed stall.

The Mistress praised her admirable sincerity but explained it was not good for a novice to be too severe with herself. Sister Mary Rose, still weak and trembling, almost told her why she was fasting, but then, shaking her head twice, she determined to keep it a secret between herself and God.

As soon as she was alone, she wondered if she might possibly be more effective following some other precept. After all, she was concerning herself with a very material affair, a transaction in property, and she wondered if the Spanish St. Teresa, a more worldly and practical woman, who, too, had been a nun, wouldn't be more likely to assist her than little Theresa of Lisieux. So she began to think of talking, herself, to Doctor Stanton and had a kind of a vision of herself easily persuading the old man to be sensible about a business matter, and then modestly and shyly explaining to the joyful Mother Superior that she had only been an instrument because she so dearly loved the convent. But she heard that the doctor was sick, and anyway, he was supposed to be a harsh, domineering man.

At the recreation hour one day she was walking by the high brick wall, past the statue of the Virgin. Some of the novices were playing catch with a tennis ball. Sister Magdalene of the Cross was tossing the ball to Sister Dolorosa, who turned and tossed it to Sister Mary Rose. It was in the forenoon before the sun began to shine too strongly and the three novices kept on tossing the ball to each other, laughing gleefully whenever one of them missed it, finding extraordinary delight whenever one had to assume a quaint or awkward posture. The Mistress encouraged them to do that; laugh readily and joyfully, for they had their long periods of silence which often left some of them moody and depressed. They were tossing the ball wildly and Sister Magdalene of the Cross, the plump girl, tossed it far over Sister Mary Rose's head, over the brick wall into Doctor Stanton's garden.

The three young novices remained absolutely silent, looking at each other. Then, the ball came in an arc back over the wall again. Sister Mary Rose knew that the gardener, a man with a long brown moustache, who limped, and whom she had often seen from the window, bending down over Dr. Stanton's flower beds, had returned it. At that moment, she got the idea she afterwards attributed to the goodness of her Spanish St. Teresa. She walked off by herself and would not catch the ball when it was thrown to her. It bounced away into the flowerbeds and Sister Dolorosa had to go and get it.

Alone in her bedroom, she looked out the window at the doctor's garden and saw the gardener bending over a flower bed, holding a rake upright with one hand, the other patting the earth at the base of a flower stem. The sun was shining brilliantly through the narrow window. The gardener was close to the iron fence between the street and the garden. Sister Mary Rose detached slowly from her neck a sacred medal and holding it in both hands closed her eyes, telling herself that if she carried out her plan she would be both deceitful and disobedient, but her excitement and determination only got stronger. So she assured herself earnestly, while holding the medal tightly, that her notion might be the cause of so much goodness the extent of her disobedience would be trifling compared with it. Then she said a long prayer, asking for St. Teresa's help, and urging her to be an advocate for her, in case her trifling disobedience should be misunderstood.

She asked permission to visit an aunt who lived in the city. Since she rarely asked for any kind of a favor, she readily received permission. She was told that Sister Magdalene of the Cross would go with her, for neither a novice nor a nun ever went any place alone outside the convent.

The afternoon she was to go out she first of all looked nervously from the window into Dr. Stanton's garden and sighed thankfully when she saw the gardener picking weeds by the fence. It was entirely necessary, if she was to be successful at all, that the gardener should be somewhere close to the street fence.

Trembling and pale, but filled with an exhilarating excitement, Sister Mary Rose walked out sedately with Sister Magdalene of the Cross who was prattling gaily, glad of the opportunity to be walking in the city streets. They had come out the main entrance, down the steps, and were past the convent, almost to the iron fence, walking demurely, their hands folded under their little black capes, their eyes turned down to the sidewalk.

The gardener did not even glance up at them as they passed. He was bending down, his back to the fence. He had on blue overalls and suspenders over a gray shirt. They were ten feet past him when Sister Mary Rose said suddenly to Sister Magdalene of the Cross, "Please, just a second, I want to ask the gardener if he found a tennis ball I lost the other day."

"Oh, you shouldn't do that."

"Please, just a minute."

"But somebody will see you from the window."

Sister Mary Rose turned and before the startled girl could detain her, left her abruptly and walked over to the fence. The gardener, hearing her, straightened up, surprised, and said, "Good afternoon, Sister."

"Good afternoon," she said timidly, hardly above a whisper, "How is the doctor?"

"Poorly, Sister, very poorly."

"Would you do something for me," she said shyly, smiling nervously. "I mean . . . Are you a Catholic?"

"No, Miss. I'm sorry though." She looked sweetly pretty with her round smooth face and her blue eyes and little black cape.

"But just the same you're a Christian, I'm sure of that," she said.

"Oh, I guess I can say that all right," he said, smiling apologetically.

"Will you take this?" she said cautiously, handing him her sacred medal, her back hiding it from Sister Magdalene of the Cross.

"What'll I do with it, Sister?"

"Please bury it in the garden there. Please promise me." Her cheeks began to flush a little.

"It'll be a pleasure to do it for you if it'll amuse you," he said, smiling.

"Oh, thank you very much," she said, smiling and flustered, turning away quickly. "I'll say a prayer for you."

Sister Magdalene of the Cross, who had become impatient and a little offended, said, "What on earth were you talking about?"

"He was saying he'd look especially for the ball, that's all. To be polite I asked him about the doctor."

"The doctor isn't a good man, and anyway, you know I'll have to tell Mistress."

"Please, please promise me you won't tell Mistress."

"But I ought to. That's what I'm here for."

"Please promise, little sister."

"All right," the good natured girl said reluctantly. "I'll promise."

They went on talking seriously as they walked along the sidewalk, their heads held at the same angle, their hands hidden, their long black skirts swinging easily.

A week and a half later, Doctor Stanton died. He was an old man and it was inevitable. The executors of his estate wished to dispose of his property quickly and the convent made much the most attractive offer. So they were assured of getting the property.

Sister Mary Rose was ecstatically happy when she heard the convent would get the fine old house, and she was not bothered by the doctor's death. At first she prayed fervently, thanking St. Teresa for interceding and obtaining her favor. She could hardly resist telling the other novices about her special prayers and how she had persuaded the gardener to bury the sacred medal in the doctor's yard. She suffered the ecstasy of feeling she had been an instrument, but dared not tell the Mistress about it because she had been both sly and disobedient.

It occurred to her at collation hour, when eating a thickly buttered slice of bread, that she might, in a way, have been responsible for the doctor's death by wishing for it. Though she hadn't actually wished the death, it amounted to the same thing. When she first had this thought she said, as she was sure her strong St. Teresa would have, that the good of the whole convent was more important than the life of one man. But suddenly she felt weak and left the other novices, and went up to the bedroom, depressed and disturbed, wondering about her guilt or innocence.

All night she lay awake, tossing on her hard bed,

rubbing her shoulders and elbows on the board till they were scraped and sore. She was wondering whether this feeling of depression and sorrow wasn't an intimation that she really had no vocation and ought to leave the convent, as two of the novices were doing at the end of the week. It was plainly her duty in this first period of her novitiate to be watchful of every circumstance indicating that she really did not have a vocation. First, she thought miserably she ought to leave the convent at the end of the week because she was a deceitful worldly woman interested only in material affairs. Then she thought uneasily just before she went to sleep that perhaps, if she waited a week, she might become reconciled to her own conscience, and then no one need ever know.

Hello, America!

IN THOSE DAYS, TIMES WERE TOUGH AND GETTING WORSE. In the winter men were still wandering across the country looking for work, and so old Herrmann, who ran the little white diner down near the station, got hold of Henry Stevens. The young Englishman came in shivering one night and offered to wash dishes for a meal. He had no overcoat on and no socks. His fair hair hung down on the back of his neck. His voice was soft and polite, but his blue eyes showed how discouraged he was.

Old Herrmann was always on the look-out for someone who would work for nothing. Sometimes he picked up a man on the highway when he was driving along in his old car with his wife, and sometimes he got them when they came in looking for a hand-out. Being a very suspicious man, he had it figured out that anyone who was completely discouraged and easy to browbeat would be too scared to be dishonest. His big round face actually glowed when he saw Henry, though he tried to look just a little sad. He had been working day and night himself and was so tired he had even thought of paying someone to help him.

"Sure you can wash the dishes," he said. "Come on, kid. Go to work and get warm and get it off your chest."

As Henry washed the pile of dishes and talked a little brokenly, old Herrmann listened like a rough, affectionate father. He wrinkled up his fat face and made clucking, sympathetic noises in his throat. The kid sounded just right. He hadn't worked for four months. He had come from England after his mother had died and there was no money left in his family. He had come, he said, because he had read so much about the friendliness of the people of North America. All the lovely names of the places he had wanted to see – Colorado, Algoma, Tia Juana, Sault Ste. Marie, and Oregon – he recited them to Herrmann, with a dreamy, eager look in his eyes as he stirred the brush in the water and scrubbed the dishes.

Listening with his hands on his big hips as he eyed the kid shrewdly, Herrmann said, "I know what it's like. Stay here awhile, kid. Maybe I can let you sleep on the couch in the back room there. Maybe you can wait on the counter a little. Of course I can't afford to keep you around long. I'm a poor man," Herrmann said, wanting Henry to go on feeling terribly insecure. "But you can eat, see, and by jingo, maybe I can give you a couple of dollars."

"I'll do anything you say, sir," Henry said.

Herrmann liked the way Henry had called him "sir." Leading him into the back room when he had finished the dishes, he had him hang up his coat. He didn't seem to have any possessions but a little brown book of Edgar Allan Poe's poetry and a picture of his father and mother. To show what a deep personal interest he was taking in him, Herrmann got a pair of scissors and gave him a hair-cut and promised to bring him down a pair of his old socks in the morning.

Henry started working behind the counter in the morning. Every little while Herrmann kept bobbing in from the back room to make sure he was treating the customers right and putting the money in the till. But after a few nights, old Herrmann was so tired he simply had to go home and get some sleep. A little after midnight, his wife, a big-boned, surly woman, who looked at Henry as if she had seen a hundred like him around the place, called for Herrmann in the old car and took him home. For a few hours Henry was alone.

The late shift from the station yard came in at that time, powerful-looking men in overalls and grease-marked faces, who shouted at Henry for their hot bowls of stew and took turns putting coins in the slot of the big juke box. They soon started calling Henry "Limey." But he liked them for their friendliness. He liked their rough, free, laughing conversations.

After the last of the night shift had gone out and Henry was alone at the counter, a man in a long brown overcoat, so long at the sleeves it completely covered his hands, came in and sat down at the counter. He was grimy and bristly and his face was smeared with soot, but he grinned at Henry. "How about it, buddy?" he asked.

"How about what?" Henry asked.

"Slip us a bowl of soup, eh, pal."

It was a very cold night outside, the place was still full of the smell and the warmth of the well-fed night shift from the station yard, and this fellow looked as if he might have come from the other end of the earth on an empty stomach. He certainly looked as if he needed companionship even more than Henry did.

"All right," Henry said, getting him a bowl of soup. "Where are you from?"

"St. Paul, brother," he said, and then while Henry waited eagerly, he wolfed the hot soup down. Then he took a paper napkin, wiped his mouth, grinned broadly and took out a tiny cigarette butt from his pocket. "Okay," he said, expanding. "You're swell, kid." So they started talking like two old friends. "Jimmy Dyes is the name," he said. He was a carpenter by trade, trying to make his way to Boston, where he had a brother. Off and on he had been working at jobs all over the country. Sometimes the jobs didn't last, he said. Sometimes he just got restless. Holding up the sleeve of his coat, he said, "See that, it belonged to Overcoat Charlie. Never did a day's work in his life. Died in the box car on the way east. Maybe he's been in here and put the touch on you." They went on talking about what it was like in different cities. Henry's face was glowing with friendliness and excitement.

"If you're ever in St. Paul you go and see my cousin, Dave," Jimmy Dyes said. He was writing the name on a paper napkin when Henry looked up and saw old Herrmann coming in.

Herrmann was unbuttoning his coat and taking out his handkerchief as if he had begun to sweat as soon as he got out of the icy air. He had a sad and disappointed expression on his face. Jimmy Dyes took one look at him and went out.

"You gave that bum a hand-out," old Herrmann said to Henry.

"Well, I guess I did," Henry said, nervously.

"Put the cash in the till."

"I haven't got any cash, Mr. Herrmann."

"Henry, I guess I'll have to throw you out," Herrmann said. It seemed to worry him. It seemed to touch his gentle heart. He said nothing more to Henry that night, though. Then in the morning, he was almost indulgent. "Don't be worrying, Henry," he said. "Maybe I'll let you stick for awhile." Around midnight, when his wife called for him in the car, he slapped Henry on the back. "What the hell. Don't look so scared!" he cried. "I trust you. Come on. I'm going to buy you a glass of beer."

They left his wife behind the counter, and they walked along the street together to the tavern that was a few blocks away. They took a short cut through the little square behind the church, and the path was lined with benches, and on every bench was a huddled-up, shivering man. "Just look at those poor guys," Herrmann said. A cold wind was blowing dust and twigs along the path. The men on the benches were wrapped up in old sacks. One had his coat lined with dozens of newspapers that stuck up around his ears and kept the wind from his neck.

"Ain't it terrible?" Herrmann said. "Don't tell me they haven't got it tough."

"Don't I know it," Henry said, his voice breaking.

"And just think, maybe some of them have got an education just like you, Henry," Herrmann said.

Henry didn't have much chance to enjoy the glass of beer they had together in the tavern. Not that Herrmann talked of throwing him out. The old fellow simply sat there with a sad, wondering expression on his face, as if he never would be able to forget the row of benches in the square. The lonely, frightened look came into Henry's eyes. Herrmann's warm little white diner began to seem like the most beautiful spot in the world.

Back in the diner, Henry worked all night, and then in the morning when he was lying down, in spite of himself, he found he was thinking of the friendly, eager conversation he had had with Jimmy Dyes. He tried to put it out of his head. It only made him feel insecure. Then he lay on the bed, his face burning with shame. He knew he was scared even to dream. It made him think of his father and mother and fellows he had grown up with in England, and his eagerness to come to America. He got up, wanting desperately to prove to himself he was still like what he had been, and he sat down and tried to read a few of the poems in the little book. In a while he found that all he was hearing and thinking of was the sound of engines shunting in the station yard and the cry of the freights skirting the hills beyond the city.

Later, at the counter, he was so servile with his "Yes, Mr. Herrmann, as you say, sir," that the old man was delighted and almost tender with him. Henry told himself he had no right to have dreams about seeing the country. But every night men kept coming up from the station yard when he was alone. They kept coming in, independent migratory workers with water frozen on their caps, or just bums speaking with twangy accents and drawls, covered with box-car dirt and with cinder-torn faces. He tried hard to drive them all away. But he was lonely and longed for their free and easy and exciting conversation.

Herrmann hadn't given him any money since he had come, and he found himself figuring out that even if he gave away as many as twenty bowls of soup in a week it would only amount to change out of Herrmann's pocket. Surely, he told himself, he earned much more than his food and the right to sleep on the little iron bed.

So, when a kid came in one night with a coat-sleeve frozen stiff by water and steam from the engine, he handed him a bowl of soup. Leaning across the counter, they talked eagerly to each other. The kid was independent and footloose, and very American and sure of himself and just hungry. It was funny how many were like that. None of them were really scared. Henry learned in these nights that most of the men were just trying to get from one place to another on the continent. He had a collection of names written on paper napkins they had left with him.

One night two fellows in leather jackets, bricklayers out of work for the winter and making their way south, came in and hung around and got warm and kidded each other and Henry, and obviously expected a bowl of soup. They had just got Henry interested in them when a young black came in and stood at the door sniffing the aroma from the steaming pots and looking desperately at Henry.

"Get out, black boy," the red-headed bricklayer roared.

"Who says so?" the black boy pleaded, coming closer.

"Move it, coon," the other bricklayer said, giving the black a push.

"This place ain't yours. You just came here, too," the black whined. Then the big redhead swung the back of his hand and let him have it on the mouth. "Butt out," he jeered, "and stay out."

"Gentlemen, maybe you're making a mistake?" Henry said, politely. "Would you mind leaving this to me?" He spoke with all the dignity of an offended host. The bricklayers were a little sullen and sheepish. Henry called the young black to the counter and gave the three of them a bowl of soup, and they all talked together.

When old Herrmann came in the next day, he noticed at once that Henry was moving around as if he had pride in himself. "Business is getting worse," Herrmann complained, eyeing Henry thoughtfully. "Sometimes I think I ought to close the joint up." He could see by the way Henry was mopping up the counter that he had begun to get a little self-respect and he couldn't understand how it had happened. He watched him suspiciously all morning. When his wife came around at noontime he asked Henry to come with him down to the warehouse to get some supplies, and on the way he drove him past the mission, where there was a soup kitchen and a long line of men.

"It breaks my heart every time I pass these places," Herrmann said. "Can you imagine what you'd feel like in that line?"

"I know how they feel," Henry said, uneasily.

"That's right. You probably know better than I do," Herrmann said, apologetically. "It just goes to show a man can't feel too sure of himself these days."

He spoke so grimly that Henry was sure someone must have tipped him off about him handing out the soup. He began to feel sick. If Herrmann ever caught him again he knew he would throw him out, and Henry began to pray that nothing more would be said and they would get back to the diner all right, and that there never would be any trouble between them.

But Herrmann's wife didn't call for him after midnight and Herrmann went back and forth from the kitchen, watching everyone Henry spoke to and listening for the noise of the cash register opening. Henry went on praying that no one would come in. But at a little after two in the morning, a kid about eighteen showed up. His face was coal black, and he was so cold he could hardly drag himself to the counter, yet he looked as if he had never wheedled from anybody in his life.

As soon as the kid sat down and put his swollen and beefy red hands on the counter old Herrmann came in from the kitchen and stood at the edge of the counter. While the kid was taking a minute to get his breath, Henry felt his heart jump. Then the kid said, "How about it, pal, a bowl of soup, eh?"

"Nothing doing," Henry said, wiping the counter with a wet rag and not looking up.

"No? No, eh? Well, I knew it. I knew it was a lot of

crap," the kid said, bitterly. "Only a guy from St. Paul, Jimmy Dyes, said if I was passing through here . . ."

"Jimmy Dyes, sure," Henry whispered. Looking into the kid's eyes, he remembered the man in the long overcoat and the good-will and warmth and friendliness he had felt in him. Then he was so stirred he could hardly speak. It seemed to him that in many other places in America that night men meeting on the road or sitting around a fire were saying, "If you get that far, there's a place near the station. There's a guy in there . . ." He turned miserably to Herrmann.

When Herrmann saw the misery in his face he sighed and relaxed. His fat face lit up in a contented smile. "That's the boy, Henry," he said.

"Wait a minute," Henry whispered to the kid.

In Herrmann's smug, self-satisfied expression Henry suddenly realized how it pleased the old man seeing him feeling wretched and scared. Henry got a bowl of soup, and his hand trembled when he put it in front of the kid. "Here you are," he said, as Herrmann leaned a little closer, waiting to see if the kid would pay.

"Which way are you going, buddy?" Henry asked the kid, who was lapping up the hot soup.

"I know a bunch of guys in St. Louis," the kid said, pushing the bowl away from him and grinning.

"Like a little company?"

"Okay. Who's that?"

"Me," Henry said. "You wait outside for two minutes."

"Sure," the kid said, enthusiastically.

Taking off his apron, Henry tossed it at old Herrmann, who looked baffled.

"I want to thank you, Mr. Herrmann," Henry said with dignity.

"Listen, Henry," Herrmann cried.

"You've helped me make a lot of friends and I feel I've sort of got to know the country. I like it," Henry said as he went into the little room to make a bundle of his few things.

Rendezvous

HAVE YOU EVER KNOWN A MAN YOU COULDN'T INSULT, humiliate, or drive away? When I was working in an advertising agency in charge of layouts, Lawson Wilks, a free-lance commercial artist, came in to see me with all the assurance of a man who expects a warm, fraternal handshake. As soon as I saw him bowing and showing his teeth in a tittering smile, as if he were waiting to burst out laughing, I disliked him. Without saying a word I looked at his work spread out on my desk and, though it was obvious he had some talent, I wasn't really interested in his work. I was wondering what was so soft and unresisting, yet so audacious about him that made me want to throw him out of the office.

"I'll get in touch with you if I ever need you," I said coldly, handing him his folder.

"All right. Thanks a lot," he said, and stood there grinning at me.

"Is there anything else I can do for you?" I asked.

"Oh, no, nothing. But I've wanted to meet you, that's all."

"You honor me."

"I've heard about you."

"What have you heard about me?"

246

"I know people who know you, and besides, I've admired your work a lot. I can open a newspaper and spot a layout that you've had a hand in at once."

"Thanks. Now you flatter me."

"Are you going out to lunch?"

"I've a very important date. I'm meeting my wife."

"I've often talked to my own wife about you. She'd like to meet you sometime," he said.

"Please thank her for me," I said. "And now if you'll excuse me . . . "

"Listen . . . . let's have a drink together sometime. That's one of the two things we have in common," he said, shaking with soft laughter.

I was so enraged I couldn't answer for a moment. All my friends knew I had been drinking hard and couldn't stop and in the late afternoons my nerves used to go to pieces in the office. Sometimes it was terrible waiting for five o'clock so I could run out and get a whiskey and soda. Every day it got harder for me to go to work, and besides I was doing crazy things with friends at night I couldn't remember the next morning, that used to humiliate me when they were mentioned to me. I thought he was mocking me, but I waited a moment and said, "Drinking, yes! And you might be good enough to tell me what the other thing is we are lucky enough to have in common."

"Why, I thought you'd notice it," he said. He was so truly, yet goodnaturedly embarrassed, that I was astonished. I stared at him. There he was about my size, plump, dark, overweight, wider across the middle than across the shoulders and with a little black moustache.

"What is it?" I insisted.

"People have always said I looked like you," he said with a deprecating, yet easy swing of his arm.

"I see, I see, I see what you mean," I said, and got up and was walking him toward the door.

"I'll phone you sometime," he said, and he wrung my hand very warmly.

As soon as he had gone, I looked in the mirror on the wall and rubbed my hand softly over my face. It was not a flabby face. I was fat, but my shoulders were strong and heavy. I began to make loud, clucking, contemptuous noises with my tongue.

One night a week later my legs went on me and I thought I was losing my mind. My wife begged me to take some kind of a treatment. It was about half past eleven at night and I was lying on the bed in my pajamas trembling, and with strange vivid pictures floating through my thoughts and terrifying me because I kept thinking I would see them next day at the office and I would not be able to do my work. My legs were twitching. I couldn't keep them still. My wife, who is very gentle and has never failed me at any time since we've been married, was kneeling down, rubbing my bare legs and making the blood flow warm and alive in them, till they began to seem as if they belonged to me.

Then the phone rang and my wife answered it and came back and said, "A man says he is a friend of yours, a business associate."

I didn't want any business associate to know I couldn't go to the phone so I put on my slippers and groped my way to it and said with great dignity, "Hello. Who is it?"

"It's Lawson Wilks," the voice said, and I heard his easy intimate self-possessed laughter.

"What do you want?" I yelled.

"I thought you might want to have a drink with me. I'm not far away. I'm in a tavern just two blocks from your place."

I suddenly had a craving for a drink and felt like going out to meet him, and then loathed myself and shouted, "No, no, no. I don't want a drink. I'm not going out. I'm terribly busy. Do you understand?"

"Okay," he said. "I'll call you again. I was just thinking about you."

I saw him in October, about a week after I had taken three months' leave of absence from the office, trying to get myself in hand so I wouldn't have to go away to a nursing home. I really wasn't making much of a fight and sometimes I was ashamed. I looked shabby, twitching a lot. I sat for hours smiling to myself. I couldn't bear to have anyone see me.

On a dark windy day, I was sitting in the Golden Bowl Tavern with a whiskey and soda, promising myself I wouldn't have another drink, not until I had read the Sunday papers at least. Then, I looked up and saw that Wilks had come in and was grinning at me with warm delight, as much as I've ever seen on a man's face. While I turned away sullenly, he sat down, ordered a whiskey, and nodding at my glass, said, "The same thing, you see. Didn't I tell you?"

"Didn't you tell me what?" I said. He looked pretty terrible to me. His dull eyes were pouchy, and he seemed heavier and softer. As he raised his glass his hand trembled. When he noticed me staring at him, his face lit up with fraternal goodwill. I wanted to insult him. "You better watch out," I whispered. "The heeby-jeebies'll get you. They'll have to take you outa here soon."

In a tone that maddened me, because he meant no offence, he said, "We're taking the same trip, my friend."

"How so?"

"You don't mind me sitting here, do you?"

"Sit here if you want," I said. "I'm reading the paper." It was a pleasure to see him looking such a wreck. I was delighted sitting there turning the pages of the paper slowly, never looking up at him while his voice droned on, patient, friendly, dead. Surely anyone else in the world would have found it too humiliating, sitting there like that, yet he said, "Do you mind letting me have the comics?"

"Take them," I said, letting him pull the paper from me.

"I thought I might as well be doing something while I waited for you," he said.

I folded my paper. "Sorry," I said, "I have got to go."

"Let's walk together to the corner," he said.

He was so contented on that dark and windy October afternoon that I decided to mock him. I began by asking questions and he told me he really hadn't been happy for some years. He didn't make much more than enough to live on and besides, his wife wasn't very sympathetic to his work. On the nights when he wanted to drink and be surrounded by jovial companions and talk about his work and about art, literature and the drama, his wife, a matter-of-fact woman, wanted to go out with the ladies and play bridge, and it was a game he couldn't stand.

"How about you? Does your wife play bridge?" he asked.

"She can't stand the game," I jeered at him.

"Maybe my wife and I got married too young. Sometimes I feel that she doesn't really love me at all. How about your wife?"

Full of gratitude to my wife for giving me another chance to widen the gulf between this man and me, I said crisply, "It's entirely different with us, thank you." Then I started to laugh openly, showing I had been mocking him with my pretended interest in his wretched affairs. Chuckling, I left him standing on the corner, with that puzzled yet overwhelming smile of goodwill still on his weak and puffy face.

I didn't see him again for a month. There were nights when I had some terrible experiences and I grew afraid for my wife and myself. I let them put me in the nursing home.

The first weeks were hard, terrifying, yet fascinating. I had a little room to myself and when I was normal and quiet I had the freedom of the house and the grounds, and I had some good conversations with the male nurses. Sometimes they locked me in. The door leading to the corridor had bars on it.

In the morning I often felt that I had floated out of my body at night and had remarkably interesting encounters in space with friends who were dear to me, interesting because they seemed to enlarge the borders of reality for me.

Then one morning one of the nurses said, "We have a patient just across the corridor who knows you."

"Who?" I said.

"A Mr. Lawson Wilks."

"How is he?"

"Very bad for the most part."

"Look here," I begged. "I don't want to see him at all, you understand?"

It seemed terrible that he should be there making me hate him when I was better and looking forward to getting out of the place. I refused to go to the door to look across the corridor. I knew he was standing there looking across at my room and I had a truly savage pleasure in never letting him see me.

During one very bad night, the last bad night I had, I felt that part of myself that was truly me hovering around overhead, right overhead from where I was, except of course that I wasn't confined at all. I was smiling at Lawson Wilks, who had joined me, and we were having a very friendly and easy conversation about many simple things. We laughed a lot and liked each other and I was happier than I had been in years.

In the morning when I woke up I lay in the bed a long time remembering the night and growing, bit by bit, more puzzled. Then I couldn't help getting up and sneaking over to the door and peering at Lawson Wilks' room.

When I got to the door I saw Lawson Wilks standing there looking over at me, and when he saw that I'd come at last to the door, he nodded his head in encouragement. His warm smile seemed even kindlier now. "You and me, we had a good time, didn't we?"

"We did?" I said, with a little cracked smile.

Pointing high over his head, he grinned and said, "It was wonderful last night, wasn't it?"

DRAWING BY GEORGE GROSZ